Yesterday's Shadow

Yesterday's Shadow

A Novel

Ray McElhaney

iUniverse, Inc.
New York Lincoln Shanghai

Yesterday's Shadow

iUniverse books may be ordered through booksellers or by contacting:

iUniverse
2021 Pine Lake Road, Suite 100
Lincoln, NE 68512
www.iuniverse.com
1-800-Authors (1-800-288-4677)

ISBN: 978-0-595-48130-9 (pbk)
ISBN: 978-0-595-60228-5 (ebk)

Printed in the United States of America

1

Ian

He'd probably been involved with more wars than any other man, alive or dead. Had not only led men in combat and bore battle scars, but had studied wars, also ... their successes and failures, the victims and devastation, the tragedies. War had been good to him, put money in his pockets, he'd even come to view it with a strange fondness, as a security blanket of sorts.

Ian had just turned east off I-95 headed toward the Atlantic Ocean when that annoying little you-need-gas light caught his eye. He spotted a service station with a faded red and white winged horse sign out front and two ancient gas pumps. *Thought that company with the flying horse logo went out of business years ago?* He got out of the black BMW, automatically adjusting his tie and pulling on his dark gray suit jacket in spite of the 95-degree blast that enveloped him. A panting, mangy dog with an obviously infected ear sauntered up to him, looking tired but curious. Ian felt sweat forming on his face as he grabbed the hose handle from the premium pump, filled the tank, and went inside to pay.

The clerk had a friendly, bucked-tooth smile. "Afternoon to you, suh."

"Hello, how are you? Man, is it hot out there."

"Not too bad today. Hit 101 yesterday. That'll be thirty-six dollars and twelve cents. Going to Charleston?"

Ian handed him two twenties. "Yes, I am. Ever heard of the Old Battery Inn there?"

The clerk's eyes went wide as he spit some brown liquid into a paper cup. "Well shit, I guess. Sweet Jesus, that's big bucks fancy. Y'all goin' there?"

"Yeah, I'm booked there. How far is it from here, time wise?"

"Hour and a half. Maybe an hour if you go fast." He handed Ian his change. "Damnation. Stayin' at the Old Battery Inn. Sheee-it." He grinned and shook his head in awe. "Y'all come back now, ya hear."

"Uh, yeah. Good-bye."

Ian glanced at the flying horse sign fading away in the rearview mirror. He liked the South—owned a house on Hilton Head Island in South Carolina and another in Atlanta. But he never got accustomed to the striking dichotomies of rich and poor, educated and ignorant. He puzzled over why the stark differences made him feel uncomfortable. He'd known penury, and he knew rich. There was no contest in his mind. Money might not be life's ultimate answer, but it surely made things better. Much better.

At age 33, he felt he had come a long way. He dressed well, had an overseas villa and three cars. Recognized as an expert in his field, he spent successes' rewards as he saw fit. He absent-mindedly checked his image in the 700 series BMW's rearview mirror and grinned. He saw nothing wrong with self-reward and pride, if it was justified and self-earned.

As for his unapologetically healthy ego, he saw it as a first cousin to confidence, which he saw as vital for success. He loved his work but knew that all the intellect, goal-setting, honest self-criticism and hard work he put in were only pieces in the equation. He was very good at what he did, and he knew it. Confidence won the battle and the war. So, if certain people thought him arrogant or egotistical, screw the simplistic bastards.

Even a confident and confessed workaholic like Ian Michael McBride had burnout limits and he was quickly approaching his. He'd left the man he, with tongue in cheek, called his *boss* in Boston, and had been on the road for thirteen days, filled ten audiocassettes with observations, scribbled a stack of notes, and had roughed in an outline. Twelve nights in motels or hotels, some great, some not exactly five-star. Thirteen days and seven states of working his way south included: far too many burgers and fries; three lecture appearances; and seven Civil War battlefields, complete with museums and U.S. Park Service walking tours, in the heat and humidity of July. Actually, he didn't mind the heat. It was the cold he hated.

The Old Battery Inn was a four-star hotel on old Charleston's Battery, a historic street fronting the Atlantic. It was Charleston's signature area. The local Chamber of Commerce always used the lovingly restored, pastel-colored houses of the Battery to depict Charleston's laid-back, classy Southern charm.

The hotel had originally been a pre-Civil War military storehouse for arms and explosives. Cannons on the roof, called an artillery battery, gave the building its name. Now, the guns were gone and the building was considerably expanded. The pale pink, stucco inn offered an array of comfortable rooms and suites that oozed Old South elegance and seemed to say, "Stay and relax for a while, in expensive style."

Ian checked into his suite just after 4:30 PM, handed the bellman his keys to have his car washed and polished by morning, and asked for a 5:00 AM wake up. His suite, with its twelve-foot ceilings, was a study in function and exquisite taste. An antique brick fireplace, cherry furniture, thick off-white carpet, and a pastel floral duvet that matched the draperies covering the king sized bed. Signed lithographs and oils decorated the walls and a working desk with a cleverly concealed state-of-the-art computer blended beautifully with the suite's soothing décor. Because Bob had called ahead, the suite's thermostat was preset at 78 degrees and a tumbler of frosty vodka martinis arrived with Ian's luggage.

He loosened his tie and mulled over the phone call he'd received a few hours earlier from his business manager and publisher. However, he didn't let the disturbing call stop him from setting straight to work, dictating thoughts, sending and reading e-mail and scribbling project ideas that, for the moment, flowed like a river.

When he next looked at his watch, it was 9:10 PM, and he was hungry. He changed his shirt, cuff links and tie, and headed downstairs, thinking the dining room would be thinned out at that time of night. Instead, it was packed. Third in line for a table, he gave the hostess his name and a $5.00 bill and headed toward the bar, which was jammed, too.

Ian was scanning the smoky room for a place to sit when his eyes came to rest on an attractive woman sitting alone at a small table. *Hmm ... Very nice.* A smile curled his lips. Why not?

2

Shannon

Her father said she always marched to the beat of her own drummer, never coped well with bureaucracy, rules, or authority figures. And today, for a well-educated, intelligent woman, she was slow on the uptake. Hungry, tired, running behind, and frustrated with herself, she was in no mood for this delay.

Blowing through the State Police radar at 89 MPH was bad enough. Defiantly handing over a Connecticut driver's license amounted to two big strikes against her. She should have been polite and hoped her striking, blonde-haired, blue-eyed good looks would buy her some leniency. But, no, such reserved practicality seldom defined the in-your-face Shannon Elizabeth Collins.

The tall South Carolina state trooper stood by the driver's door of her shiny Mercedes convertible and looked down at her through pilot-style sunglasses. He slowly shook his head as she finished her tirade.

"... and then I have an asshole hick cop pull me over for some bullshit traffic thing."

"Mizz Collins, here's the way it's gonna work." The trooper spoke in a slow, deep drawl. "I'm gonna give y'all this citation for speedin' and reckless drivin' and allow y'all to continue on your trip. But …" He paused, pushing the sunglasses down his nose and fixing her with a firm look. "If one more nasty word comes out of your sweet mouth, I'll put you in handcuffs and haul your pretty behind off to jail. Are we clear, Mizzz Collins from *Connecticut*?"

The significance and gravity of this total no win situation dawned on her, along with a bit of common sense. Shannon bit her tongue and said, "Yes, officer. We are clear. May I go now, please?"

She drove away crumpling the $400 ticket in her fist. "Stupid! Really, lamebrain, stupid …" The propelled paper ball ricocheted off the dashboard onto the empty passenger seat. "Acting like a condescending, spoiled bitch to a state trooper." She shook her head. "Calling him an asshole, for God's sake … Jeez, get a grip."

She sighed, forced herself to refocus, and reached for a map—sure didn't want to lose him now, not after five days. What kind of man worked until midnight then was on the road and gone at 5:00 AM? Thanks to the chatty Marriott desk clerk who couldn't stop ogling her breasts, she at least knew he was booked into a hotel in Charleston for a few days. Unfortunately, the clerk didn't know which hotel. How far to Charleston, anyway?

At age 30, she'd accumulated substantial practical work experience. Some might say too much work experience, since departing Yale with her bachelor's degree nine years earlier. She had become an excellent journalist and photographer, much to the chagrin of her well-to-do parents, who had planned to fit her into the template of a proper socialite daughter. Smart, hard working, ambitious, and aggressive, she had a nose for offbeat, interesting stories.

What Shannon wasn't, is what employers often call a people person. Her reputation for intelligence, talent, and beauty, was eclipsed by abrasive hardheadedness. She'd been a print reporter for two small newspapers in New Jersey and Pennsylvania, and her stunning good looks and polished speaking voice had landed her TV reporter jobs in two more cities in New York and Connecticut. However, in each position, she had managed to frustrate and ultimately infuriate her managers to the point of her dismissal or forced resignation.

Therefore, for the past two years, Shannon had been a nomadic free-lance journalist and photographer, a fringe member of what is commonly known as the paparazzi, a word she despised. Earnings had been sporadic, at best. Only when one of her stories caught the eye of a major newspaper, magazine, or TV network, had she lived well. However, there had been multi-month gaps between good stories and not even a whiff of that big exclusive, the career maker. Spending money from her trust fund set Shannon's teeth on edge, went against her independent nature and her pride. However, following leads to get stories meant traveling, which was aggravatingly expensive, sleeping in the car had gotten old very soon, and she was fond of eating, at least every now and then. Regularly tapping the multi-million-dollar fund had been necessary.

Two months earlier, she'd had her last date with Richard Billings, a divorced middle-aged attorney. Handsome, witty, and fun, he also bought her lavish presents. However, she had discovered he used drugs and was far too dependent on alcohol. It had also become evident he was looking for sex on demand, payback for the expensive dinners and presents he provided. The kept woman concept was disgusting and repulsive to Shannon, something she would never be.

Late that last Saturday night, after far too many drinks and a bout of unfulfilling sex, Richard had bragged to her about a hooker he had as a client in a potential blockbuster paternity lawsuit. The woman, a longtime street whore, claimed that one of America's most eligible bachelors, whose name Shannon recognized immediately, had illegitimately fathered her estranged teenage daughter. Shannon realized this could be a huge story, the career-making story she'd sought for years … if she could verify it with facts and photos.

Although she knew how to handle men quite skillfully, it was time to move on. She left Richard and New York City and for six straight weeks exhaustively researched records and interviewed sources about her new subject. There was a wealth of information about his professional successes and achievements, as well as numerous newspaper and magazine gossip pieces about his high priced tastes and fondness for women. He was often pictured with beautiful women in exotic spots, drinking champagne or dancing; he was described as smooth, arrogant, and wickedly handsome.

She studied the news photographs and thought that as a boy he must have been almost too pretty, but oh not now. His sun-bronzed face had weathered handsomely. Thick, chestnut-brown hair that was just a bit too long, lent a roguish touch to his overall image of polished sophistication. Although news photographs always showed him in a suit or a tuxedo, never in casual dress, Shannon had deduced he was no poser. Her research indicated he'd served in the Marine Corps and saw combat during Desert Storm—heroic acts, medals awarded for valor, and battle wounds. He had later obtained his bachelor's degree in English at night, while working full time; and had then earned his master's in history, graduating with honors.

Shannon had scribbled in her notes, *strong-willed, rich, talented, and interesting*. Nope, no poser; this one was as advertised ... all male. However, while looking at his green eyes and windblown hair in a photo she had mused that while some women might find him attractive this was business. He was business. She assured herself it didn't matter how he looked.

She could find no trace of this man's childhood or early teenage years. No school records, birth records, no records of any type earlier than age 17 or 18, when he joined the Marines. Very odd—he didn't seem to exist before that. Her diligent efforts had hit one brick wall and dry hole after another. Quite strange, since she knew her way through the public records maze, was normally quite good at research. Frustrated, but sensing the records gap was somehow significant, she began following and photographing him.

Five days and four states later, Shannon had noted that her surveillance subject was a fastidious dresser; seemed friendly and outgoing with all classes of people; worked hard and long; ate irregularly and little; and, without ever trying to do so, drew women to him like flies to sugar. She also conceded that he was quite good-looking, and well ... damn sexy.

Last night she watched him check into an upscale Marriott, go to dinner quite late, and then return to his room where his lights were on until midnight. Thinking he would be tired and sleep in, she set her own alarm for 7:00AM, to be safe. However, when she checked out the next morning at 7:45, the desk clerk told her that Mr. McBride had left about 5:00 AM. That eliminated her breakfast and had her roaring down I-95 in an effort to catch up.

"Damnit!" Didn't this guy ever get tired? She was almost three hours behind him and had no idea where he was staying in

Charleston. The welcome to South Carolina encounter with the oversized trooper had only added to her problems, now she hungry, almost out of gas, and had to pee something awful. Shannon had certainly had better days.

The Charleston exit sign caught her eye. Turning off I-95, she pulled into the first gas station she saw, one with a faded red and white winged horse sign out front. A necessary stop, she reasoned. But she'd never overtake him at this rate. She grimaced. *Mr. Green Eyes probably filled his gas tank last night.*

Bubba spit tobacco juice into a paper cup and absent-mindedly viewed the cranberry metallic Mercedes convertible roll to a stop at the gas pump island. He was admiring the sleek convertible when the driver's door opened—Bubba's bucked teethed mouth dropped open. The two longest, most perfectly formed female legs he had ever seen, extended to the pavement, followed by the remainder of the blond beauty's 5-feet-10-inch body. Her legs and shapely butt appeared to have been sprayed with faded denim that stopped on tanned hips several inches below her exposed navel. A pink, half-length T-shirt covered large, well-sculpted breasts obviously unencumbered by a bra. The shirt had two strange letters Bubba didn't recognize and the words Delta Gamma arched in pale blue across its front. Long, honey-colored hair broke over her shoulders, and moved seductively as she strode toward the office.

Bubba's eyes fixed on the two swaying peaks distorting the pink shirt's lettering as Shannon came through the front door. Accustomed to the stares and their usual target, Shannon smiled and nodded to the nearly comatose Bubba. "Point me to the john, sweetie. Then be a good boy and go fill up my car with premium."

He pointed wordlessly and disappeared out the front door to do as he was told. Shannon walked over to the dingy door marked *girls* and closed it behind her.

Shannon knew what many men saw and thought when they looked at her. It didn't upset her however, because she lived within strict personal proscriptions and prided herself on being an intelligent, principled woman. Still, she was well aware of her physical gifts and saw no reason to hide that particular light under a bushel.

The Mercedes was filled with gas, and Bubba had regained his ability to speak. Shannon handed him her credit card. "What would you say are the three best hotels in Charleston?"

Bubba adopted a pained expression and scratched his head, pondering the question requiring a multi-part answer. "Well, let's see ... That there Marriott Ocean is big-bucks fancy, and that there Charleston Omni is one of them expensive, high-riser types. But, mostly they say the Old Battery Inn is the best around." He paused. "Yes'um, that's what they say. Matter of fact, some rich lookin', business-type guy in a big-ass black Beemer, jest here couple hours ago, said he was gonna' stay there."

Shannon's hand froze in the middle of signing the credit card slip. "Oh, yeah?" Looking up, she gave Bubba her best man-melting smile and said, "What'd he look like, sweetie, this business-type guy?"

"A real dude. Yes'um, movie-star face, wearin' a dark suit and tie. Kinda' weird in this heat."

"Yeah, sure is. Thanks."

Shannon hurried out the door.

3

Paige

She was a romantic at heart, striving to see the good in people and in life. She'd always loved to write, and had received compliments on her writing ability since before high school. While attending Vanderbilt University she'd been a principal contributor to the university newspaper and its editor during her senior year. She had heeded her mother's stern cautions about promiscuity and followed her father's philosophy of setting goals and working hard; she'd eschewed sorority membership, written a lot, studied diligently, and dated little. Her first novel was published while she was in graduate school at Duke.

Now, with a bachelor's and master's degree in English and a Phi Beta Kappa key five years behind her, she had five published novels to her credit, three of which had been on *The New York Times* list of best sellers. She had worked selflessly, telling herself she was temporarily subordinating her personal life for her goals. Success was now at hand, and life seemed like it should be good.

For the last five years, her publisher, Fred Williams, had pushed her to seek public exposure, saying that, in the sale of romance novels, author name and face recognition counted almost as much as plot and character. He'd often reminded her that readers of her genre wanted to believe their favorite authors led adventurous, romantic lives as did the characters in their books.

Fred was a near genius at devising gimmicky situations to tantalize the gossip media to write about her. He leaked information of her swimming with a royal prince, golfing with a millionaire playboy, and dropped hints of intimate relations with an unnamed politician. Fred had manufactured an image of a fashionably cool, sexually sophisticated, fun-loving jet setter. Even though the façade was largely bogus, the fact that she was a pretty, naturally sensual woman made it an easy sell. Paige Ann Brittany had become a recognizable, popular author of torrid romance novels, and she and Fred had consequently reaped considerable monetary rewards.

She had expected fame would bring life changes and even some restrictions, but she had significantly underestimated the personal tolls. The endless cycle of interviews, personal appearances, book signings, and charity events was draining. In addition, her mother who always insinuated that sex was dirty, something men compelled wives to do, and should only be for family reasons, was demonstrably embarrassed by her fame. Paige had not spoken to the woman since she described Paige's books as "shameful and almost pornographic" to a *New York Times* book critic. That was three years ago.

Paige sat in her hotel suite, looking into the large, dark blue eyes of the face in a wall mirror. Wasn't this what she wanted, what she'd worked so hard to achieve? Paige reminded herself she had arrived; she'd made it. However, much of it was a tapestry of lies—no romantic relationships with princes, millionaire playboys, or politicians, and certainly no sexual ties to such men. She remembered how her mother had repeatedly told her that men only wanted two things from a pretty and affluent girl, her virginity, and her family's money. Once they had the first, they would take the second.

That couldn't be universally true. Not all males could be that way. There had to be some good men out there. However, aside from an occasional working dinner with Fred or arranged appearances with a celebrity, she had been on no more than a handful of real dates in the past three years. It seemed her life had been spent with others setting her goals, living up to other peoples' expectations, and allowing them to meter out her happiness on their terms. Someone else had always defined her, told her what she should be. Here she was twenty-eight-years-old rich and famous ... yet feeling very alone and unhappy.

Paige dropped the plush, oversized towel and stood nude in front of the full-length mirror, turning, examining, and evaluating. She critically viewed her 5 foot 5 inch, 110-pound body. Smooth olive skin and a petite, almost delicate, build. Pert breasts ... not large, but shapely and firm. Her stomach was board-flat, waist small, and her long legs strong and lean from running and aerobics. Her heart-shaped face featured full lips with a deep Kewpie doll curve.

"It's not the package," she mused. Brushing back shoulder-length, blue-black hair, and pursing her lips, she turned her back to the mirror and checked out her butt with an approving nod. She sighed. "No, it's what you're not doing with it." She shook her head and gave the mirror a wry smile thinking how millions of women considered her an expert on steamy sex. She sighed again. What a sad joke—she was a lonely, frustrated, creeping-up-on-thirty, virgin.

Anger surged through her. "Well, enough of this!" She looked at the blue eyes in the mirror and defiantly set her jaw.

"It's high time I put Paige first, loosen up, and yes, have some fun. I'm going to meet a handsome man and become a real woman with him, like the imaginary me in the tabloids." She nodded resolutely. *And, soon.*

She looked at the clock and muttered, "Now, if I only had a clue of how to loosen up ... or how to find a man in 'real' life instead of my novels." It was just after 9 P.M when Paige donned a conservative, light blue suit and went downstairs to dinner. The elegant dining room of The Old Battery Inn was full and there was a waiting line. She gave her name to the hostess and went to the bar to wait. She would have one drink in the bar and possibly a glass of wine with dinner, but absolutely no more. She needed to be sharp at 8:00AM tomorrow morning when she faced that group of aspiring authors and graduate students at the College of Charleston.

The bar was as crowded as the restaurant, but she moved quickly and snagged a chair at a tiny round table as a couple got up to leave. The waitress had just delivered her Manhattan and Paige was placing her wallet back in her purse when she sensed a presence.

He stood quietly, sipping a vodka martini, looking down and admiring her silky black hair, delicate hands, and sleek legs. She hadn't noticed his approach but felt she was being watched. She turned and looked up and into the most penetrating, sensual, sea green eyes, she'd ever seen. Paige felt her stomach clench and her breath catch. She jerked her hand, sloshing ice cubes and whiskey onto the table and knocking her purse to the floor. Her only lucid thought was, *Oh, my.*

4

Fateful Decisions

The sign on the door read Richard E. Billings & Associates. Of course, there were no associates or partners—hadn't been in the last five years—not since Richard Billings became partners with the white gold. His addiction, although largely secret, had cost him dearly ... his wife and children, his house, two cars, and a previously thriving law practice. The four associates in his firm, one by one, had become tired of late paychecks and empty promises and moved on to pastures providing upward mobility in more stable environments. Yes, cocaine ruled his life yet Billings steadfastly denied the drug's damaging affects.

He was now a one-man-band with no more prestigious clients or their guaranteed retainers, reduced to taking court-appointed defense cases and any contingency suits he could scrounge. That is how he came to represent a prostitute alleging a well-known, wealthy author had illegitimately fathered her teenage daughter. He knew only an ambulance-chasing bottom feeder would take on such a client. Still, it had seemed like an okay idea a couple of months ago, now he wasn't so sure. But, he desperately needed money, a lot quickly, and any way he could get it, to pay people who were extremely demanding.

The gray New York day matched Richard's mood and disposition. He paced in his office, lit another cigarette and shook his head. How the hell did he get himself into these situations? He couldn't figure out a way to handle the compounding mess that seemed to circle back onto itself. Never had he owed this much, and he sensed the chances of getting any more time to come up with the money were slim. Sweat beaded on his face as he drummed his fingers. His stomach clinched, bile burning his throat as if he might throw up.

Okay, first things first. The client was always the primary consideration, but Martha McDonald had disappeared. He hadn't heard from her in two weeks and hadn't been able to find her. Their last meeting had been surprising and disturbing—she changed her story, now claimed to be the playboy writer's half-sister, and said her tale about him fathering her daughter was "just made up." Nevertheless, she insisted they sue Ian McBride for paternity anyway, because "He's rich and will buy me off." She had demanded he, as her attorney, give her an advance against the paternity suit money.

"It doesn't work that way," he had explained. We need a valid reason to file suit and credible evidence in order to secure a monetary settlement."

"Screw all that legal mumbo jumbo," she'd countered. "I want money from him. He owes me, damnit. Money that's rightfully mine."

"That doesn't matter to a judge. We need evidence."

"Well, if you don't have the balls to sue him … I'll get the money my way."

She had stormed out of his office, convinced newspapers would pay thousands for the salacious information. Outlandish as that seemed, it had planted a seed in Richard's brain. The stupid bitch could be right; a lawsuit wouldn't be necessary if McBride was convinced paying her off was a good idea, his only viable alternative. That could mean big money, exactly what he needed. He wasn't thinking about extortion, a serious federal felony. No, more like heavy lawyer-to-lawyer jawboning, saber rattling with inferred threats. Hell, he had attorney friends who did it all the time. Besides, he knew Robert Fowler, McBride's publisher. Pragmatic, logical Fowler ... Bob would see the wisdom in paying to keep this allegation quiet and out of court. After all, McBride was his meal ticket, his cash cow.

But what of the would be plaintiff, his client? The private investigator he'd hired using advances on one of his VISA cards reported that Martha McDonald, a prostitute for many years, had been arrested numerous times, mostly in California. An on again-off again junkie, she had a reputation for making up stories, had committed actual perjury on two occasions.

But what if she was telling the truth this time? If she was McBride's half sister, he might pay handsomely to keep that from becoming public. Proving such a relationship would take hard evidence, DNA results, probably. But, a match between McBride and the woman could equate to a huge payday. Yeah, he'd confront Bob Fowler with a strong but veiled threat. But, what if Fowler balked at a payoff idea, insisted on going to court ... Oh, that could be bad.

His options seemed few, the need critical—his back was to a wall, wasn't it? Already two weeks overdue in paying his cocaine supplier ... hell, his life was in jeopardy. Sweat trickled down his back, his mouth was dry.

Yes, he would meet with Fowler tomorrow or Wednesday at the latest. Nevertheless, he needed to find his client and make a couple of heavyweight decisions. Richard dialed a private number and thumbed through the Yellow Pages as he waited for the man to answer. It was decision time, time to act.

Mark Redding had kept a journal ever since his days with the NYPD ended. He didn't tell anyone about it, figuring that one day it might earn him a big chunk of money. Of course, there was also the risk that the information in the journal could land him in jail. Writing and rereading it from time to time reminded him of how far he had come, in terms of income, and how far he'd fallen as a human being since that cold January night.

He didn't like the term Private Investigator, nor did he particularly like being one. Didn't like the title of Private Detective any better. However, the public understood both handles, and that brought in money to augment his NYPD pension. *My pension. What a joke!* $18,500 a year in disability payments didn't seem like near enough for losing a kidney, his spleen, and walking with a permanent limp.

He once again wondered why. Why'd he have to take two bullets from a low-life junkie? Hell, there were liquor stores all over the city. Why did the asshole have to pick one in his patrol area to rob? Oh, sure, Redding had shot and killed the miserable son of a bitch, but not before he and his partner were both hit. Jimmy Williams, his partner and friend, died on the frozen asphalt that night. That was ten years ago, but he still thought of it far too often, both when he was awake and when it woke him at night.

The shooting had changed everything. He'd been an idealistic, hard-working police officer. Yeah, he roughed up a few suspects who deserved it, but he was never into brutality. He kept himself fit, followed the rules, was never on the take, and was scrupulously honest in enforcing the law. Nevertheless, the NYPD said he couldn't be a cop any more. Not even a desk job. Losing his badge had been almost more painful than the two bullets.

So many things had changed over the past decade. He was thirty-five, and felt more like fifty. He did not exercise. Couldn't actually, since the pain was never completely gone. Didn't eat well, an occupational hazard. And, of course, he drank too much. His wife had left him a year after he was forced out of the PD on disability. The bitch ran off to marry another cop she had been secretly screwing while Mark was in the hospital and at the rehab center. No, the last ten years hadn't been exactly sweet for Mark Redding. What he had gone through had changed his outlook and priorities. Made him darker, baser, and largely insensate.

However, he was a skilled private investigator. He never drank when he was working, had a naturally logical and inquisitive mind, and a way of getting information out of people. When his clients wanted them, his written reports were organized, concise, and detailed. But a law-abiding PI was usually a hungry PI and Redding didn't intend to be hungry or poor.

He'd bent or broken many laws in the past ten years, but he made his clients happy and that translated into big paychecks. As far as he was concerned, it was all about money. Money talked. It would get you anything and everything, including women. Morality or laws took a backseat on his priority bus. He provided what his clients wanted, as long as they paid his price. If a guy wanted pictures of his old lady humping the pool boy, Mark brought him eight-by-ten, full-color close up shots. If a divorce-minded wife wanted proof of hubby's extra-marital, afternoon delights, Mark provided videotapes that would have made internet porn sites proud. Lawyers or business executives desiring records or documents that were not exactly legally available ... Not a problem. Yep. Money talked and Richard Billings was currently doing the talking and paying him well.

Redding sat in his small New York apartment and continued to write in his journal.

This half-assed lawyer, Billings wants info on some writer. Wants it real soon. Those factors always up the ante and, knowing guys like Billings as I do, I always get the money from him up front. He promised me an extra grand to get some court records on thi s guy. It was a piece of cake, but I'll say it was risky and worth another $500, take it or leave it. Billings also wants me to start following this same guy. South Carolina, of all places. But, he wouldn't say why except that he needed either blood or hair from the guy. Sounds like he's looking for a DNA sample, but he refused to explain. I don't like following people without knowing why. Making me curious is going be expensive for him.

The two documents Billings wanted so badly were on Redding's kitchen table next to his journal. What the two papers showed didn't seem like a big deal. Some seventeen-year-old kid, named John William McDonald had changed his name—Grew up to be the author guy Billings was so hot to know about. But hell, it had been years ago. A check of PD and juvenile records on the McDonald kid had yielded a date of birth, some addresses, a long sheet of minor offenses, and one felony, a stolen car arrest. Again, no big deal. However, since they seemed so important to Billings, he'd make him pay extra to get the documents. His impatient kind would always pay more. But what about the blood and hair thing?

Billings is up to something. I'm not sure this is lawyer business he's got me doing. Maybe I'll look at what I turn up a lot closer before I give it to Billings. Who knows? Could point to big bucks to me ... without Billings ever knowing.

5

Bob

He stretched his 6-foot-4-inch, 255-pound frame to its limit, lunged, and caught the ball with a forehand swipe that sent it rocketing into the corner. It hit a foot off the hardwood floor and rolled toward the center of the handball court.

"Damnit, Bob," screamed a sweat-soaked, panting Richard Billings. "How can you hit a kill shot like that on a diving run?"

"Pure talent, Richard … Plus well-honed skills, of course," he added with a good-natured grin. "By the way, that's game, I do believe. Care for another?"

"No, damn you. A man can stand just so much abuse. Let's shower and then you can buy me lunch. The least you can do after showing no mercy to your elders." The 48-year-old attorney paused, wiping sweat from his face with a towel. "Besides, I have something I need to run by you about one of the ponies in your publishing stable."

"Okay, but I choose the place. You're on my turf here in Boston, my friend." Bob smiled amicably. "I know your New York steak and fine wine mentality and your appetite."

Forty-five minutes later the two men were in a typical Irish bar sipping dark beer and awaiting their burgers. They talked quietly, surrounded by the dim light, dark wood, and a mournful ballad playing in the background.

"So, Richard, whatever happened to that drop-dead beautiful blond with the wet dream body you were squiring around the last time you were here?" He downed the last of his beer and signaled the waitress for more.

"I don't know." Bob saw something flicker in the man's eyes. "That would be the delectable Miss Collins. What a woman. Man, is your description of her right on the money, a real looker. Smart too. But all good things must come to an end. She split, haven't seen her in a couple of months. Maybe I pissed her off. Not sure. Anyway, looks like she left town. Her work, I guess—freelance journalist."

"That's too bad. But if she should call some night looking for a man to comfort her … Well, I could probably make myself available to help her out."

Richard balled his fist in mock attack, but grinned. "You're a real prince."

Bob smiled and shrugged as two more drafts arrived. "You said you wanted to talk about one of the authors I represent. Which one? What's up, buddy?"

"It's your guy, McBride. I have a client who claims she has a teenage daughter who should be calling him daddy."

"What?" Bob Fowler set his beer mug down so hard the amber liquid sloshed onto the table. His eyes narrowed. "What's this bullshit, Richard? You know what kind of squeaky-clean people I represent. McBride's a ladies' man, for sure, but paternity? That's a crock!"

"Easy, big fella'. Look, I'm just giving you a heads up. I'd like to depose him, when it's convenient."

"You've got to be joking. No way. When did you file the papers? When will he be served? And who's your crazy fucking client?"

"Come on, take it easy. First, I haven't filed any paper yet, have no idea when or even *if* your client will be served. And ... hell, this is the embarrassing part: the woman making the allegation is a longtime prostitute. I have a PI checking her and her story out. I'm just advising you of the allegation ... as a friend."

"Okay, okay. Sorry for going off on you, but McBride's more than just a client, we're friends. This just isn't him. Hell, the man has a streak of integrity as wide as a highway. He wouldn't get some woman pregnant and take off. Not him." Bob paused, and then pressed on. "Two questions: First, didn't you say the woman making this BS allegation is a known whore? Have you gone nuts? And two, you said the so-called child is a teenager? Why'd she wait so long to make this claim? McBride's been in the public eye, high profile for years."

"I took this thing on contingency. I'm not even sure I believe her. Hell, Bob, you're a lawyer, too, not just a publisher—you know how it works. No hard feelings ... You and McBride just happen to be on the other side of her allegations. If we weren't friends, I would have ambushed you two. Look, we ... you and me, could knock this down, probably make it go away—get rid of her with a quick clean cash settlement before it goes any further. What do ya' say?"

"No. I don't like this at all." He paused. "Who else knows about her claims? Please tell me it's been closely held."

"Only my paralegal and I know about it. No one else ..." His words stopped.

"What?" Bob caught the expression on the man's face, a sick look growing in his eyes. "Who else have you told?"

"I uh … You know the looker we were talking about, the one who split a couple of months ago? Well, the last night we were together I was pretty drunk … may have told her."

"A journalist, for God's sake!" Bob Fowler smashed a fist onto the tabletop. "Shit!" He scowled across the table. "Tell me Richard … You may have told her or you did tell her? You pillow-talked this unsubstantiated crap to a damn reporter?"

Richard Billings could manage only, "Yes."

Bob Fowler threw a twenty-dollar bill on the table. "Here's for lunch." He leaned close to the other man, his voice cold as a fresh grave. "Be advised, Richard. If this hurts my friend's career or his reputation, your ass will be before the ethics committee before you can breathe. I'll have your fucking law license. That's a promise."

Richard Billings felt his stomach knot and his throat tighten as he watched Bob Fowler storm out of the bar. Bob was a nice guy, but was also known to be a hard-nosed man of his word. But Fowler's threat paled compared to the pressures on Billings from other quarters.

He had established himself as a force in the publishing business at age 35. As a vice president of one of Boston's most prestigious publishing houses, he had demonstrated a knack for recognizing new talent and nurturing it into profits. Robert T. Fowler had become a millionaire after he put up his own money years ago to publish the first manuscript of a brash, new author named Ian Michael McBride. The manuscript had been unique because men simply did not write romance novels, at least not profitably. However, the McBride war stories with their dash of sex had attracted millions of female romance novel fans as well as male readers. With Bob's business savvy, the two men had made substantial money on the six McBride novels and a three-part TV mini-series. They trusted each other, worked well together, and had become as close as brothers.

As he walked out of the bar, Bob was already hitting a confidential speed dial number on his cell phone. He was worried. A greedy fellow lawyer, a lying whore, and a reporter who would do God only knew what with this vicious rumor. Robert Fowler meant to put a stop to this. His white-knuckled fists balled in resolve.

6

The Client

He was breathing a bit easier for the first time in days. Maybe, just maybe, things were starting to turn his way. They had to be turning his way because he was running out of time. Richard Billings had made the decision—he would get the money he had to have. Convincing him to pay was the key. Only solid evidence would make Fowler believe McBride had to pay, or be ruined. That was where that leach PI, Redding fit in.

The court records Redding had obtained indicated McBride was hiding some kind of past. His true identity was John William McDonald, the same last name as the whore. Who knows? She might really be his half-sister. McBride was from The Bronx and had changed his name before he was twenty-one years old. It was normally unheard of for a judge to allow that.

If they could ID the parents, Redding could run criminal checks ... Could tell a lot about them and possibly lead to more information. He needed Redding to get documents identifying the parents of McDonald. A birth certificate would help, although birth records were normally a bitch to obtain. However, this PI seemed to have some kind of info pipeline. Billings smiled. He already knew McBride's name was a lie. What else was there? He thought it was like peeling an onion, each layer logically leading to another and another, until you reach the prize you're looking for. If all kept going well, he would soon have enough to make McBride more than willing to pay him to keep quiet.

He was becoming more confident of his plan. And why not? Bob Fowler had described McBride as *squeaky-clean*. Yes, Fowler put a great deal of importance on public image. Doubtful he or McBride would report extortion to the police. The cops would want to know his vulnerability, and the press might see the police report. Therefore, Richard was more and more convinced he could pull this off, could get the $150,000 he needed to pay off the dealers, stay alive, and keep the cocaine he craved at hand.

He leaned back and sipped his whiskey. Why shouldn't he get a little extra, a cushion to make his life easier? "That's it—I'll demand, uh ... $500,000." A broad smile swept his face as he slammed a fist into the palm of his hand. "Yeah, McBride's going to be my ticket out of this mess and back to the good life."

Martha McDonald had only been in New York for a few months, having grown up in California with two sets of foster parents. They'd treated her okay, especially the second husband and wife, whom she'd really liked. George and Tina Petruski had even talked about adopting her, although they never did. So she went her own way when she turned eighteen and ended up hooking on the streets of LA.

Four months ago, the Petruskis were killed in a car wreck. After the funeral, their adult son gave Martha a folder of papers he had found in his parents' safe. It contained an old private detective report indicating Martha had been born in New York. It identified her parents and detailed what kind of people they were. She thought it was ironic her mother had been a prostitute. The report described how the woman had deserted Martha, leaving social services to take her as an infant. That pushed Martha into the system, landed her with foster parents, and moved her to California. The folder also contained numerous photocopies of news articles, actual news clippings, and book reviews about a famous, apparently rich author, Ian Michael McBride. The clippings had been stapled together with an eye-opening note on top bearing a handwritten inscription, *Martha's half-brother. Same mother.*

There was nothing in the papers to indicate Martha's mother had done time in prison for abandoning her year-old daughter in an alley. No indication she'd only had the child because another back-alley abortion might have done her in. Neither was it stated that the woman's second husband and pimp would surely have killed her had she stopped turning tricks.

Now Martha was back in New York to obtain what she felt was rightfully hers, one way or another. She had changed her plans, hadn't seen her lawyer in two weeks, been avoiding him actually. The all-important manila folder lay on the table as if watching her, taunting, nagging at her.

Martha laid down the joint she'd been smoking, and donned what she saw as her most conservative dress, hoping it was long enough to be seen as proper. Looking into the mirror, she tugged down the hem of the dress that came just halfway to her knees. She had applied only half her usual make-up, striving to look as normal as possible—couldn't afford to project the image that brought her men and money. Not today because normal men didn't respect or believe anything whores said. At the last minute, she remembered to change out of the silver stiletto pumps and into seldom-worn black three-inch heels. She was torn between tangerine or hot pink lipstick, since both seemed conservative. It was important the men she met with today saw her as credible, and believed her story so they'd be willing to pay big for it.

She had already looked up *The Times* and *The Post* in the phone book. The scrap of paper with the two locations was in her purse as she hailed a cab. To hell with that jerk-ass lawyer, Billings. She would get some big money on her own ... and without spreading her legs for a change. Martha grinned. She got into the cab, patted the Indian driver on the cheek, and gave him a wink. "Take me to *The Times,* Sugar."

Five hours later, she had been to both newspapers, where she had spent hours in various waiting rooms and been shuffled from one reporter to another. One of them had groped her thigh, and all of them had generally brushed her off. They were supposed to jump at her story about this famous playboy author having a half-sister who was a lady of the evening.

She went into the restroom at the *New York Post* and looked into the mirror as she freshened the tangerine lipstick. Thinking how the one reporter ran his hand over her leg had her momentarily miffed—all men thought with their crotches. Her lips however curled into a sly smile. Good thing they did. Otherwise, she'd be poor and hungry. But her plan was not coming together at all. The reporters had said either they didn't care, did not believe her, or said her story wasn't worth more than a couple hundred bucks … if she could prove it. They had actually laughed at her when she asked for $50,000.

After getting the same bum's rush at the second newspaper, she borrowed a phone book and looked up the address for *The Enquirer*. She hadn't wanted to go there initially, thinking the big newspapers would pay more. So what if she wasn't certain she was his half-sister? She might be. Maybe she'd call Howard Stern. Try to get on his show with her story.

The New York offices of *The Enquirer* were in a rundown, ten-story building in a seedy part of Brooklyn. Bernard Groinstein's office was not the most impressive she'd seen, but she had gotten inside, which she saw as a plus. Bernie, the manager was a sleaze but appeared interested in her story. To Martha, he looked like a cross between Danny Devito and a greasy Mafia hit man. To make it worse, when Martha mentioned $50,000 for her story, he laughed just like the others. She was starting to think 50 grand was maybe too much. She wondered how much Bernie would be willing to give.

Bernard Groinstein held a smoking cigar between his teeth and pretended to listen while he studied her. He figured this broad was probably full of shit. But her legs weren't bad and those tits were fantastic. "What you're going to need, Babe, is DNA proof," he advised. "With that, we'll pay you for your story, and you'll have this McBride guy doing whatever you want."

"DNA like the cops do?" she asked. "How do I do DNA on this guy, don't I need blood or something? And those tests are expensive. Right?"

"You understand I ain't no scientist. But, yeah, I think so. Maybe we could give you an advance payment of … oh, I don't know, maybe a thousand until you get the DNA results."

"A thousand, huh?" Martha fought to keep a straight face while going giddy inside. *A thousand friggin' dollars! Wow!* "I guess that might be okay … for now," she said. It was going to work. They were going to give her money for this.

"You understand of course, I would need reciprocation up front to advance you the grand," he countered. His florid face bore a sly smile. The weasel moved to sit beside her grinning around the cigar bobbing in his mouth.

"Oh, that kind of reciprocation," Martha replied with a knowing smile. "Well, Bernard let's see the thousand dollars first, then we'll see about getting you … reciprocated."

She walked out of the building twenty minutes later, straightening her dress, putting a check for one thousand dollars into her purse, and shaking her head. Most guys paid her fifty bucks for a straight quickie. Yet Bernie lay sprawled on his couch covered in sweat having just paid a thousand dollars for the very same fifty-dollar special. "Stupid jerk," Martha muttered, yet again amused at how easy it was to control men once their pants were down around their ankles.

However, something greasy Bernie said had her thinking. With DNA proof, the paper would pay her, and she'd have Ian McBride in a bind. That appealed to her from a get-even point of view. He owed her, didn't he? After all, her mother had thrown her away like garbage and kept him. He should have to pay for that. If she could prove she was his half-sister, she might hit McBride up first before going back to Bernie the sleaze. She had to think about this DNA stuff, maybe ask some of the other street girls what they knew about DNA. Martha McDonald was smiling as she entered Chase Bank to cash the check.

She would make the rich playboy pay. Maybe she'd do both, shake him down and get money from the paper, too … Probably needed to ask her lawyer some questions about all of this.

7

You Come Here Often?

Her cheeks and ears felt hot and she was trembling. Paige chewed her bottom lip wishing at that moment only that she could disappear. She kept her eyes riveted on the tabletop and continued sopping up the whiskey she'd spilled with a small, already soggy paper napkin.

Ian stood watching with amused interest as she mopped with one hand and picked ice cubes off the table with her other, clinking them into her now-empty cocktail glass. He placed his hand over hers and saying nothing, stopped her clean-up efforts. She saw a hint of a smile on his face as he lifted her chin.

"My apologies for startling you, I only wanted us to have a drink before we went to dinner," he said in a low voice. He looked intently into the prettiest large, deep blue eyes he'd ever seen.

"What?" she exclaimed. "Dinner … no, I couldn't. I don't, don't even know …" She closed her mouth and her eyes widened. "What are you doing?" He had taken a burgundy silk handkerchief from the breast pocket of his suit jacket and was drying her wet fingers, while still gazing into her eyes. Paige's mind fogged; she wondered if he could perhaps read her thoughts.

"We should probably get your things off the floor—don't you think?"

Yanked back to the moment, she pushed her chair back and leaned over to retrieve the scattered items that had fallen from her purse, as he quietly watched. When she stood a fresh Manhattan waited on the now clean and dry table; the waitress was walking away. Ian lifted his martini glass into a toasting motion.

Paige raised her glass. "I'm so embarrassed. I, uh ..." He placed a finger lightly on her lips stopping her statement and then ever so gently traced her lips with his thumb.

A flash of heat tightened Paige's belly. She could almost hear her heart thudding against her ribs, as something akin to mild panic enveloped her. Was he handsome? Yes. Sexy? Oh, God yes ... although obviously dangerous, she cautioned herself. Or was she just being ...?

"Ready for dinner?" His strong whisper interrupted her internal debate. "By the way, my name is Ian. And yours is?"

He seemed so right, and there he stood, asking her to dinner. Probably just less than six feet tall, tending toward thin, with a tanned face that featured high cheekbones. She was barely able to breath but could not seem to take her eyes off him—strong mouth, an aristocratic nose, and those incredible green eyes. Her stomach was in her throat, insecurities threatening to smother her. Maybe she wasn't ready for this after all. Could she handle dinner with him? *No. Can't. Gotta' get out.*

"Well, Ian," she began hoping her voice sounded firm as she shook inside. "While having dinner with an attractive man might prove enjoyable and interesting ..." She pushed herself upward with moist palms and struggled to her feet. "I'm not prepared to provide ... what I think you believe dinner would obligate me to give." She swallowed hard, turned on rubbery legs and glanced over her shoulder. "Bon appetite, Ian."

Many men would have felt belittled, put down, Ian was only impressed and intrigued. He admired her cute little bottom and shapely legs as she walked away, then smiled and lifted his glass in a toast. "Well played, pretty lady. A cool, classy move."

Shannon watched with substantial interest from the far side of the bar in a figure-flattering low-cut black dress and strappy stiletto pumps. She'd been hit on three times during the past thirty minutes; thought is was merely the natural order of things. It was her belief that women who claimed they didn't try to turn men on were either lesbians, frigid, or liars. She hadn't however let the male advances divert her attention. She'd seen the entire exchange between McBride and the petite brunette. Now, her opening was at hand.

She stood, smoothed the short dress over her hips and walked toward the table where Ian was toasting the departed woman. She stopped behind him and leaned close to his ear. "I doubt a man with your looks gets shot down like that very often," she purred.

Ian took a sip of his martini, turned, and smiled. He'd of course noticed her earlier and suspected she might seek him out. "Are you just curious, or have you come to repair my poor, damaged ego?"

"Oh, I suspect your ego is never easily damaged," she whispered with a smile. "I was just going to dinner, interested in joining me? My name is Shannon."

Her smoky, sultry voice seemed a natural fit with the remainder of the package, but the phone call he'd received earlier that afternoon flashed in Ian's mind like an alarm bell. Bob had said a female reporter knew of a prostitute's allegations involving him, and that the reporter had dropped out of sight. He'd said she was 'a real looker,' a description that surely matched this sexy blonde beauty.

"Shannon, you say?" Ian didn't believe in coincidence. This had to be the subject of Bob's call, Shannon Collins. He decided to give her some rope, play along, and see why she just happened to be in Charleston. "My name is Ian." Her light perfume was intoxicating; a faint whiff of jasmine. "As for me having dinner with you, that's perhaps, a possibility." He shot her a mischievous grin. "Okay, a distinct probability. But, sit a moment and finish your wine."

She took note as he pulled out a chair to seat her, a naturally smooth gentlemanly move. Even his deep voice carried a subtle, but confident seductiveness. He was a charmer, all right. She slowly crossed her long legs and watched his look of approval as he surveyed them.

"So, you were watching?" he asked. "Do you enjoy watching men and women interact?"

She grinned. "Why not? She was very attractive. At least, you seemed to think so. And, you're not too hard on the eyes either, Ian." She canted her head as if to adjust her hair. "As for watching, I usually prefer participation."

"Yes, she was quite attractive." Ian raised his glass with a wolfish smile and clinked it against hers. "However, here's to *our* possible participation and interaction."

Shannon eyed him. She took a sip of the fragrant Merlot and looked over the rim of her glass, comparing his face to those she had studied in the many news photographs. Fixing him with a stare, she said, "I can't decide if she was a fool for leaving or far more intuitive than me." Yep. A silky-smooth charmer—born to please women, and he damn well knew it. "But, it would seem you don't always get what you go after, Ian."

Ian's left eyebrow went up. "Actually, I usually *do* get what I go after. Depending on how much I want it. What about you? Just what are you going after, Shannon?"

"Right now, I'm going after dinner." Her full red lips curled into a coy smile as she pushed away from the table and stood. "Want to keep me company?"

Mark Redding felt strange in the blazer and tie he wore so seldom, but the attire allowed him to blend into the background of the swank hotel's bar patrons. He'd just watched the pretty brunette leave, and was focused on the tall blonde with McBride. *Man, oh man! What a couple of fine looking babes.* He'd certainly endured rougher assignments than being paid to watch a man who attracted such nice looking women. He'd already surreptitiously taken cell phone photos to document the women's presence with McBride, information he thought his New York client would want.

On the way to Charleston he had phoned Billings to say he'd obtained birth records of John William McDonald and that it appeared, he and McBride were in fact the same guy. Billings sounded excited on the phone. Too excited. He had to be up to something illegal. He faxed the birth certificate to New York after he made sure Billings had wired another $2,000 into his business checking account.

Redding had little trouble finding McBride in Charleston, figuring a big shot would be in an upper crust hotel. He'd been right as usual. However, discovering the women factor had been a pleasant surprise, especially if McBride took one with him on his continued travels. A broad would slow McBride down, making him easier to follow.

In his office hundreds of miles north of Charleston, Billings leaned over the coffee table in a well-practiced manner. He now knew where McBride was. Blocking one nostril with an index finger, he drew a long, steady breath through the glass tube, expertly moving the thin cylinder along the small mirror on the tabletop. He luxuriated in the feel of the white powder entering his system. Once again ignoring how cocaine ruled his life, he savored the momentary rush, thinking that next to orgasm it was the most wonderful sensation he knew.

Yesterday, his client, Martha McDonald, had shown up at his office wanting him to obtain material necessary for a DNA test on Ian McBride. He didn't tell her the wheels were already in motion to accomplish her request. He also did not mention it was being done for his benefit and that she would never get what she wanted. Regardless, he obtained $500 from her on the promise that he would deliver the material, while thinking it quite clever to use her money to help pay the PI's fee and bag him some cocaine off the street. Martha McDonald apparently had her own plans to try to get money out of McBride, but Billing wasn't concerned. Stupid, inept whore was nothing to worry about.

Billings looked at the computer monitor and reread what he'd compose; satisfied the message would have the desired impact. He had installed software to make it impossible for his e-mail to be tracked back to him, and he'd bought a cell phone from a street thug for the exchange of conversations he antici- pated with McBride. Almost certainly stolen, the phone couldn't be traced back to him. All prudent preliminary moves for a blackmailer, Richard thought. Yes, he was feeling quite good about his plan.

Paige stopped lecturing herself just long enough to finish her salad and down a glass of Chardonnay. She felt the mental tongue-lashing was in order, well deserved. After all, hadn't she promised herself just a couple of hours ago she would find a handsome man, loosen up, and have some fun? But, when a drop-dead gorgeous male treated her like a desirable woman and asked her to dinner, what'd she do? She'd run ran like a scared rabbit. She sighed, shook her head and held up her empty glass to signal the waiter to bring her another Chardon- nay.

She hadn't eaten in ten hours and was beginning to feel bet- ter when the waiter placed the steaming entree and a replace- ment glass of wine in front of her. The shrimp scampi smelled wonderful and inviting. She picked up a fork, but paused. That's why she'd handled it so poorly. Yeah, it was just hunger, tiredness. With food and rest she would have, of course, handled the situation with him much better. Nothing to do with fear or panic, she rationalized.

She was indeed hungry and the scampi tasted fabulous. She'd emptied her second Chardonnay when she saw the hostess escorting them to a nearby table. The tall blonde had laced her arm through his. Nothing short of beautiful, the woman looked so at ease, so natural with him. As they approached, chuckling about some intimately shared piece of conversation, he pulled her closer. Paige asked herself how he could have found such a woman to have dinner with him so easily. *Because any normal women would have welcomed the opportunity—that's how, you twit!*

Paige was just about to look away when Ian nodded to her with a friendly, warm smile. Her stomach knotted, and her mouth went dry, she was astonished by the pleasure his smile brought. Then, compounding the emotional blow, the tall blonde also nodded and smiled. Her smile, however, was one of feminine victory, sending a clear woman-to-woman message. "You had your chance and blew it. He's mine, now."

That could have been me, Paige thought. But, oh no, she had insured that didn't happen, hadn't she? Looking away from them, she paid her check as quickly as she could, and headed straight to the bar. She ordered a double Manhattan to take back to her room where she would think this through, and hopefully find some backbone.

Paige, you idiot!

8

Rude Awakenings

"Oh, God!" she cried. Janice shook and clung to him, gasping, "Yes … Ohhh, yes …"

Bob collapsed atop her, breathing heavily, still buried deep within her clutching aftershocks, savoring the marvelous prolonged repletion.

"I love you," she whispered into his ear. "I think about us a lot … our future together."

Oh how he'd hoped she wouldn't say something like that again, especially at that moment. He felt his manhood's reactive retreat and wanted to groan. The woman was a master at working conversations around to topics he tried to avoid, marriage in particular.

Not that he didn't care for her … he did; thought she was an attractive, intelligent, woman; he admired her, enjoyed being with her. However, the simple truth was, Bob never claimed to understand the concept of marriage, the giving up of self to become a pair, the blind come-what-may lifetime commitment. Therefore, he'd never told Janice Roark he was in love with her. True, he had dated her for two years, although never exclusively, but he hadn't lied to her. In Bob's view, she had quite erroneously made certain unfounded assumptions on her own.

She was a research librarian whom he had met while working on a complicated legal project. He'd asked her out and things became sexually heated and thereafter increasingly complicated. They had fun together and great sex. However, love and marriage were very different things. Things to be carefully avoided by intelligent men.

Janice raked her fingers through his sweat-damped hair. "Did I tell you about the woman who was doing research on Ian McBride a couple of weeks ago?"

Bob's eyes flew open and he sat up. "No, you didn't. What was she researching? And, by the way, what did she look like?"

"What did she look like? Janice's lips formed a moue. "Why would you ask that?" She brushed hair from his forehead and continued when he said nothing. "Well, anyway … she was tall, blonde, and pretty. The kind to turn men's heads …" Janice's cheeks colored a bit. "You know, big boobs, nice butt, like men love to watch … and touch." She shot Bob an inviting, look and pulled his hand to her bare bottom.

He obligingly massaged her buttocks but pressed on with his questions. "What was she interested in? What was she after concerning McBride?"

"Oh, I don't know. Anything and everything about him, I guess." Janice ran her tongue into Bob's ear. "She seemed frustrated and almost angry I couldn't help her find much about his childhood or his teenage years. I guess that was really her focus since she found a lot of material about his adult life." Janice's hand moved up Bob's muscular thigh. "I thought it strange when she asked me if I knew of any way she could check criminal records, other than the police."

"Really? She asked that?" Bob exclaimed. She was nodding as he sprung from the bed, pulled on his pants, and reached for his other clothes. "Ah ... I have to run."

"Why?" she queried. Her face bore a confused, hurt look.

"Just remembered something ... uh, at the office. Important business. Sorry. Have to go. You understand, don't you?" He was out the door, never heard her begin to sob.

"Ian, that Shannon Collins I told you about ... She's a bigger problem than I thought." The cell connection was not the best, but Bob had gotten through to him, in a Charleston hotel men's room, of all places. "What? She's there—Dinner? Are you crazy?" Bob rolled his eyes and shook his head in disbelief. "Damnit, Ian! She's trouble ..." Bob took a deep breath. "This is your friend and your lawyer talking—be thinking with your *big* head, the one on your shoulders, when you're alone with her." He fumbled for the appointment book in his briefcase. "I'll get to Charleston as soon as I can. Just be careful what you say."

Midnight found Ian lying in bed, thinking. The life and identity he had carved out, created actually, was rewarding ... fulfilling. Today he'd enjoyed productive work, dressed well, traveled interstate from one luxury hotel to another, had excellent food and drink, and spent time with, not one, but two very attractive women.

The beautiful Miss Collins was interesting and he found it difficult to be angry about her deceptiveness. She was straight out of Hollywood Central Casting, a Greek goddess only in a tight black dress instead of a toga. He'd returned to his suite feeling good about their impromptu dinner date and its heated ending. Even though she'd continued to press for information throughout dinner, he had enjoyed her company. He'd simply employed conversational devices he had devised and practiced throughout his life to evade her questions about his childhood and teenage years.

He had walked her to her room, knowing they would kiss and looking forward to it, however, the passionate good night kiss had surprised them both. Remembering they were in a public hallway, he'd mustered his self-control and pushed her to arms length. They stared wordlessly at each other for a moment before she touched his cheek, said, "Good night," and disappeared into her room. Sure, she'd had him stirring with lust, but he was actually relieved she hadn't asked him into her room. She was considering doing so—he'd sensed it clearly. Not following through was telling, said something about her as a person. She might see him as a professional opportunity, but she wouldn't use her body to get what she wanted. Character and beauty. No, she hadn't disclosed her real reason for coming to Charleston, but she seemed otherwise straightforward, not a woman naturally prone to deceit and guile. Only doing her job, he thought ... believed his past would make a marketable story.

But allowing that was unthinkable. He had buried his past and spent two decades hiding its existence. Lives and fortunes were at stake, public disclosure of his other identity would be disastrous. So, naïve as it probably was, Shannon Collins' pernicious agenda had to be ended—he and Bob would derail and end her efforts, whatever the costs.

Ian enjoyed being with women, liked talking to them and exploring their femininity. He enjoyed probing their emotional depths. Girls and women had always seemed drawn to him and he'd experienced more than his share of unsolicited, sexual advances. However, he didn't usually believe in one-night stands, a fact quite contrary to the media image of the jet-setting, bed-hopping, sophisticated heart breaker Bob had constructed. In truth, he was always honest in his romantic dealings; a demanding erection and mere sexual desire not enough to tip the balance for him. No, he saw having sex as special, a valued emotional move, undertaken only when he had significant feelings for a woman—reserved for long-term relationships.

And there was the trust thing. He found trusting women, or anyone for that matter, all but impossible, and he didn't pretend to understand being in love with someone or *being* loved for that matter. Those personal deficiencies had ultimately ended each of his serious relationships.

He returned mentally to Shannon Collins, her potentially destructive objective, and how to approach it? Fatigue won out over contemplation, and he was soon drifting into somnolence thinking about her and the mystery woman with wavy black hair and vivid blue eyes. Miss Mystery was a bit of a puzzle. She'd flat-out turned him down … unusual. There was something about her he couldn't put his finger on, something different … something intriguing. Too bad. He probably never see her again anyway.

It was dark when he awoke. Drenched in sweat, heart pounding, he was disoriented, shaking, and breathing hard. The
nightmares came for no apparent reason. Vivid, repressed memories flooded over him, hideous, vile visions and recollections.
In tonight's installment, he was about ten years old although he
couldn't be sure because his birthday was never celebrated and
his parents had lied about his age when it benefited them. The
scene was another in a series of small, dirty rooms, shared by
three people and visited by a trail of men. The stygian apart-
ments were always cold, stinking of cigarettes, urine and hurried
sex. The floors, covered with torn linoleum were often slanted,
and rattling glass told of the frigid New York winter winds beating against cracked windows brown with dust.

John was cowering in a corner, his hand covering his mouth
with blood running through his fingers. He could smell the
man's fetid body odor, his cheap cigars and the whiskey on his
breath. The man towered over John, scowling down with his
big fists clenched. Almost always drunk, the mean venal, filthy
man was terrifying. John vowed he would end it some day, stop
the beatings, the terror, and the broken bones. Some day when
he'd be bigger and strong enough ... then he'd do it ... Then he
would kill his father.

"Be still, you little son of a bitch. Shut up and don't look,
damn you! How many times I gotta' tell ya'? Ya' dumb-ass kid.
Don't make no noise and don't be lookin' when she's fuckin'
for money. And stop that damn cryin'. Hell, I just split your lip,
didn't break nothin' this time. Now shut up or I'll smack you
good, knock out some teeth, mess up your face."

"Don't hit me again," John pleaded. "Please, I'll be quiet. Won't make any more noise. It was a mistake."

"Mistake? You're the mistake of my life." He burst our laughing at what he saw as a joke. "Yeah, that's you all right, a mistake of a kid your momma never meant to happen."

John drew himself into a protective mental shell. But, he couldn't block out the familiar squeak of bedsprings, continuing on and on, finally ending with the exit of his mother's latest trick.

The red-faced, panting fat man had been gone only a few minutes when she began her daily ritual. The bent spoon, the white powder and liquid … She mixed it carefully while holding the spoon above a Zippo lighter flame. John William McDonald sat on the cold floor and watched her suck the mixture into a smudged syringe before injecting it into her arm. She released the tourniquet on her arm, allowing the heroin into her system, and sighed anticipating the temporary euphoric escape to come. She'd be nicer to him for a while now, might even fix something for him to eat. He hoped so. He was hungry, oh so cold, and his mouth hurt.

"Don't go gettin' your ass all comfy," the man commanded. He belched and sneered at her through broken, rotten teeth. "Gotcha 'nother trick awaitin' downstairs." He laughed, coughed, took a swig from the bottle, and staggered to the dingy couch. "He's a big black buck prob'ly hung like a mule."

"I'm tired and sore." She lit a cigarette and a coughing jag followed her first deep drag. "I'll be plum wore out, 'nother year or two, for sure." Emboldened by the drug's rush, she glared and spat at the man. "You ever gonna' work again, you lazy, good-for-nothin' bastard?

He was up in a flash, hitting her hard in the stomach. "Shut up, bitch, and get ready to spread 'em again." As she doubled over gasping for air, he laughed. "Goin' downstairs to get that black dude. Stupid mother's gonna' pay me fifty bucks to hump your sorry ass."

As the door slammed, John tried to think of anything other than his situation. He thought of school where he felt safe. John loved school, even looked forward to the free lunches the other kids ridiculed. Sure, they poked fun at his one set of dirty, ragged clothes, but that was okay. The teachers were nice to him, told him he was smart, and his grades were excellent.

When the 5:00 AM wake-up call came, Ian had been working at his laptop computer for two hours. He'd found that immersing himself in work usually dispelled the gloom that followed the nightmarish dreams. Hell, he was never able to go back to sleep anyway. He had all but finished an outline for his new book, a tragic, yet sexy Civil War tale he would show to Bob on Saturday when the big guy got to Charleston. Ian clicked *save* and was into his shorts, running shoes and T-shirt within a few minutes. Downstairs, he strode out onto the deserted, pre-dawn streets and fell into his usual seven-minute-mile pace. The air was cool but thick and heavy, promising another steamy summer day.

Her hands groped to find and stop the terrible ringing noise. "Hello?" Paige mumbled.

"Good morning, Ms. Brittany." The absurdly cheery male voice on the other end of the phone continued. "This is your six o'clock wake-up call. Have a wonderful day."

The line went dead and she fell backward onto the pillow. The landing shot a stabbing pain through her skull. A hammer beat inside her head, her mouth was dry cotton, and her tongue was fur. "Oh, my Lord ... what have I done?" Her stomach churned like an angry sea, throwing up was a distinct possibility. Her eyes felt puffy, wouldn't open fully ... Surely, her breath was toxic to all living things. Why had she drunk so much? Why? And wasn't the last one a double? How could a well-educated woman be so stupid?

Six A.M.? Half of her brain had decided to go back to sleep while the other muddled half struggled to register a scheduled reality. *The College of Charleston ... the panel ... today.* Her eyes flew open, and she bolted upright in bed. "Good Lord!" Pain again jabbed the inside of her head. She had to sound intelligent and answer an audience's questions in two hours. "Ohhh," she groaned, grasping her head with both hands, hoping to stop the pounding.

Last night's events started to come back to her ... his beautiful face. No man had ever affected her like that, his sexuality pulling at her like a magnet. A wave of momentary warmth was eclipsed by embarrassment and pangs of regret and missed opportunity. Feelings that had to be the result of the hangover, she told herself. Besides, he was probably gone now anyway. Off to another city, another woman, like that tall blonde.

She grimaced at the thought of the haughty other woman, then sighed, and raked her hands through her sleep-tosseled curls. She'd blown it.

She had to stop thinking about him, focus on today's events, forget yesterday's fiasco and get going. But there was some indefinable something about him ... something special. "Damn. Damn!" She stumbled to the shower feeling nauseous, but vowing that when the next Ian showed up, she'd be ready.

9

A Growing Awareness

She drove her rental car through the main gate of the College of Charleston campus at 7:30 AM, squinting through slitted eyes. Four Tylenol tablets, a piece of dry toast, and black coffee had brought her around. Her stomach was still argumentative but no longer in full revolt and the pounding in her head had been reduced to a slow-pulsing pain. She had foregone her regular morning run deciding it would constitute cruel and unusual punishment. Feeling better, she had donned dark sunglasses and thought she might live after all. She could hear birds singing. Yeah, the day might be okay.

To Paige, The College of Charleston campus seemed a cross between Colonial Williamsburg and a plantation scene from *Gone With The Wind*. The downtown campus covered several city blocks and was surrounded by an old twelve-foot wall. The aged red brick barrier was partially covered with ivy that kept company with dark green moss in the many shady areas. The security guard checked her visitor's pass as she took in the beauty of the main campus road ahead of her. Scores of huge live oak trees formed a colonnade to the three-story administration building at the road's end. Spanish moss draped many of the trees adding to the visual splendor. The administration building, like all the buildings on campus, was dark red brick and sported huge white columns and ten-foot windows. The quintessential prestigious Southern college campus, academically welcoming, yet laid back.

She parked where her guest lecturer packet had instructed, finished off a large bottle of spring water, along with two Rolaids tablets and began walking toward the designated building, briefcase in hand. As she was about to enter, a gleaming black BMW sedan came speeding down the main campus road and stopped in front of the administration building. The college president, a wealthy alumnus, a visiting politician? Needing directions to Dean Richardson's office, Paige didn't pause to find out.

Ian locked his car and walked into the administration building, shooting a friendly smile at the receptionist. Five minutes later, he stood at the back of a small auditorium awaiting the other panel members and his host, Dean Roy Richardson. Many students were already seated, but others were trickling in. Ian estimated the audience of graduate students and seniors at 200 or so, all aspiring writers. He adjusted his blue foulard tie, pulled down his starched French cuffs, and strode down the center aisle toward the stage, where a long table with four chairs faced the audience. The presence of the lean man in the Armani suit didn't escape the students notice, especially the women among them. Some nervous giggles and whispers of "Wow!" and "Nice butt" could be heard as he climbed the stairs to the stage. He liked to size up an audience and had found an entrance was a good way to gauge the mood. This group would not be dull.

"Ah, here he is," intoned Doctor Richardson from behind him. "We have found the other member of our illustrious Romance Writers Panel."

Turning, Ian saw the dean's smiling face and the faces of two people he was escorting. One, a portly, bald, middle-aged man in blue jeans and a Jerry Garcia tee shirt, the other, to his surprise, was dark-haired, petite Miss Mystery who'd rejected him the night before.

She too was surprised, he saw it in her face, but he saw something more … female interest. As nice as he'd remembered, maybe better, her glossy black hair was pulled back into a twist emphasizing her pretty face. Tanned skin that looked soft as silk, a neatly tailored, teal green suit with an above-the-knee skirt that covered but didn't hide her feminine curves—a professional yet subtly sexy and very appealing package.

It's him! Inexplicable heat flushed through her. Lord, he looked even better in daylight. A tingle ran up her spine, and her stomach tightened. Here she was, Miss Puffy Eyes. Probably looked like a frog. But … what was he doing here? Surely, he couldn't be …

"I'm very sorry; we have no time for personal introductions," Dean Richardson said, looking at his watch. "Let's take our seats." They found desk-style nameplates on their chairs, placed them on the table in front of them, and sat down.

Dr. Richardson stood and addressed the audience. "Ladies and gentlemen, we are fortunate to have with us today, as a special part of our ongoing Writers' Workshop, three of the best-known authors of romance novels in the United States. These three cover the genre's span. One with traditional stories from a woman's perspective, another ads the dangers and fears of war to the mix, while the third presents rather graphic tales featuring strong men and submissive women. Since their books contain not just romance but also sex, I will allow more latitude in your questions than I normally would. Nevertheless, let us maintain some decorum. To my far left is Mr. Jeffrey Freeshay, the prolific author of more than twenty novels in the continuing series *Hard Rock and Rock Hard,* novels which reminds us that sex, drugs and rock'n'roll are an inseparable trio."

"It's twenty-three novels, actually," Ian said into his microphone.

"Oh, another fan, I see," Freeshay said, smiling smugly.

"No ..." Ian looked at him and then smiled at the audience. "More a critic of crude writing."

Freeshay's face tightened and flushed as the audience broke up into hoots and applause. Dean Richardson raised his voice over the din and took control. "In the midst of these two rogues we have the lovely Ms. Paige Ann Brittany. With five novels to her credit, including some *New York Times* Best Sellers, Ms. Brittany's novels feature successful, strong heroines who are also softly romantic creatures in torrid affairs with take charge men." There were some lascivious smiles, mumbled sexual comments, and a few low, male whistles from the audience.

Freeshay leaned into his microphone. "Her stories are a bunch of sentimental crap."

Paige bristled and shot him a frosty look. "Well, at least none of my sentimental books, as you call them, have been banned from libraries, nor have they resulted in my being prosecuted for lewd content, as yours have."

Again, the audience laughed and applauded. Ian smiled at her, wet his index finger with his tongue, and gestured as if marking up points for her on a scoreboard.

Undaunted, Dean Richardson pressed on. "And, last, but not least, we are pleased to welcome Mr. Ian Michael McBride, author of numerous best selling, sexy, romantic war stories, and the now famous, TV mini series, *The Flames of War.*"

The audience applauded as Dean Richardson took his seat. Ian nodded to her and lifted his water glass in a mock toast. She felt her cheeks heat, as the previous night's embarrassing encounter flashed in her brain. Still, she smiled and raised her glass in a return toast. Well, how about that? Ian from the bar was Ian Michael McBride, one of her chief competitors. She had embarrassingly botched their first meeting, but could life be giving her a second chance? She felt a surprising surge of self-confidence, and decided then and there to make an uncharac-teristically bold move. She would ask *him* to dinner. Could be fun ... Okay, so he was experienced with women ... no, very experienced probably ... and a little dangerous, most likely. He seemed nice enough ... even though his smile and those green eyes should be registered with the police. She averted her eyes, unable to suppress a grin. Now, if she would only not wimp out.

The program was going well. After twenty minutes, all three panelists were enjoying the spirited question and answer session, verbally sparring with each other and with the audience.

Then they saw her, walking down a side aisle, carrying a pro-fessional looking camera bag over her shoulder. All male eyes focused on Shannon Collins with her skin-tight white Capri pants and snug, overflowing tank top. She took a front-row seat, selected a lens for the 35-mm camera, and turned on a small tape recorder.

Although Paige didn't know her name, she certainly recog-nized the woman. She sighed deeply and looked over at Ian, expecting to see the same empty-headed lustful smile she saw on other male faces in the auditorium. He was indeed focused on the tall blonde, but his cold determined countenance was light years from a smile—a dark, tight-jawed expression that both surprised Paige and made her strangely uncomfortable.

That tears it! Ian was willing to excuse the woman trying to talk information out of him in a bar or at dinner. But this was an inexcusable intrusion into his professional life. He locked his eyes on her. *I'm not tolerating this shit!*

The woman looked up from her equipment bag and directly into Ian's icy penetrating glower. Paige watched the blonde's face go pale as she seemed to actually shrink backward into her chair. The man staring her down was not the suave charmer of the night before. This Ian McBride was angry, defiant, and obviously dangerous.

After a student questioner sat down, Ian spoke into his microphone. "Dean Richardson, if you would indulge me, I would like to introduce someone in our audience." His voice was controlled, almost deferential, but his cold eyes never left those of the targeted woman.

"Well, uh, certainly, Mr. McBride ... by all means."

"Ladies and gentlemen, I direct your attention to the woman who recently took a seat in the front row. Yes, you miss." His arm extended, pointed directly at her. "She is not one of you, not a C of C student, nor is she one of us. Not an author. Please stand, miss."

"What?" Shannon's jaw dropped. "No, I was just, uh ..." Her face flushed. She looked like a child caught with her hand in the cookie jar, but she seemed to realize she had no choice.

She slowly stood, clasping her hands together, color rising in her face, pearls of sweat on her forehead.

"No, this woman is a member of the Fourth Estate, a freelance journalist and photographer who has been ... well, stalking is perhaps too harsh a word. Let's say, following and secretly photographing me for several days and in several states. Meet a real live member of the ambush press. Meet the paparazzi's own Miss Shannon Collins."

The auditorium was totally silent and Shannon appeared stunned. After a pause, the audience began to murmur, some pointed their fingers, and a few booed. Shannon looked to her left then her right, as a deer caught in headlights.

"Perhaps Miss Collins would address the topics of surveillance techniques and journalistic ethics for us," Ian continued. A growing chorus of epithets boos, and jeers rained down on Shannon. Dean Richardson looked questioningly at Ian, then stood and tried to restore order.

Shannon grabbed her equipment and retreated, no ran up the aisle and out of the auditorium. She didn't slow down until she reached the parking lot.

Paige was shocked and perversely impressed by this man's handling of, no, dismissal of Shannon Collins. He was the classic Alpha male, and unapologetically so. She felt that should put her off and wondered why it didn't. To the contrary, strong, articulate and intelligent, he was a package she couldn't help but admire. Nevertheless, he was not one to be pushed. But, wow, did he ever have style. She felt even more determined to spend some time with this interesting man.

"Idiot," Shannon screamed at her image in the rearview mirror.

Fear and panic were not a part of her makeup, why hadn't she stood her ground? She knew the answer. Ian McBride had knocked her completely off balance, cleverly used the crowd against her. "You just had to sit in the front row, didn't you?" She had known he was smart. Yet, she'd screwed up and given him a clear shot. "Stupid, Shannon." She wanted to hate him but couldn't seem to do that.

She started her car to drive away. Then it hit her. "Wait a minute ... how did he know?" She was almost positive he hadn't spotted her following him and she had told no one she was working on this story. "Damnit!" She pounded the dashboard. Only one person could have guessed ... Richard Billings. But how? She had no reason to think they knew each other. "Oh, no ..." Another thought hit her. He had known last night? Had he known and let her talk, played her like a violin?

She resolved to not underestimate him again. Shannon raked her hands through her blonde hair and felt her composure and control returning. What was he hiding? What was so mysterious in his past? This was not over by any means. She looked into the mirror. "We'll see who has the last laugh, Ian McBride."

By the time Dean Richardson took the microphone to announce the end of the discussion, the scheduled one-hour session had lasted an hour and a half. He was just beginning to thank the panel when the audience erupted in wild applause, shouts and a few whistles.

Ian leaned over to Paige and said, "You think they got their money's worth?"

She smiled, gave him the thumbs up sign, and noticed he was gesturing for her to look to her right. They both choked back laughs. Jeffrey Freeshay was bowing deeply as if taking all the credit.

Dean Richardson thanked them together and separately. "I think the students had a great time—you three gave them one hell of a show. If they didn't want to be writers before, they should now. Don't forget about the faculty reception?"

Paige and Ian agreed the coffee reception with the English Department faculty was dull. Freeshay however, seemed content delineating the subtleties between his writings and outright pornography.

The sun was bright and very warm as Ian walked with Paige toward the parking lot. She stopped and turned to him. "About our first meeting, I feel that I owe you …"

Ian smiled and cut her off. "Oh, yes, I'm still removing darts from my wounded ego. Any chance we could push rewind and do it differently?"

"Possibly," she said coyly, feeling tremendous relief and some curiosity. Had he sensed her discomfort? "What would you change, Mr. Ian Michael McBride?"

"Well, Ms. Paige Ann Brittany," he replied in a mock serious tone. "Now that we've been formally introduced, may I suggest we try going to a first name basis?"

Stroking her chin, she mimicked his serious tone and demeanor. "Done. But on one important condition."

His left eyebrow went up, accompanied by a grin. "And that would be?"

"Although your approach last night had the tact of a velvet steamroller, you were kind enough to invite me to dinner, and I turned you down. In retrospect, my decision may have been hasty, and it was certainly ungracious of me."

"Uh-oh ..." Ian put up both hands in a defensive move. "Why do I feel like I'm going to have more darts in my ego?"

"Because, you're a man. Men always worry about their egos." She was shaking inside but mustered up courage that had previously been evanescent in his presence. "My condition for a first-name-basis relationship is that I take you to dinner ... Tonight." She held her breath. "Gee whiz, Miss Paige." Ian laced his fingers, looked down, and shuffled a foot in a circle. "The nerve of you, you brazen hussy, being so forward with a naïve young lad such as me. Aw, shucks, I might just swoon here in the mid-day sun."

Paige's eyes narrowed then went wide a moment before she erupted into uncontrolled giggles. Covering her mouth, and snorting, she tried to regain control. Still chuckling, she wagged an index finger at him. "Oh, you're bad. You got me good."

"You should do that more often," he said, smiling warmly. "I like that look. Your face and eyes light up when you laugh."

He was holding her by her shoulders and gazing at her with those sea green eyes. Her laughter faded, and her mind began to fog as it had the previous night.

"You are a very attractive, interesting woman." He saw her blue eyes change, growing darker, going dreamy. "I'd love to have dinner with you ... but I too, have a condition."

"Huh?" Her voice sounded far away to her. "Yes, dinner," she said slowly. "A condition?"

"I pick the place. There's a special restaurant I think you'll really like."

She couldn't stop looking into his eyes. His fingers had dropped from her shoulders, now held her hands. "Okay by me," she heard herself say. "I guess."

He raised her hands and touched them to his lips, without breaking the intense eye contact. "Pick you up at seven. Don't forget your credit card. I'm not a cheap date."

Before she could object, or even consider it, he had pulled her into an embrace and kissed her, hard and deeply. Just as quickly, he pushed her away and ran a hand lightly down her cheek, grinning mischievously. "See ya' at seven, Paige."

Dumfounded, she watched silently as he turned and walked away. She ran a finger over her still warm lips wondering what she had gotten herself into.

"What the hell?" Ian stopped abruptly about fifty feet from his BMW. He had been whistling and his stride had more spring than usual. He looked back at the parking lot and saw Paige's rental car pulling away. Smiling, he thought of her shocked look after he had kissed her. He was glad he'd followed that impulse. What was it about her? He raked fingers through his hair, assuring himself that the jolt he'd felt both times he'd been with her was nothing. He'd just been surprised, he argued. However, he knew differently, he'd been pleased to see her, quite happy actually. But he picked up mixed signals from her. She was friendly, had an open smile, yet she was also ambitious, coolly professional, and aloof. Maybe 'aloof' was the wrong word. Could she actually be shy? Yeah, possibly, but he found that odd.

Discipline, habit, and routine took over; it was time to get to work. He slid into his car and headed back toward the hotel with many thoughts cluttering his mind, hazy images of her face, her wonderful laugh, and those deep blue eyes all danced along the fringes of his mind. No, not the hotel; he turned off the main road and headed toward a place he knew where the food was greasy, the coffee great. Comfort food—he would eat, think, maybe jot down some notes.

He ordered peach pie and black chicory coffee. Quickly into the pie, Ian was intently scribbling down plot-line thoughts and bits of potential dialog when his mind started to drift. Shannon Collins ... Savvy, sexy, had all the moves. Then there was Paige Brittany ... not his type at all, he suspected. Sure, she was pretty and intelligent, even interesting in her own way ... but probably one of those focused on the C word. Commitment wasn't his thing. His type of woman knew how to play the social game ... conversation, dinner, entertaining, sexy company, maybe heavy making out, but no dangerous involvement. Some had cursed his attitude, said he just led women on, even called him a tease. Not so, it was just that he'd struck out with long-term relationships, had screwed up every one he'd had. He was wary, weary even of allowing emotions into the mix.

Paige Brittany ... He doubted she had a clue about playing that game, and that could make her boring. Hadn't he circled right back to the point? She was cute but not his type? Besides, they were both leaving town the next day, so that was that. He downed the last of his coffee and shrugged. She would probably be dull but attractive company for dinner. But hell, it would be better than eating alone ... he hoped.

10

Uncharted Waters

Why so fidgety? Why was she feeling so uptight, reacting like a junior high school girl invited to the senior prom? The answer, of course was obvious … Ian McBride. She'd felt ridiculously nervous since leaving him at lunchtime; had tried writing, her normal refuge from stress … proved useless, only added to her frustration. She had to get a hold on herself, needed to redirect her thoughts—how could an afternoon last so long?

She decided to handle something she had been avoiding, a call she'd been putting off for two days. Dialing, she took a deep breath and prepared herself. Sure enough, her publisher, Fred Williams was annoyed she was taking an impulsive vacation, just as she'd expected. He ticked off events that would have to be cancelled or postponed, and talked of potential PR fallout. But she held firm. "No, I don't know where I'm going. I'll let you know when I decide." She was determined to keep the promises she'd made herself, to make herself happy and finally experience sexual intimacy as her novels' heroines.

Paige walked to the window, thinking yet again about Ian McBride, who both intrigued and frightened her. She hardly knew him but found herself wondering if he could be *the* man; was fantasizing about … "Going to bed with him?" she mused aloud. That did it, the nerves and doubts returned in full force. "Come on!" She blurted, berating her twin reflected in the window. "Jeez! Get a grip—you're a twenty-eight year old woman."

She would have been okay if he hadn't forced that hard, fast kiss on her. It just wasn't right, not in broad daylight in a public parking lot. Well, maybe he didn't exactly force the kiss on her. Still, it was wrong of him. However, she knew the truth of it ... He'd taken her by surprise and she had absolutely loved it—thought her knees might melt. Then he just grinned and walked away. She couldn't wait to be with him again, and yet she was afraid.

Her guilty conscience said she should be writing, but this called for thought. She allowed herself the womanly prerogative of spending an inordinate amount of time deciding what to wear. He had only seen her dressed in professional business attire, tonight needed to be different, a non-conservative look. *But not like a slut,* she cautioned. She decided to go for subtly sexy and caught herself wondering what her prudish mother would think of her trying to look that way.

After choosing the dress, she soaked in a bath, which helped her nerves, but only a little. Room service brought up a Manhattan, which she'd sipped like liquid Valium. She'd painted, trimmed, plucked, shaved, or made up every inch of her body until she felt like a harem odalisque. Yet, she still ended up being ready twenty minutes early. Be calm, she kept telling herself.

She jumped when she heard the knock. Taking a deep breath, she opened the door and could only stare. Lord, he looked like something out of a magazine, as if he belonged on a yacht in that navy blazer and off-white linen pants.

He flashed a quick, warm smile. "Hello, Page, are you ..." Stopping mid-sentence, his expression changed dramatically.

Paige watched his eyes, and held her breath, as he put his fist to his chin. Her stomach churned as he looked her up and down in a slow, unapologetic masculine appraisal. Still not speaking, he gave her a turn-around sign with his index finger and nodded as if evaluating a painting. Her nervous system was in overdrive.

Ian swallowed hard. The dress was a short column of some silky red something that slicked her hips and pert breasts like rainwater. Cut high, it was secured by a tiny thin strap behind her neck. The bare back dropped off to nothing from neck to waist, exposing her entire tanned back, confirmed she was bra-less. Strappy high-heeled pumps completed the image, making her long legs look nothing short of delicious. "Elegant. Classic elegance, and with all that flowing black hair you throw in a blast of sex appeal. A man's dream date." He watched her stumbled for a reply, had already decided he liked making her that way.

"Elegance?" Had he said sex appeal? "Uh, thank you." Struggling for composure and attempting light conversation, she blurted, "Do you always wear a coat and tie?"

"Usually. I'm comfortable dressed this way." Ian chuckled, laced his arm through hers, and walked toward the elevator. "Besides, we have to keep up our PR image. Right?"

His BMW was waiting at the curb in front of the hotel. As the attendant opened the door for Paige, Ian leaned on the fender enjoying the way she slid onto the black leather, her shapely calves lifting and drawing into place. They chatted as he drove.

"You seem pretty familiar with Charleston," she observed. "You must come here often."

"I've known Dean Richardson for a few years and have spoken to his grad students a couple of times before." He glanced over at her. "I suppose your schedule is pretty hectic. Where does duty call you next?"

She enjoyed watching him, and turned half sideways for a better look as they talked. How could he always be so relaxed, so smooth, and engaging? "Actually I'm taking some time off for personal R and R, to recharge the mental and emotional batteries."

"Interesting. I'm about to do the same. My publisher just flew in today. We're off to Hilton Head Island tomorrow, about two hours away. Ever been there?"

"No, but I hear it's beautiful; lots of golf and tennis."

"Yep, that's Hilton Head. However, you didn't mention the beautiful beaches. Talk about R and R, it's great to lie on the sand, soak up the sun, and just watch the ocean."

"Well, I'm not sure where I'm going, but I plan to kick back, relax, and pamper myself."

"Whoa, you scared me." He smiled at her. "I thought you were about to add 'and read a good book.'"

"No, that's one thing I'm not planning." Paige smiled. "But, I have read three of yours."

"I'm flattered, I think. But I'll take the coward's way out and not ask for a critique."

"No reason to shy away. You have a unique and original style. I enjoyed them …" She paused. "But I was shocked when you killed off the main character in *Bengal Lancers and Black Satin.* I actually cried."

"I was right." He snapped his fingers, looking pleased with himself. "I had you pegged as a romantic."

Seeing into her that easily made her uncomfortable. But she had sensed sagaciousness in those green eyes when they'd first met. "I think we're both making a good living thinking like romantics."

"Don't try to be slippery. You know what I meant. It was a compliment, not an indictment."

The drive to the restaurant took them about fifteen miles out of Charleston, across a river, and ultimately onto a narrow, unmarked side road. It ran through woods and ended in a small parking lot paved with broken oyster shells, seemingly in the middle of nowhere.

However, the place was peacefully quiet and unlike anything she had ever seen. An osprey swooped overhead and she caught the smell of honeysuckle floating on the heavy summer air. Beautifully desolate, it was surrounded on three sides by saltwater marsh that seemed to stretch for miles, quite a stunning vista, with the July sun still shining at 7:40. It was like a painting with a sort of melancholy intriguing feel, high tide with an orange sun starting its downward arch toward the marsh's edge.

Ian studied her, admiring her petite profile as she stood, shading her eyes against the setting sun with a delicate hand, taking in the view with the concentration of an artist.

"It's beautiful … a fabulous place."

"Yeah, I first saw it a couple of years ago, fell in love with it." He extended his arm to her. "I'm glad it pleases you. Shall we go to dinner?" She looked at him quizzically but said nothing.

Huge live oaks festooned with Spanish moss framed the tiny parking lot, seemingly pointing to a planked, narrow walkway that stretched across fifty yards of reeds to a house on high ground rising out of the marsh. "Is that the restaurant, that little house?" she asked incredulously.

"Yep. Wait and see what you think. You do recall what they say about books and their covers. Right?"

"Okay ..." She grasped the crude handrail and took an uncertain high-heeled step onto the wooden catwalk. "I guess ..."

The one-story, white frame house's exterior with its green shutters and red door was anything but impressive. However, once through that red door, the change was dramatic. A gray-haired, tuxedoed man with a trace of a French accent greeted them, addressing Ian by name. "Good evening, Mister McBride. Nice to have you with us again."

"Thanks, Jules. This is Ms. Paige Brittany."

"Oh, yes. A pleasure, Miss Brittany. My wife is a big fan of your novels."

"Well, how nice. It's a pleasure to meet you, Jules. The place is lovely. Please give your wife my regards."

"I will, indeed. She'll like that."

The manager's finger snap brought a tuxedoed waiter, who also greeted Ian by name. He took Paige's arm, and led them to a secluded corner table. There were only ten tables in the entire restaurant, each with a waiter, an assistant, and a busboy. The restaurant's wall facing west was almost entirely of glass, turning the vast expanse of marsh outside into a living mural. The flickering candles on each table and in numerous wall sconces set off the fine china, sterling silver, and delicate crystal arrayed atop royal blue linen. Highly polished, yet obviously old pine plank flooring made for a dramatic contrast. Judging by the dress, and demeanor of the other patrons, Paige thought this was an exclusively private place, known to few, off limits to most. "Ian, this is quite something. I'm glad I'm taking you to dinner in such a nice place."

"Wait until you try Joseph's special dishes. The man is both genius and devil. Your cholesterol level and caloric intake will skyrocket tonight. But you'll die happy."

Paige grinned. "Bring it on, Mr. McBride. So far, I'm impressed."

"So am I ..." He looked into her eyes, and took her hand. "Impressed and intrigued."

Averting her eyes to buy time was probably cowardly, however, his directness had thrown her, and she needed to formulate a response. Uncertain of what to say, she decided to go her honest reaction. She looked back up. "I'm flattered, Ian. But, intrigued? You? I can't imagine a man like you finding me intriguing."

Not expecting a discussion on this point, he searched her countenance wondering if he'd just seen a hint of insecurity. He looked up at their waiter who had just come to the table. Without consulting her, he said, "James, the lady will have a Jim Beam Manhattan, and make it a dry Absolute vodka martini for me. Thank you."

Without missing a beat, he began addressing her last statement, or was it a question? "Okay, first things first. I say what I mean, sometimes to my detriment. I don't lie to impress women, to curry their favor, or coax them into my bed. Next, I think you are an attractive, impressive woman. And yes, I find you intriguing, in a variety of ways."

She shot him an enigmatic look but made no immediate comment. For lack of something better to say, she tried humor. "Okay, Sir Galahad." Grinning over the rim of her glass, she looked up through long thick lashes. "So you wouldn't lie to me for those reasons, but I'll bet you'd fib to me on some occasions, now wouldn't you, Sir Knight?"

"Of course." Ian grinned. "I'd lie like a rug. Ask me if a certain dress makes you look fat and I'll lie to you in a heartbeat. I'm no idiot. If you said you kissed only Hispanic men, I'd lie to you in fluent Castilian Spanish, swearing to you I'm from Madrid."

He'd done it to her again; she was struggling to stifle a fit of unexpected giggles while trying not to spill another drink in his presence. Control restored, she smiled at him while slowly shaking her head.

"What is it?" he asked.

She paused, and then ignored the potential consequences. "I've laughed more with you in one day than I have with other men in the past year. I enjoy your wit and your sense of humor." She paused again, looked off across the restaurant, and then focused on the menu. "I probably shouldn't have told you that."

Her complete lack of artifice charmed him. Ian was beginning to think he was right about her. Watching her all but hiding behind the leather bound menu, he thought further about what made her tick. She was a paradox, a public figure, a woman who wrote hot sex scenes, yet she seemed shy and uncomfortable with men. Or, was she just uncomfortable with him? "Bull," he blurted. "You're a strong, intelligent woman. Say what you want to say." He paused gathering his thoughts. "You're also independent, cunningly romantic, and stealthy erotic."

"I am not." She seemed to actually recoil. "I'm not those two … things." He was entirely too relaxed and he was making her damn nervous.

"Oh, yes, you are, Paige." He leaned across the table, lowering his voice and smiling with knowing assuredness. "I have more: You're a sensual, fascinating, complex, shy ... fraud." He waited a beat. "Does that insult you?"

She was shocked by his words and bluntness, he had touched a nerve, seemed to be able to see right into her, right through the multi-layered public image Fred had constructed. In two short meetings, he had pierced the façade that had fooled critics, millions of readers and gossip columnist for five years. Why him?

Their waiter returned and addressed Ian. "Are we ready to order appetizers?"

Paige spoke up, causing the waiter to turn toward her. "Yes. The gentleman will have the shrimp cocktail and I will have the fried green tomatoes." Ian just raised an eyebrow and nodded to their waiter.

Her response to his fraud statement was slow, deliberate, and contemplative. "Of course, your appraising me as a fraud disturbs me, but no, it doesn't insult me."

Again, his eyebrow went up, a questioning gesture. "Why's that?"

"Because it's very close to correct." Why she wanted to tell him more about herself, she didn't understand, but she pressed on. "I'm not insulted, but I'm embarrassed you've seen through me so easily."

His voice rose in frustration. "Don't be ridiculous." He reached across the table and gently took her chin in his hand, focusing his eyes on hers. "I understand, even empathize. My public image is also bogus, fabricated by my publisher and his staff. We're both frauds."

She knew what he was about to do, felt it coming and didn't at all want to stop it. He stood, leaned across the table, and touched his lips to hers. A quick spear of heat hit her belly and her heart rate took off like a rabbit. When he ran his hand down her cheek, her nipples turned to hard points pressing against her dress. *Good Lord!* An astonished sigh escaped her lips as warmth blushed her cheeks.

He sat and drew her hand to his lips kissing her palm. She jolted, thinking the sensual gesture might turn her brain to pudding. His were a poet's hands, yet surprisingly rough and hard for a man who worked with sentences and paragraphs. Hands with a touch so warm and tender.

Ian noticed her aroused nipples. He had also felt his own unexpected stab of sexual energy. She had surprised him with a powerful combination of independence and vulnerability he'd never encountered. Emotions were moving in him, feelings he wasn't sure he welcomed or wanted to handle. He wondered if similar confused feelings were pulling at her.

"Paige?"

She looked at him through dreamy eyes, her voice thick and slow. "Yes, Ian?"

"I have strong feelings about something."

"Strong feelings?" she muttered.

"Yes. I feel strongly that we should order our entrées and some wine before we do something deliciously wicked and embarrassing right here on this table."

Snapped back to reality, she began snickering and shook her head at him. "I was right this afternoon. You're bad. But ..." Letting out a long breath, she smiled. "In spite of my conservative instincts and best judgment, I think I like you. I sure enjoy being with you."

Ian Michael McBride was proving to be a bundle of different, enjoyable surprises, and a fascinating man. She took a second bite of the fried green tomatoes, amazed at the wonderful taste. Ordering them had been a whim, a shot at loosening up and trying different things.

"I like hearing that," he said while flashing a smile that she thought was blatantly sensual. "But you take yourself too seriously. You have a great laugh and I can see the fun hiding behind your eyes. I'll confess however, that I enjoy knowing I can make you nervous."

"Oh, is that so?" She shot him a mock scowl. "How can you stand up with that heavy ego weighing you down? You're pretty sure of yourself."

"Oh, I don't know about that. But, you've got me damn curious and determined to figure you out. By the way, how do you feel about Chateaubriand? Joseph's is to die for."

"I give up." She held up her hands. "You're making me crazy with all this analysis. Let's order some food and wine. Don't get me wrong, I'm having a good time. But, you talk about me being intriguing and trying to figure *me* out. Well, that cuts both ways. You're a curiosity also, not exactly simple or dull." She began looking around the restaurant. "That last part was a compliment, by the way. Now, get James over here so I can order entrées for me and the man I'm taking to dinner."

"Yes, ma'am, Miss Brittany." He grinned and saluted. "Right away, ma'am. Will do." He raised his hand, getting James's attention. "Yes, I'm glad you like me. Because I've decided I like you, too, Miss Brittany."

Smiling at him, she said, "How do you feel about Cabernet Sauvignon with your Chateaubriand, Mr. McBride?"

The entire dinner experience had been wonderful, although the bill took her breath away. She remembered him warning her that he was not a cheap date. Thank God for credit cards, she thought.

It was dark when they picked their way across the dimly lit catwalk to the parking lot. Reaching around her to open the car door, he accidentally brushed a hand over her breast. The slight touch sent a tingle through her. He placed his hands on the car, effectively caging her—she could see both question and challenge in his eyes. The feel of his hand on the nape of her neck, ignited heated shocks down her spine, and she was shocked to feel a rush of warm moisture between her thighs. Had she just moaned? "Is this part of figuring me out?" she whispered.

"Sort of, yes ... but it's your turn to kiss me."

Her voice deepened and slowed as she touched his cheek. "I've already kissed you."

"Not so. I've kissed *you,*" he breathed hoarsely into her hair.

Her conservative nature said to ignore the silly, puerile challenge. However, on impulse, she leaned forward and touched her lips to his, intending it to be a light, quick kiss, a measured risk, nothing more. But warm pleasures were coursing through her, and as her lips parted on a sigh, his mouth closed over hers, changing the kiss, taking it deeper. The warning voice was saying, 'back off, it's dangerous.' She ignored it, laced her hands behind his neck, and explored with her tongue. In an instant, she was lost in the kiss ... lost in him, her breath coming too fast and hot sensations swamping her.

She was left feeling weak when he broke the kiss, her breasts felt swollen and she was gulping air. His eyes were serious, his countenance perplexed.

"You do something to me," he said. "I felt it the first time I saw you. But tonight has made it intense." He paused getting his breath. "I don't claim to know what it is ... but it's strong and volatile."

She was shocked by her aroused state, and the old feeling of near panic had return, although not as controlling as it had been during their first meeting. That warning bell was ringing again in her head, but she went with her heart. "I feel something for you, too ... It confuses me, scares me a little."

She had to regain control, needed to find the courage to stop where she thought this was heading. Pushing his arms away, Paige took a few steps. She turned and gave him a firm look. "Ian, I just don't do casual sex. Sorry."

His movement was cat quick. It hurt, surprised, and frightened her when his strong fists clamped onto her shoulders. "My statement wasn't casual." He glared at her. "And I said nothing about sex, Damnit." There was anger and frustration in his eyes and ice in his voice.

"I know, but ..."

"But what?" His voice went louder, sounded angrier. "Look, when I want to make love with you, you'll damn well know it. And it sure as hell won't be casual. You got that?"

Her lower lip was quivering, and the scared look he saw in her eyes hit him hard. "God, I didn't mean to frighten you ..." He felt awful, angry with himself. "But I felt insulted. Paige, understand this ... I would never force you into anything."

Saying nothing, she opened the car door. He noticed her lips were drawn into a moue as he got in and slammed the door.

The atmosphere in the car was chilly during the drive back into Charleston. She sat in silence, mulling it all over. He shouldn't have yelled at her. True, but she was surprised her assuming he wanted sex, would 'insult' him. She conceded that was probably a point in his favor, but still … Contemplation exploded into an angry outburst. "You hurt my shoulders," she blurted. "And you shouldn't have yelled at me." She continued, her chin jutting defiantly toward him. "You're arrogant, presumptuous, frustrating, and egotistical." She folded her arms and huffed.

"And those are my good points." He stopped the car and turned to her. "No, I shouldn't have done or said what I did. It was wrong. I apologize." Without waiting for a reply, he looked away from her and pulled back into traffic.

She continued to brood … and think. He troubled her, this quick-tempered, beautiful man, she hardly knew. Why was he responding so forcefully? She knew she would miss him when they went their separate ways. That was silly, wasn't it? Nevertheless, so many things about him felt so very right. Did she want him to stay the night? No, of course not—what reckless thinking, she'd only known him two days. She should play it safe.

With the car parked in the garage, they rode the elevator up to her floor in silence until he finally spoke. "Has everything in your life always been structured, controlled, and so organized?"

She looked at the floor; that was none of his business. Normally, she would not even consider answering such a personal question, but for some reason she wanted to answer. "Yes, I suppose so," she said with a note of resignation. "My parents sought to create the perfect daughter. They taught me to strive, showed me the values of dedication and hard work. They also smothered me with rules, moral standards, labeled many fun things as sins, made me prim and proper … and suspicious of men."

Ian could see, almost feel the years of suppressed anger … and an underlying sadness. He was even more drawn to her. They had a lot in common, albeit for different reasons.

She didn't regret telling him and she did not want him to go when they reached her door. Surprising herself, she charily said, "It's not like me to say something like this … But won't you come in? I've enjoyed being with you, and I'm not anxious for you to leave."

He had a sense of what it had taken for her to say such a thing. It moved him, but he wasn't sure accepting her invitation was a good idea. He had already lost control with her once, still, he could not say no.

Once inside her room with the door closed, she looked up into his eyes as if searching for something. Was it prudent to take another risk? "I'd like to kiss you." Her voice was barely above a whisper.

Ian stepped backward as if under the force of an unexpected punch. "Oh, Paige …" Shaking his head, he smiled and paused, looking into her questioning blue eyes. "Men seldom use the word sweet, we struggle to even say it. But, you are just so damn sweet."

She took his face in her hands and brought her mouth to his, parting Ian's lips with her tongue. What she had thought would be a gentle, tender kiss flamed into pure passion, a raw needy sensation that was all new to her, scorching through her body like lightning. A hot persistent pulse drummed between her legs as a wave of emotions and sensations washed away her panic, fear, and reserve. She gasped in sharp recognition as Ian's rigid readiness pressed firmly against her belly—felt his hunger and went with it.

Ian pulled her tightly to him and ran his hands up her bare back and down to cup her buttocks, the increasing heat of her flesh almost unbearably arousing. He could feel her petite body trembling, could almost taste the desire in her mouth, and heard her sigh then moan his name. God she smelled good. He wanted to pull that red dress up and take her, right there. But something was screaming in the back of his mind, telling him to show restraint, be patient. His breath was coming in pants as he pushed himself away. Shaking with desire, he held her at arms length, telling himself he was doing the right thing. But that didn't dampen the ache and lustful need to have her.

Her dreamy eyes popped opened. "You stopped," she gasped, fighting to fill her lungs. "What's wrong?" She breathed. Was he cursing under his breath? "I've never felt such ..." She closed her mouth, seeing the stern look on his face.

"You're just not ready," he said. He took a ragged, but determined breath. "Not ready for what I want to do with you." Exhaling audibly, he stuffed his fists in his pockets and muttered another curse. Another deep breath; he let it out slowly. "Paige. I want you want to make love to you. But, as I said earlier ... I will not push you into anything. It's almost killing me, but I'm trying to do the right thing here. I'm not going to force this."

Paige stood flushed and drawing air in gulps. Wasn't she supposed to be the one with the tough decision? She wanted him, desired him ... very much. Yet Ian was pushing her away. *He* was deciding ... and saying no. His caring restraint hit her hard. She could see the lustful want in his eyes, and sensed it must be difficult for him to hold back. Knowing that had her wanting him more than she ever thought it possible to want a man. But she was adrift in uncharted waters—what was she supposed to do now?

Paige plopped down into a chair and raked her fingers through her hair. "I don't know what to say, Ian." His next words stopped her cold.

"Come with me to Hilton Head Island tomorrow. Stay with me for a week. Give us a chance to get to know each other, to let whatever this is between us go where it will. The island is a beautiful place."

"What?" She eyed him as if he'd gone crazy. "I enjoy being with you … really do. But … I cannot … can't just go shack up with you in an island hut for a week."

He sighed and sat on the bed. "First, I thought we'd dealt with the casual sex discussion. This is not at all casual for me. Second, my place is no hut. It's a five-bedroom, two-story house—you'll have your own private bedroom and a private bath. You'll love it."

"Stop. Just stop." She clamped her hands over her ears, and said, "You've gotten me all worked up. I want to get to know you better …" She shook her head. "But I can't just go with you, just like that. It's not me." Her voice rose. "I don't know … You confuse me."

"Come on, Paige." He wanted to hold her, but he kept his hand in his pockets. "Take a chance."

Everything inside her was yelling *no*. "I can't believe I'm even discussing this. Doing such a thing would be imprudent madness." She stood and began pacing, feeling as if she was looking over the edge of a precarious cliff, hearing and ignoring a hundred alarms. She closed her eyes and muttered, "Okay. I'll go." She shook her head again, looking bewildered. "God only knows why, but it feels right to me, like I should let it happen."

It took Ian a beat to absorb it. He had hoped she would say yes, but thought the chances were slim, at best. "You said yes …" He was shocked, surprised. Actually, he was delighted. "That's great!" He crushed her into a tight hug and gave her a hard, fast kiss. His excited words gushed out. "Well, go to bed. We'll meet Bob downstairs at eight for breakfast and be gone by nine. I'm not going to risk kissing you again. I have to go before I …"

She grabbed his wrist. "This has been a confusing, exciting, wonderful evening." She paused. "I'll say this for you, Ian McBride … You scare me a little, but you're sure not dull." She brushed her lips on his and ran her hand over his face.

Her warm touches sent a charge through him and most of the blood in his head straight south. Ian groaned and stuffed his hands back in his pockets. "My scruples could be the death of me. I don't want to go, but for your sake, I'm outta here."

She smiled at his uncomfortable demeanor. "Good night, Ian."

Once he was gone, she fell backward onto the bed, mentally exhausted but feeling so very much alive. Not at all, what she had expected, but oh had she enjoyed the evening. God had she *ever!* She was secretly delighted that he was sexually attracted to her, and that she, a twenty-eight-year old virgin, wanted him, too. Very much. She clamped her legs together and sighed.

This was all unexplored territory. It wasn't that she had *zero* experience with men. A few had tried to get her into their beds, although she never gave that serious consideration. She'd been touched and fondled, and had even done some exploratory reciprocal touching and fondling herself. But never had she experienced anything like tonight; not emotionally or physically. Such heat and intensity and the unquenchable desire for more. And what was she to make of these out-of-the-blue emotions bubbling inside her? There were certainly many more questions than answers. An unsettling, mind-muddling situation, for sure, however, it was undeniable that Ian McBride made her happy. Sleep was out of the question so Paige decided to pack. She stared into a wall mirror, conversing with the woman looking back at her. "What a night. An interesting, handsome, complex man." She grinned. "And, Lord, is he sexy."

She looked back into the mirror wondering what she'd gotten herself into.

11

The Name's The Thing

For Robert Fowler the thought of flying out of Boston's Logan International Airport on a Friday evening was right up there with Chinese water torture or being tied spread eagle on an anthill. He planned to go straight to the nearest airport bar before boarding his flight. He had already spent more than an hour in traffic just getting there. If ... and Friday flying out of Logan, was definitely an *if,* his flight to Charlotte was on time, and if his connecting flight to Charleston wasn't delayed, it would *only* take six hours to get to Charleston. Then he still had to rent a car and get to the hotel, which would take another hour. One could drive more than halfway there in seven hours.

"Thank you, sir." The Delta Airlines ticket agent handed Bob the driver's license he had just shown for identification. "That'll be Gate 47 in the E Concourse. Looks like it's right on schedule. Have a good flight, Mr. Fowler."

This was supposed to be the first day of a one-week, laid back, working vacation with Ian on Hilton Head Island. However, there was the serious business awaiting him in Charleston. He tossed down the remainder of his drink and began walking to Gate 47, chewing an ice cube and trying to whistle. A week on the beach, ocean breezes, women in bikinis and first-class golf was sounding better and better.

Incredibly, Flight 514 left at its appointed time. Bob reclined in his first class seat and began going over the problem in his mind. True, he was looking forward to playing golf and tennis and sunning on the beach, but he was going to Charleston specifically to derail Shannon Collins' project that could damage Ian and his career. There was no reason to believe her intent was to be destructive. However, if she were to somehow find out about Ian's past, the harm could be enormous. Although he doubted she had made any progress in that regard, he wouldn't take any chances.

They had met a year ago at a party. He remembered her being quite attractive. However, he had recently learned Shannon Collins was far more than just a pretty face and a shapely body. She was smart and tenacious, and that scared Robert T. Fowler. He drummed his Waterman pen on the armrest as he thought. Yep, the two different names were the key. As long as she didn't tie Ian's two names together, she was essentially stymied.

He considered the best way to approach her and decided to try a soft sell, perhaps dinner and some drinks. Then he'd appeal to her logic, but on a personal level. That could work, and it might even be enjoyable, too. What harm would there be in dinner? Then, over after-dinner drinks they'd discuss the problem and come to a mutually agreeable solution. Bob closed his eyes, exhaled and imagined how well it would go. Yeah, she would agree to his terms, and then she'd go to his room, where she would probably ask, no, insist that they have sex. Her body would be silky-soft yet toned and firm. She would grasp his ... Bob's eyes flew open. "What the hell?" he muttered.

He felt the color rising in his face as the man seated next to him looked over. "Did you say something?" Bob ignored him. Erotic daydreams? Hell, what was he doing? *God, Get a grip, Bob.*

He asked the flight attendant for a vodka and lime and stared out the window at the tops of puffy clouds. His lips involuntarily curled into a faint smile. Shannon Collins was certainly a looker. There was no denying that. However, this was all about Ian, protecting him. That set him to thinking about their friendship. Neither of them had siblings, and through the years they had grown so close that they felt and acted almost like brothers.

They'd met at Boston College where Bob, at twenty-three, was just starting law school and Ian, a veteran of Desert Storm, was just beginning his undergraduate studies. They literally bumped into each other in the campus library foyer on a snowy day in December. Both dropped an armload of books and responded with a mutual outburst of epithets. A partially finished manuscript Ian had been working on fell to the floor, scores of pages scattering in all directions. Bob began to apologize, as did Ian, while they picked up the pages of what, some years later, would become Ian's second published novel.

"You a writer, an author?"

"No, man, I just mess around with it. Like a hobby, ya' know."

"Bullshit." He was reading a page he'd picked up. "I read a lot and can tell this is good. Any chance I can read the rest sometime?"

"I don't know." Ian's brow wrinkled. "I guess. If you really want to."

"Yeah, I do. That is if you promise to watch where the hell you're going the next time we meet."

"Me? It was you ..." Ian smiled and put out his hand to the man who would become his closest friend and only confidant. "By the way, I'm Ian McBride."

"Nice to meet you, Ian. Bob Fowler."

Bob sipped his drink and savored the nostalgia, recalling how he'd encouraged Ian to continue submitting his manuscripts to publishers, even after scores of rejection letters. Bob took a job as a corporate attorney as Ian was nearing graduation. By then, Ian had become discouraged about fulfilling his dream of becoming a successful author.

A couple of years later, Bob had finished reading Ian's sixth completed manuscript, *The Flames of War,* and he knew it was his best. Without telling Ian, he submitted the manuscript to a subsidy-publishing house and paid to have it published. A few months later, he watched Ian's eyes fill with tears when he handed him the first hardbound copy. He didn't learn for a year that that was Ian's first ever experience with unselfish kindness, and that trust was all but unknown to him, as were true friendships.

They marketed the novel themselves, were obnoxiously aggressive, and somehow made it work. The novel took off, sold six million copies, and led to a TV miniseries for Ian and a prestigious publishing job for Bob. He became Ian's manager, lawyer, and publisher during his friend's meteoric rise as an author, and the two of them became an acknowledged force in the romance novel segment of the market.

As their friendship deepened, Ian revealed details of his childhood and teenage years, and the reason he'd changed his name. One rainy night over pizza and beer, he recounted how his father had taught him to pick pockets and run small-time con games on the streets, and how he demanded that thirteen-year-old Ian bring in money to finance the SOB's warped needs and pleasures. Ian told how he'd learned to skim some of the money before he turned it over to his so-called father. Although he never used or sold drugs and never pimped women, he fell in with an organized car theft ring. By age fifteen, he was spending most of his time either at school or on the streets helping to steal cars.

Bob rattled the ice in his drink and looked at a recent photo of the two of them. He remembered Ian telling him about the last beating at the hands of his father one night when Ian was sixteen. He recounted how it started as it had so many times before, but that night Ian had reached his limit and fought back with a vengeance, beating and kicking the man until he thought he was dead. His prostitute mother stood by half-naked screaming curses at both of them. Ian never saw either of them again and was disgusted to learn his father had recovered and would live.

For the next two years, young John William McDonald lived by his wits and his fists in the Bronx, secretly sleeping in the boiler room of the high school where he excelled academically. At age seventeen, he became editor of the school newspaper and graduated a year later, with a 3.7GPA. A week after he graduated, however, Ian and the entire auto theft ring were arrested—Grand Theft Auto, a felony and his inexperienced, court-appointed attorney persuaded him to plead guilty and accept a prison term.

Ian was sitting in his cell one night when he was handcuffed and taken to the presiding judge's chambers. The judge, a plain-spoken man who believed that criminals should be punished for their crimes, said John's high school principal and no fewer than three of his teachers had interceded on his behalf. They had told the judge about John McDonald's background, his excellent grades, and pleaded for him to be given a second chance. The judge made young John McDonald a one-time, take-it-or-leave-it offer, saying it wasn't open to debate or revisions—he either took the deal or would go to prison for five years.

The proposal was unorthodox but simple: The judge would emancipate him, legally making him an adult. He would officially change his name and immediately enlist in the United States Marine Corps for a period of four years. Finally, The judge warned he would be monitored ... any crime, any arrest, he would be returned to serve his full prison term in New York. However, if he stayed out of trouble, all facets of the proceeding would be sealed for twenty years and his entire criminal record would be expunged.

He chose *Ian* for his first name after his favorite author, Ian Fleming and Michael as a middle name simply because he thought it sounded cool. For his last name, he looked to his English teacher, Mrs. McBride, who had encouraged him and praised his writing. At 10:37 PM that night, John William McDonald ceased to exist, and Ian Michael McBride was born. With the judge's influence cutting through the red tape, Ian was sworn into the U.S. Marine Corps the next morning.

Once he started basic training at Paris Island, South Carolina, and realized he was going to live through it, he grew and matured. He said becoming a Marine had changed, reordered his life, made him a fit, self-confident and ordered individual ... gave him self-respect. The Corps transformed him into a man, one of honor and inner strength.

12

Just A business Dinner

Bob made the call on his cell while waiting for his luggage to appear on the carousel. The plane had arrived in Charleston on schedule, and he thought the timing would work out well for a dinner. "Hello," she answered. He asked if she had plans, reminding her they had met in New York one night when she was with Richard Billings.

His name didn't ring a bell with her. She barely remembered briefly meeting him, had only an overall favorable impression and that he was maybe tall, large. She wondered briefly how he knew she was in that hotel. However, she was desperate for information about Ian McBride's past, and he'd said he was Ian's friend and had some information she needed to hear; she accepted his invitation. Could his being in Charleston be mere coincidence? Not likely.

She picked an electric blue dress cut high in front, not paying much attention to her choice since this was only a business dinner where she would be interviewing Robert Fowler. She was checking herself in the mirror when the knock came at precisely eight o'clock. Shannon braced herself for a necessary dinner and a boring man. She pasted on a smile and opened the door.

Her breath caught in her throat at the sight of him. *Oh ... my ... God!* He was huge, well over six feet and built like a bull with chocolate eyes and thick blond hair. There was a gut-slamming sexuality about him that any woman would have notice instantly—strength and power covered him as well as the obviously expensive suit he wore.

"Shannon, I'm Bob Fowler."

"Hello, Bob." She extended her hand to shake his, but she could not seem to stop staring into his dark eyes. "It's nice to see you again."

Instead of shaking her hand, he brought it to his lips while looking into her eyes. "A pleasure, Shannon." He smiled. "By the way, you look lovely. I like the dress."

"Thank you. Shall we ... uh ... go down to dinner?" The touch of his lips on her hand and his rugged good looks had gotten to her.

"This your first trip to Charleston, Shannon?"

"Huh? Uh, yes ... my first trip."

As they walked toward the elevator, he placed his large hand at the small of her back, a move that seemed natural yet subtly controlling. She tried to ignore a chill that went up her spine. When the hostess led them to a table, she felt his arm glide through hers as he led her along. Their drinks arrived while he made small talk about Boston and airport traffic. She watched his intense eyes over the rim of her glass of Chardonnay. His smile could be classified as a lethal weapon. He had all the qualities that cause women to make mistakes, made them eager to make mistakes—good thing she knew the pitfalls of men like him.

Bob's memories of her had been accurate, a walking sexual fantasy. But his private investigator's report was also correct;

this was no empty-headed blonde. However, as long as he kept protecting Ian's best interests in mind, why couldn't he enjoy being with her? He smiled inwardly. Any man looking at her would have difficulty keeping anything in mind. Well, except the one obvious thing.

They ordered appetizers, and Bob told the waiter they wanted some time to talk before they chose their entrées. "So, I understand you're working on a story featuring Ian McBride?"

"Yes, I've been doing research for a while, but no writing yet. You two are friends?"

"Yes, close friends, and we also work together."

"You've known him for quite a while then. Did you grow up together?"

He grinned at her question. "Yes and no."

She gave him an indulgent smile. "Explain, please."

"We met at Boston College about twelve years ago, just after he got out of the Marines."

Disappointed by his answer, she feared another dead end. "I haven't been able to find much background about his youth. What can you tell me about his childhood?"

"I'm not going to be able to help you there. He's pretty closed-mouth about his personal life. Truth is I was hoping to get your cooperation regarding your research in that area."

"My cooperation? You said you had some information about him you wanted to give me."

"No, I didn't say that. I said I had something you needed to hear about Ian."

"And what kind of *cooperation* do I have to provide for you to share this information I need to hear?"

"Look, I know what you're up to. I'm aware you've been working on this story for a couple of months, and the angle you're pursuing because I have a strong vested interest. I also know your work history; know you graduated from Yale near the top of your class; know you're honest and you're good at what you do."

Her hands curled into fists under the table. "You checked up on me?" She struggled to hold her temper. "My background is none of your business, and I resent you poking around in my private life."

"Understandable. Poking around in Ian's past and spying on him would seem to fall into the same irritating category. Wouldn't you agree?"

Her eyes narrowed, her white-knuckled fists were now on the tabletop. "It's different, and you know it!"

"No, it's the same," he said in a calm matter of fact voice. "Look, I'm not critical of you or your work. I disapprove only of your current project, and you must stop."

"How dare you?" She glared at him, his message, or threat clear. Leaning across the table, her voice went cold. "You son of a bitch," she all but snarled the words. "No one tells me what to do. Screw you, Fowler."

He lifted a brow and smiled. "Any time you like, Shannon. Any time at all."

"You arrogant ass!" She was pushing away from the table to stand when he grabbed both her wrists with a grip like steel bands.

"I'm going to apologize for prying into your background." He looked directly into her eyes. "But I won't let you damage Ian's reputation, life, or his career with some sleazy, bullshit story. Now sit down and listen to me."

She saw the challenge in his dark eyes. Never being one to turn her back on a challenge, she sat down and a bit of anger left her voice. "For someone who wants my cooperation, you're being very unfriendly."

He put a hand under her chin. "Ian told me he had dinner with you and found you to be a very interesting woman. I think I agree with his appraisal."

She wanted to pull away, but didn't. "Your appraisal of me is not the issue." She shot him a chary but curious look, unable to ignore how his touch and his voice were affecting her. "I want information about Ian McBride and you have it."

He leaned toward her, his large hands covering hers. "Are you always all business?" His mouth curled into a smile and his gaze went first to her eyes then to her lips and lingered there, a look as powerful and as physical as a kiss. "Most women think I'm a splendid conversationalist and enjoy my charm and masculine magnetism."

Egotistical bastard, she thought. However, he did have style and that made a difference in her book because she believed arrogance as such was not necessarily bad. Men who were devoid of style gave it a bad connotation and made it unacceptable. "Who said I was all business? You do have your share of masculine magnetism." She felt his thumb rubbing languorous patterns on the back of her hand.

"I think it's working."

"What's working?" she asked.

He looked down at his thumb moving lightly over her hand. "The magnetism."

Warmth was rising within her. The clever jerk knew exactly what he was doing to her. She leveled a seductive smile at him—time for a counter-attack. Shannon speared half a shrimp and dipped it in cocktail sauce while slowly licking her lips.

Then she extended the small fork toward him. "Want a taste, Bob?"

The blatant double entendre hit him like a fist, sending an instant bolt of heated arousal below his beltline. "I uh ..." He cleared his throat to steady his voice. "Lucky me ... I've imagined how good you ... yours might taste. We men, uh ... appreciate luck, you know."

She shot him a coy smile, knowing she'd gotten under his skin. "You mean you men are always hoping to get lucky, don't you?"

"Getting lucky with you wouldn't bother me a bit." He paused and smiled. "First, however we need to negotiate a truce of some sort. Otherwise I'll have to continue to keep an eye on you, for Ian's sake."

"For Ian's sake?" She cocked her head and grinned. "Uh huh ... Right." He was conceited and overbearing, and it irritated her that she wasn't still furious with him. Instead she was finding him increasingly desirable.

When he squeezed her hand and dragged a finger across her palm, another charge fired through her. "I'm still angry with you. I'll just wait for the right time to show you."

He adopted a hurt look. "Spoil sport."

What was going on here? She was used to controlling the social dance with men, and always steered things. But she was feeling strange emotional tugs and Bob Fowler was taking control of the dance. Yes, she was attracted to him and wondered how he might be as a lover, but she thought that putting a curious toe into this sexually charged water could end in an emotionally deadly whirlpool.

"Bob, I'm enjoying this banter as much as you are, but give a girl a break. Get us some wine, and let's order the main course before I starve to death."

"I think I'm starting to like you, Shannon. I especially enjoy you frustrated and turned on."

"I'm neither of those things."

"Oh, I believe a woman of your poise seldom experiences those emotions. But for you to say you are not feeling both now … Well, we both know that's BS. How do you feel about a good French Merlot, Shannon dear?"

She harrumphed. "Merlot is fine. If I'm frustrated, it's because you still haven't answered my questions about McBride. That's all. No other reason."

"Uh huh, sure," he said as if distracted. He looked up from the wine list, his eyes serious. "About Ian … He's a man of integrity and honesty, dedicated to his craft, and the quality of his work. Speaking for him, I can say he's worked very hard to establish his career and his reputation; and he, no *we*, would be displeased with anyone knowingly damaging either." Then his look softened. "He's a good man, Shannon, and he leads a clean life." He paused. "I give you my word." He squeezed her hand again.

"You said 'speaking for him'." She eyed him with suspicion. "Are you his attorney?"

"And his publisher and business manager; he's also my best friend. We're like brothers."

Surveying his face for warning signs, Shannon searched his eyes for deceit, found none. She was still unnerved, but now wondered if he had intended to sound threatening at all. "Bob. I'm even inclined to trust you, although I'm not sure why." She let out a long, slow breath. "So, tell me the truth, why are you asking me to back off my Ian McBride piece?"

"How would you feel about me answering that over a bottle of champagne in my suite? Perhaps there are also other things we could talk about."

So he was making his move already. She gave him a cautious but not at all negative look. His self-confidence and ego were the size of Nebraska. She smiled, wondering if that size applied to other parts of him. "You don't back off, do you?"

"Nope. Not when my interest is piqued."

"So I pique you, huh?" Shannon decided to show him he wasn't the only one with a determined personality. "Champagne sounds good. Lead the way."

13

Well, Maybe Just a Taste

She understood being wanted by men as well as she understood her own desires. However, high standards, professional and personal ethics and making good choices were important to her—Shannon wasn't the promiscuous woman she assumed some believed her to be. It wasn't that she didn't enjoy sex, she loved it, but with one big qualification. It was on her terms or not at all. Choosing the right man was vital, and she was usually quite skilled at doing that, Richard Billings being her most glaring error. In addition, she saw to it that *she* was always the one to decide on the when, where and how. However, most men she met weren't intelligent or attractive enough to even bother ... before tonight and Robert T. Fowler that is.

He stood beside her in the hotel elevator. Her eyes trailed over him and she breathed in his warm masculine scent remembering it had been two-and-a-half long months since she'd been touched by a man. Bob was smart, charming, and handsome, but things had progressed so quickly, so unusually. Something aberrational had been happening that evening. She'd been with him less than three hours and he had already made her furious ... suspicious and curious as well. He seemed straightforward but was complex, and she didn't know quite what to make of him or the inexplicable draw he seemed to have over her. She looked down at the bottle of champagne and the two flutes he held. They were on their way to his suite, and there was no denying why they were going there.

This was anything but normal for her. She told herself she was in control, reassured herself that her personal standards were intact. His suave ways and raw sex appeal were irrelevant considerations. *She* had chosen him. Right? No, that was a self-serving load of defensive crap—truth was he had hit her libido like a runaway locomotive and surfaced emotions she knew were premature and shouldn't be there. And all he had to do to get her up to his suite was ask. She didn't understand it, yet there she stood feeling an almost obsessive desire to see him naked. How had he taken control and why didn't she care? She knew why, it wasn't rocket science. She wanted him, pure and simple; wanted to run her hands over every inch of him. Yes, Bob Fowler had an inexplicable almost aphrodisiac affect on her. But she planned to be coy, would stay under control and give him no indication of her feelings.

"You sure seem pensive," he said. "What's going on in that pretty Yale-educated head of yours?"

"Uh ... just thinking." She looked into his eyes, unthinkingly running a finger over his hair, and then yanked her hand away as if touching a flame. What was she doing? She averted her eyes downward only to see a growing distention in the front of his trousers. She gulped, glanced away. "Just mulling over questions," she stammered. "... About McBride."

"You could go to hell for lying." He gave her a wolfish smirk, but swallowed hard, working to ignore the flare she'd sent through him by merely touching his hair. Where was his control? He cleared his throat. "What you're thinking about has nothing to do with Ian."

He shifted uncomfortably, reminding himself that pacing was essential to bedding women. Hopefully she hadn't noticed his arousal. Letting her know she could affect him so easily played into her hands, ceded a degree of control. Oh, but she did affect him. What was it about her?

He opened the door to his suite and guided her in. "How do you like it?" He watched her lips curve into a knowing smile as he locked the door, and then spread his arms encouraging her to look around. "What do you think?"

Her room was nice but Bob's suite was lavish. "I think you're trying to seduce me, that's what I think." She'd meant for it to serve notice that she was in charge, but the only change in his expression was a raised eyebrow and a confident smile.

"And you accused *me* of being egotistical and arrogant," he said, folding his arms and canting his head. "Besides, you know we've both been in the process of seducing each other."

She shot him an enigmatic smile feeling both irritated and aroused by his sangfroid. Although still puzzled by her flagging control and aberrant behavior, desires and anticipation were building in her like steam in a teakettle. She chewed her lip as he busied himself opening the champagne. By the time he turned with two glasses of bubbly, her last vestiges of self-restraint had vanished. Her rapacious fingers seemed to move on their own, loosening his tie and working the buttons of his shirt. Impatience had her exploring lower, one hand grasping that now prodigious bulge in his trousers while her other moved to cup and caress below it. His deep groan made her tremble.

Bob ground his teeth and fought for control under her heavenly ministrations. Damn, if he didn't stop her soon he would

… Champagne splashed as the flutes he'd been holding hit the lush carpeted floor. Without even a kiss, he ripped down her zipper. He heard her moan, felt her shiver as he pulled her dress and bra down to her waist. But her eyes remained locked on his, her fingers fisting his shirt. "Jesus," he exclaimed. Her symmetrical feminine splendor was stunning. He could barely breathe. "What a body you have."

Her hands tore at his shirt. There was a rip, he saw a button fly, and heard her gasp in awed delight. She raked her nails through the hair of his chest, tracing ridges of hard muscle.

"Oh, my," she muttered almost reverently. "So fine …"

His mouth crushed down on hers until she was reeling. Pulse rates spiked, breathing became ragged, and clothes soon littered the floor. They fell together onto the bed in a frenzied tangle, sharing a hot branding kiss that drove them both faster and farther than either had expected.

He had lowered his face to her breasts, his tongue and teeth doing wondrous things when she felt a large warm hand skim over her belly and go lower. "B—ob!" She sucked in a gasping breath, as he tantalized and probed for just the right spot—found it. "Th—ere. Oh … God." She was panting and shaking, realized she was not being coaxed but driven toward the peak. His incredible moves had it approaching so quickly … so sharp and strong.

Her spine suddenly bowed then abruptly straightened, her heels dug into the sheets, and her mouth fell open in a silent scream. She shuddered, jerked, and moaned against him, riding the jarring marvelous spasms to breathless repletion.

Watching her come had ignited a primal firestorm within him—erased all control—there would be no finesse. He rolled atop and pinned her wrists above her head. She cried out as he plunged into her, but she held on and pulled him deeper. She arched up and they moved together her meeting his thrusts with her own, each taking greedily racing toward the mutual finale both so wanted. She soon tensed, shuddered, and cried out beneath him moments before he clutched her shoulders and followed her over the brink in bursts of groaning triumph.

Bob sagged against her, content to be drowning in her feminine scents. He lazily stroked silky blonde hair as he kissed and nibbled on her neck and ear. Neither spoke for some time as they lay embraced, quiescently sated, getting their breath back.

"You still alive?" she whispered into his ear. He didn't answer but she saw his foolish grin of pure male satisfaction and broke into laughter.

"That was one hell of a ride," he said, pushing himself up on an elbow. "I can barely move."

"Same here. Not exactly what I expected from a stuffed-shirt Boston lawyer and publisher." She smirked. "So, I wore you out, huh?"

"Just wait. We'll see who gets worn out."

Her smirk morphed into a self-assured grin. "Yeah, you macho men," she taunted. "Lots of big talk with no real follow-up action."

"You've obviously been with inadequate men, sweetheart. I'll have you begging for rest within an hour," he said.

True to his word, an hour later, Shannon was covered in sweat and dazed from repeated bouts of mind-blowing pleasure. She looked into his determined eyes, trying not to whimper. "Good Lord. Again ... all ready?" And so it was. She soon collapsed, blissfully sore, limp as a rag doll, and bewildered.

After their first round of passion, Bob had changed things dramatically. He was tender, showed infinite patience and a wide variety of pleasurable techniques. She'd lost count of orgasms, but knew for certain she had never been with a more skilled lover. And stamina? Lord, his stamina was scary. Wonderfully, deliciously, scary. But far more important was that she had no doubt his goal was to satisfy her.

Oh, he enjoyed it too, she saw to that. But he insisted on bringing her to climax before taking his pleasure, each time delaying and subordinating his needs to hers. Very telling, in her view ... Shannon's experience was that if a man was selfish, it would always show in his lovemaking. Drifting in sweet lassitude, she smiled up at him and ran her hand over his sweat-dampened stubble. She liked the comfortable, masculine feel of him, physically and otherwise. The draw was undeniable, the sex wonderful, but something else was also going on that left her unsettled. She did like him and unwelcome emotions were tugging at her, worrisome feelings she'd long guarded against.

He swatted her bare bottom just hard enough to draw a yelp. "Shannon, darling, I think I could grow to like you. Maybe a lot." Aside from their lovemaking, he'd decided she was somehow special, and that he wanted to get to know her. "Come with me to Hilton Head Island for a week."

"What?" Angry and obviously insulted, she spit a reply at him. "Why, because we're good in bed? You give me a roll in the hay and I'm supposed to go all starry-eyed and trot off to an island with you?" She glared at him. "Think you've sized me up? Well, forget it; I'm literally not that kind of woman."

The sharp rebuke stung. "That didn't come out right. Wasn't what I was trying to say, at all. Hold on, hear me out." He paused. "We could spend time together, doing things. I'd like that. It would give you a week to get to know Ian. Maybe we could work a deal for some kind of exclusive piece that would benefit both of you professionally."

"That's bull, and you know it. The man hates the sight of me. I don't think a week of cozy with Ian McBride is in the cards, island or no island."

"You don't know him like I do." He was thinking as she spoke, glad she hadn't said no, completely. He tried again. "Question one is, how would you feel about spending a week there with *me?*"

"I think you can guess the answer to that." She was tempted and having second thoughts. "But getting McBride to stomach me is another issue altogether. He doesn't trust me any farther than he can throw me."

"Say yes to a week with me on Hilton Head, and I'll take care of negotiating a truce between you two ... one that will allow all of us to have a pleasant week."

It could be pleasant, and it might be her best chance to learn about McBride. She gave Bob a chary smile. "Of course, I'd love to spend more time with you, and Hilton Head is a beautiful place. But, I just don't think ..." Questioning her judgment, she relented anyway. "Oh, all right. It sounds like fun." She waggled a warning index finger in his face. "But, if there's no truce with McBride, it's no Shannon on Hilton Head. I'll leave. I mean it."

"It's a deal. Breakfast at eight o'clock tomorrow morning." He shot her a lascivious grin. "Now, come here, woman. All this talk has rejuvenated me."

"I should go to my room," she equivocated. Trying hard not to, she smiled anyway. "We both should get some sleep." She didn't dare let him know how much she wanted him again or about the disturbing emotions she was feeling. She sank into his arms with a smile and a thought, *Never, never, challenge this man's sexual prowess again.*

14

Off to Hilton Head

"What?" Ian couldn't believe his ears. "You've got to be kidding me."

Bob grimaced and made a hold it down sign with his hand, glad the hotel coffee shop wasn't crowded. He'd requested a corner table, hoping it wouldn't go this way, but suspected it would. "Now Ian, calm down," he said without looking up, all the while stirring his coffee. "Why would you say something like that?"

"Oh, this is rich ..." Ian shot his friend a wry smile and continued, "You call to warn me, saying how dangerous this woman is, and you end up in the sack with her the first night you're here? That's beautiful, just beautiful."

"I didn't say I slept with anybody." Bob's eyes stayed riveted on his coffee, continuing to swirl the spoon.

"You don't have to. That shit-eating grin on your face says it for you. I can only imagine she was fantastic." He smiled. "Come on, give. Let's have the details."

"Damnit, Ian, I'm not doing that, and I haven't said anything about sleeping with her. I only said that Shannon Collins is going to Hilton Head with us."

"Spoken like a true lawyer, Bobby boy." Ian rubbed his chin as if in deep thought. "Wasn't there a movie called *Sleeping with the Enemy?*"

"Okay ... enough already, asshole." Giving him the finger, Bob was forced to chuckle. "Little guys aren't supposed to pick on big guys—screws up the natural order of things."

They talked for another fifteen minutes about Bob's dinner with Shannon and her interest in Ian's past, both men agreeing that must remain off-limits. Ian explained the incident at the College of Charleston and his anger with her. Bob smiled and wrote it off to poor judgment on her part. He said he thought she was honest and could be trusted. Ian remained suspicious, but admitted he had noticed indicators of character in her. Ultimately, they settled on terms to allow Ian and her to get along. A truce with mutual respect but no apologies required. They would explore the idea of her having a series of informal, yet restricted interviews for a possible media bio piece.

Thinking turnabout was fair play, Ian waited until Bob took the first bite of English muffin to announce that Miss Collins wouldn't be the only woman accompanying them to Hilton Head. He only grinned as Bob's eyes goggled, and he almost choked.

"Paige Brittany," he croaked. "What the ... Where'd this come from? Hell, she's a major competitor of ours."

"Don't tell me you're about to admonish me about another woman who could damage my career," Ian countered. "As I recall, you cautioned me to think with my *big* head, not the other one." He smirked. "Which head was guiding you last night, Bobby ... when you had Miss Collins for dessert?"

Bob was raising his hands in surrender when the two men noticed her enter. Paige looked pretty and fresh in navy slacks and a yellow silk top, the morning sun casting almost blue high-lights in the silk of her wavy black hair. Bob, who'd never met her, saw a smile sweep across the petite woman's face and her large blue eyes go bright when she spotted Ian. He flashed Ian a look of male approval along with a wolfish smile, and silently mouthed *"Very nice."*

Both men stood Ian seated Paige and handled the introductions. Curious, Ian glanced at his watch. Exactly eight o'clock. He grinned, remembering Paige's admittedly regimented lifestyle. Hell, she probably made daily outlines for her writing.

Paige and Bob seemed to hit it off from the start. Their conversation about writing and the publishing business was in full swing when …

Shannon entered the coffee shop dressed in tight pink shorts and a white tank top with a plunging neckline, instantly capturing every male eye in the place. Ian saw Paige go tense as Bob stood to greet the tall blonde.

"Shannon, this is Paige Brittany," Bob said. "Paige, meet Shannon Collins." The women said nothing only nodded coolly. Bob's left eyebrow rose.

"We've met, so to speak … acquainted," Paige finally said.

"Uh huh," replied Shannon.

Ian looked from one woman to the other, musing about the tensions that often seemed to exist between women. Paige's lips were set in a tight plastic smile and Shannon had that edgy look beautiful women get when there's another attractive woman in their proximity.

Shannon looked at Ian, wondering what Bob may have told him. She was both puzzled and surprised to see Paige. Eyeing her with the two handsome men, Shannon was suddenly awash in inexplicable jealousy. She'd subordinate the little sylph to her proper place. "Why, if it isn't Little Miss Muffett, the drink-spilling klutz … Looks like things have improved for you, dear, after that embarrassing bar episode Sunday night."

Uh-oh, Ian thought. He and Bob exchanged glances. Knowing Paige's conservative shy nature, Ian wondered how she would react.

"Ah yes, the famous Shannon Collins," Paige countered, her jaws taut, eyes suddenly narrow and dark. She stepped resolutely toward the taller woman. "The stalker with the camera bag," she added with a syrupy smile. "And, oh yes, those strong legs …"

Taken aback, Shannon unthinkingly looked down at her legs. Ian's brow wrinkled. *"Strong legs?'* he thought. Both men just stared, waiting for the next shoe to fall as the two women glared at each another.

Paige was churning inside. "Yes, gentlemen, strong legs I last saw sprinting up an auditorium aisle to escape boos and jeers of an angry crowd." Paige smiled sweetly. "I do so hope that wasn't as embarrassing as it appeared, *dear.* But, my, can you run when times get tough."

"You self—righteous little bitch," Shannon fired back.

The ongoing catfight had turned the coffee shop's patrons into an audience. Bob stood and put an arm around Shannon. "Why don't we just sit and …?" His arm was flung angrily away.

"What's going on here?" Shannon snapped. "Why's Little Miss Muffett here?"

"Miss Muffett, my butt!" Paige all but screamed. "What's this silicone-injected bimbo doing here?"

Shannon bristled—her face reddened. "They're real, dammit," she yelled.

For one brief, foolish moment, Bob actually considered confirming that statement as the foursome fell silent. The women continued to glower and the men looked at each other considering solutions. Finally, Ian spoke up, smiling, as if nothing at all had happened. "Well, since we're all going to Hilton Head together I suggest we have a nice breakfast before we shove off."

Both women's heads snapped around to focus on Ian. Shocked surprise, then grim realization, showed on their faces. They, of course, could leave. However, that would mean forfeiting a week with the men they desired and conceding defeat to the other woman. Acquiescing on the other hand, would preserve the week on Hilton Head, but meant accepting a very uncomfortable situation. Each pondered the situation while all but snarling at the other.

"Okay ladies, enough of this," Bob said in a low firm voice. He was tired of holding his breath and not happy being part of the coffee shop's morning floor show. "You're going to shake hands and agree to not kill each other … at least for the time being." Neither woman moved. "You two are beginning to piss me off. Shake hands." He gave each a hard look and added, "Now, Damnit."

Shannon's eyes shot daggers at Bob, but she extended a tentative hand toward Paige and sighed in resignation. "Okay, Muffett?"

If she calls me Muffett one more time … Paige slanted an icy look first at Ian, and another at Bob, then reluctantly took Shannon's hand. "Okay, I guess … Sprinter."

Breakfast ended without bloodshed, and seemed to have served as a cooling off period for the women. At least the catfight rhetoric had ceased while their mouths were full. They checked out after breakfast. Paige and Bob dropped off their rentals and the couples split up into Ian's BMW and Shannon's Mercedes.

The drive from Charleston to Hilton Head Island took slightly less than two hours but seemed longer with the chilly atmosphere that was carried over from the coffee shop's combat.

"Couldn't you have warned me?" asked Paige. "That wasn't nice … springing the Shannon Collins surprise on me like that."

"I wasn't aware she was coming along until I met with Bob this morning. He didn't know I'd invited you to Hilton Head either until then."

Paige was still not happy with him, nor was she excited about spending a week with bitchy Miss Big Boobs. "I don't know what it is about her. She just irritates me."

"If you'll allow a man's observation …"

"Oh, this should be good," she said. "Please enlighten me."

Ian sighed, but forged ahead. "My experience is that two really good-looking women seldom get along. It's that weird female competition thing."

Paige was amused by his crude insight, although reluctant to consider its potential validity. Was it competition she felt? Could she be jealous of Shannon Collins? *No way!* She was tall, beautiful, and had a body that drove men nuts—not a problem. So what if she drew handsome men like flies? Those assets were no reason for jealousy. Grounds for total hatred, yes, but not jealousy. Then she remembered Ian having dinner with the woman, and grimaced considering he may have kissed her and maybe … Thinking of Ian comparing that body to hers had the old feelings of self-doubt back in full force.

"Earth to Paige, Earth to Paige," Ian was saying. She looked over at him. "You still with me? What are you pondering so hard?"

Paige took a calming breath. "With your healthy ego, I sort of thought you'd see yourself as an expert on women's feelings."

"Uh-oh. Here we go. I'm in trouble again, aren't I?"

"Oh, I don't know about that …" Her insecurities weren't diminishing, she needed to know. "But tell me … was your observation about two really good-looking women perhaps a backhanded compliment? Are you saying that a man would find me to be as attractive as a tall, big-boobed blonde?"

"How'd I get myself into such a mess just making conversation?" Ian asked with a smile. "I feel like a rat in a trap." He thought he saw something in her eyes and his smile faded.

"That's not an answer; I want to know what you think."

Ian swerved the car over onto the shoulder, skidded to a stop in the gravel, and grabbed her by the shoulders. "You're an intelligent, interesting, and pretty woman," he said before yanking her halfway across the console to kiss her. Ending the hard, deep kiss, he pushed her away, forcing her back into her seat, and leaving her wide-eyed. "You have a natural sensuality that you're not even aware of. It's subtle yet very powerful." He ran a hand through her hair. "You and Shannon are not the same types, but the answer to your question is a clear, unqualified *yes*. You match up to her any day of the week in the good looks department."

Before she could regain her wits, he had pulled back onto the highway, crushed the gas pedal to the floor and was looking straight ahead as if oblivious to her presence. Feeling warm, weak-kneed, and a little lightheaded, she'd been surprised by his actions, but was once again shocked by how he affected her. Emotions and questions raced through her mind.

"Thank you," she said in a quiet voice. "It may sound silly …" She paused. "But I like what your kisses do to me. Really like it a lot." She noticed his knuckles whiten, his grip on the steering wheel much tighter than before. She smiled.

"You're doing that *sweet* thing again … and it drives me crazy." He looked upward, as if to the heavens. "I don't know how I'm going to keep my hands off you. But I'm going to."

Her voice was little more than a whisper. "I'm not sure I want you to keep your hands off me, Ian."

"There, right there. You're doing it again. Now, stop it. A guy can't be driving down a highway in an aroused state. It's just not right."

He seemed edgy, fidgety to her, not at all his usual smooth self. This was new, heady stuff for her. And she liked it. Liked him. "I wasn't trying to arouse you."

"I know, I know … and that's just it. Be quiet, look at the scenery, read, do anything. Just leave me be for a while."

She turned quickly to face the window, unable to restrain her smile, astonished *she* could be affecting a worldly man like Ian McBride that way. It was going well with Ian, but so fast. It was a little frightening. But, oh, how she was enjoying it. It was one thing to infuse female characters with such feelings in a novel, but experiencing them was something else altogether. Lord, she'd thought about nothing but Ian the previous night had barely slept at all. However, she had to be cautious, needed to remember she knew so very little about him. It was odd he hadn't talked at all about his past. Most men went on and on about themselves, but not Ian. Instead, he seemed interested in knowing and learning about her, always encouraging her to open up. However, she hadn't really encouraged him to talk about himself, had she? Paige envisioned walking hand in hand on a deserted beach with this fascinating man, having long intimate conversations. She wanted to know all about him, everything.

Driving onto Hilton Head Island was a delightful surprise. It was indeed an island, although only about a mile from the mainland. A concrete causeway running above marshy lowlands connected to a beautiful, yet simple, arching white bridge spanning the Inter-coastal Waterway. The view from the bridge's center was as spectacular as any she had ever seen.

Saltwater tidal marshes extended to the left and right, their grasses bent in a stiff breeze and surrounded by sparkling water that stretched for miles in both directions before emptying into the Atlantic. Smiling people waved from boats with brightly colored sails that skimmed through the water. At the end of the bridge, visitors spilled onto the island's main road, a welcoming, palm-lined parkway with blooming crape myrtle and flowering oleander in its median. Everything was lush and green with not one flashy commercial sign to be seen. Even the buildings' designs and muted colors appeared to blend with nature's plan. There seemed to be manicured golf courses everywhere, with greener than green grass accented by large splashes of white sculpted sand. Huge oak trees with their shawls of Spanish moss and hundreds of palm trees put icing on the inviting visual cake.

Ian turned off the main parkway and drove a mile or so down a tree-lined road, past a small pasture with a few horses, and into a storage facility. He opened one of the garage doors, and there, waiting under a canvas cover, was a bright yellow Porsche Boxster convertible.

Boys and their toys, Paige thought. However, there was no denying the sports car was a thing of beauty, and it seemed to almost ooze testosterone. She watched Ian transfer the luggage and carefully park the big BMW in the garage. The Boxster's throaty racing engine roared to life. Paige smiled—this just kept getting better. They drove away with the top down, her black curls streaming in the wind. And to think she'd almost said 'no' to coming here.

When they pulled up to Ian's driveway, Shannon's Mercedes convertible was already there. That and the sight of the statuesque blonde on one of the balconies had Paige's stomach tightening. But, she'd vowed to be civil, would make a sincere effort to get along and not let Miss Big Boobs' presence spoil the week.

Ian's beach house sat with a few other houses amid grassy dunes at the end of a narrow road in Sea Pines Plantation. The light tan stucco exterior blended perfectly with its surroundings. The wave-stroked edge of the Atlantic, only a few hundred yards away, was accessible via a wooden walkway running above what looked like sagebrush.

The house's interior was done in earth tones, and furnished with obviously expensive but comfortable furniture. The great room had a twenty-foot cathedral ceiling and a wall facing the sea that was almost entirely glass. The view was spectacular. Paige surmised there had to be a housekeeper; the kitchen was fully stocked and a large arrangement of cut flowers was on the coffee table by a stone fireplace. Yes, it was a man's house, but a man with taste and style. Paige thought it felt warm, relaxed, and very inviting.

"So, what do you think?" Ian asked. "Not bad for a hut?" He kissed Paige's nose and held her by the shoulders, grinning. "I think that was your word, right?"

"It's a nice hut." She smiled. "Quite the beach cottage; it's huge, perfect, actually. My room is lovely … and the balcony, what a fabulous view."

"I'm glad you like it, but you'll have to vacate your room for a while, right away."

"Okay, I guess … But, why?"

"The locksmith's coming to put an iron bar and big locks on the door so I can't get in and take advantage of you."

"How do I keep letting you set me up like that?" she asked laughing. "Either you're very good at it or I'm a simpleton."

"Miss Brittany, you are many things …" He brushed his lips over hers. "But a simpleton is not one of them. You're cute and sexy. But simple? No way."

With that, she pulled his face to hers and kissed him with surprising passion.

"Wow!" Ian pretended to stagger backward. "What was that for? Not that I didn't like it, you understand." He flashed a wicked grin.

"Just seemed right. I like your island hut, and I'm happy I came here with you."

"Keep kissing me like that and you might change your mind."

"That's my call, Mr. McBride," she said with a coy smile. "I think I'll kiss you like that, whenever I have a mind to, and I doubt I'll change my mind. So there!" She stuck out her chin, balled fists on her hips.

"Great. I'm stuck with an obdurate, troublemaking female." He stroked her cheek. "How'd I get so lucky?" Ian took her hand and tugged. "How about some iced tea? Sound good?"

They walked into the large kitchen and found Bob and Shannon locked in an obviously serious kiss. Speaking in a stage whisper, Ian said, "Now, children, show some control." The kiss continued, but Bob's right hand went up behind Shannon's back, giving Ian the finger. Turning to Paige, Ian said, "I must apologize for my oversized friend's manners. I can't take him anywhere."

Paige raised her voice to answer. "Oh, I don't know. It's not that embarrassing. Besides, their technique looks pretty good."

Bob broke the kiss, leaving Shannon's lips parted, her eyes closed. Through irregular breathing and a faint smile, Bob asked, "Are you two trying to be pains in the butt, or did it just sort of happen?"

"Hello, you two." Shannon opened her eyes with a lazy, satisfied smile. "I see you're still working at stirring things up, McBride."

"Out—all of you, out on the balcony." Ian gestured toward the ocean. "I'll bring the iced tea."

He stood studying the two women, pleased the truce between them seemed to be holding. Both looked relatively relaxed as they listened to Bob's stories of his college football exploits, named NCAA All-American, et cetera. Ian had heard the tales numerous times and had witnessed their impressive effect on most women. However, to Bob's obvious puzzlement, these two women reacted with the equivalence of a collective yawn. Ian wondered if Bob considered Shannon just another transient bed partner. She wasn't his usual type. Stubbornly confident, tough and beautiful, just as smart and strong-willed as Bob. Ian decided this could be interesting to watch.

Although the two women were no longer glaring at each other, each was certainly sizing up the other, reevaluating first impressions. *Maybe she's not such a total bitch after all,* Paige mused. *Have to wait and see.* The heated kiss in the kitchen had gone a long way toward easing one of Paige's concerns. Shannon Collins appeared plenty interested in Bob's body and affections, seemed to have no designs on Ian. *But, she's still bitchy.*

Shannon listened to Paige carefully, watched her jab and tease Bob about being a big no-neck jock. *Maybe if she wasn't so uppity and irritating ...* She had reluctantly decided that this snooty little slip was quite smart and nobody's fool. *Little witch has grit, too.* Her aggressive counterattack in the coffee shop had proven that; no shrinking violet, this one. *But she's still a pain in the ass.*

There was just something about her. Bob couldn't seem to stop staring at Shannon and wondering about her. She was different, somehow special. He watched her blonde hair blow and focused on her pale blue gray eyes. Exactly the kind of woman who made men do stupid things, he cautioned.

"Guys, I'm enjoying this, but duty calls," Bob announced. They were all feeling it; work was as much a part of these four as breathing. "Need to check my e-mail and make some calls. I'm going to hit it for a couple of hours. How about a late lunch? Say, about two?"

Ian, Paige, and Shannon all agreed. They also had business to handle.

None of the four had noticed the green Ford Taurus shadowing them all the way from Charleston to Ian's beach house. The one now parked half behind a bushy tree, a block away, its driver watching the house intently through binoculars.

15

Shifting Currents

The 35-millimeter camera with its powerful lens rolled off shot after shot. Redding was running through his mental list of to do's, as he reached for a new roll of film. He took another bite of his Milky Way and a swig of Pepsi.

A veteran of many stakeouts, he realized McBride's neighbors would take note of his car. There was also the possibility that McBride or Fowler had noticed the Taurus behind them on the highway. He'd turn it in for another vehicle and locate at least one other spot where he could observe McBride's house. He also had to find a way into the house to get the needed DNA material. Contrary to Billing's belief about blood, Redding knew human hair made for an excellent DNA test vehicle. A brush or comb used by McBride would be all he'd need, but blood on his razor wasn't to be ruled out either.

Richard Billings believed he would soon have McBride where he wanted him, felt he had covered all contingencies, had left nothing to chance. Still, he sat vacillating. Considering extortion was one thing, but committing the federal felony that could get him twenty-five years in prison was something else entirely. He poured more bourbon into his glass.

Thirty minutes later, he sat before the computer screen rereading the demand note for what seemed like the hundredth time. With trembling fingers, he took a deep breath and clicked the mouse cursor. The threatening blackmail note was sent. He looked down and saw his haggard face in the small, square mirror on the coffee table. *There's no going back now.*

She wasn't feeling at all in control as she always strived to be, didn't want these feelings, this gnawing hunger for a man. Shannon grimaced. She'd tried to work but her brain wouldn't cooperate, and the emotions pulling at her heart refused to diminish. Cursing under her breath, she continued a self-deprecating, shoulda, woulda, coulda debate with herself, a finger absent-mindedly twirling in her hair as she chewed her bottom lip. All the symptoms and signs pointed to one thing, but it just could not be that. It couldn't be happening again. She stamped her foot. "Damn! Damn!"

Love had first enveloped her when she was a naïve, virginal nineteen-year-old who thought she knew all about men and everything else. He was twenty-five, a tall Navy pilot who seemed perfect. Mature and take-charge, he looked so good in that uniform. She'd been lost in love, and he … well, he was enjoying their regular sex. Oh, how stupid and used she'd felt when the truth hit. She had told him how much she loved him, and he'd just laughed. Said only what a great body she had. The pain had stayed long after he was gone. She had vowed no man would ever have that power over her again.

Proving a college degree and experience were no bars to bad judgment; she had blithely ignored peril and gone down the same road again when she was twenty-five. She'd refused to heed her friends' warnings and her own misgivings, trusted her heart. The humiliation, pain, and emotional scarring had been as severe as the first time.

That was when she established her ironclad personal rules and protective barriers for dealing with men. Five years, yet the pain was still very fresh in her mind. So, why had she tumbled mindlessly into bed with Bob Fowler like some vacuous slut? What had she been thinking ... or not thinking? She could blame it all on him, except she'd sent strong signals, and all but pounced on him. Stupid seemed an inadequate adjective. Asinine? Sex-crazed? Insane maybe? Lord, she was obsessing.

Whatever. She could not get him out of her mind. Why him? He wasn't Mr. Perfect by any means, what with all that bravado macho stuff. Conceited and pushy, not to mention controlling and self-centered ... and oh, so, arrogant. Yeah, but ridiculously handsome, could be sensitive and tender, and was sexy enough to stop a clock. Yes, he was flawed and no, she shouldn't be so attracted to him. But she was. Way too damn much.

She'd tried telling herself it was just physical, only sexual need that night. However, she knew sex wasn't the only motivator in play here, she'd felt those unbidden but strong emotional tugs, then and now. She should get out of this, but they'd been so good in bed. *Good?* Mind-bending, heart-stopping sex, the greatest orgasms of her life was light years past good. Yes, Bob Fowler had gotten to her, *really* gotten to her. Nevertheless, she wouldn't lower her guard again without knowing his true feelings and intentions. But that was the question, wasn't it? How did he feel about her? If her intuition was wrong, she needed an exit strategy. But, how was she to know?

It came to her in a mental flash. She smiled into the mirror, a mischievous, knowing smile. "Bobby boy, you are about to go on a diet." She would cover him with every feminine kindness and gift—everything except sex. That she would withhold. Shannon didn't feel entirely right about this, had always prided herself on being honest with men. But she cared for this man more than she wanted to admit. So, even though she was uncomfortable with the tactic, it seemed a sure fire way to divine his real innermost motivations. And knowing his true feelings was essential to protecting her heart.

Ian climbed the stairs, briefcase in hand, thinking. He really enjoyed being with her, and was certainly attracted to her. No doubt about that. But what about the other feelings? No big deal, he'd argued. He'd had feelings for a few other women before, but these feelings were unique, different, and stronger. He was experiencing a kind of happiness with her, he'd never felt before. However, he was unsettled about this, found it all troubling. Why? What was he to make of all this? What did it mean?

Ian shook his head, admonishing himself to just enjoy the week without thinking things to death. He removed his laptop from the briefcase and logged onto the Internet to check his e-mail. Struggling to concentrate on business, he was already looking forward to seeing her over lunch. He saw there were scores of e-mail messages to go through. On impulse, he shook his head and made a decision. "No! I'm on vacation. No e-mail."

Logging off, Ian went straight to work on the new novel he had started and was soon engrossed in the Civil War story.

Paige was turning over the same thoughts and questions she'd been evaluating for three days. She hadn't been cautious enough, must have mishandled things because this surely didn't happen so quickly with other women. Maybe it was because of the promises she had made to herself. After all, she'd made those decisions only hours before Ian McBride walked up to her table and into her life. Was it fate? Coincidence? Regardless of how it came to be, she had to approach this logically, start being guided by her good sense, not emotions. She needed to maintain control, proceed at her own pace.

This was stupid. It had only been three days, and she knew so little about him. Nevertheless, she knew she cared for him. She liked his smile, the way he moved and spoke, even the way he smelled. And Lord his kisses—making her go brainless and limp each time, always leaving her wanting more. Incredibly, the one decision she would have thought to be the toughest was made—Ian was to be the one, her first. She would soon convince him they were right for each other.

"Whoa," she exclaimed. "Right for each other?" She was so stunned by the magnitude of the unbidden phrase that had jumped into her thoughts she had to sit down. She shook her head as if to clear it. She looked in the mirror. "No ... that's impossible ... isn't it?" She sank into a chair on a sigh. No. This was only about the promises; just loosening up, a good time with a handsome man, and finally experiencing sex like other women.

She stood and walked to the window. Making love and maybe having an extended relationship, that sounded okay, didn't it? "Oh, I don't know what I'm doing ..." She held her head in her hands. "What's wrong with me?"

She only made things worse, created even more questions and had come up with no answers. Clamping her eyes shut, she let her forehead go against the wall with a thump. "Why does he have to be so handsome, so witty, so nice ... so everything?"

Ian glanced at his watch and remembered they had agreed to meet for lunch. He had just enough time. Tearing off his blazer and slacks, he was soon in the shower, loving the feel of the hot water hitting his head and shoulders.

As he stepped out of the shower, he heard a knock on the door. "Be right there," he yelled. That would be Bob with some business thing. Pulling on an old pair of Levis that hung low on his hips, he opened the door with water still dripping from his hair and bare chest.

Her mind went instantly blank at the sight of him. "Oh!" Paige sucked in an audible gasp. "Uh, I uh ... "Struggling for composure, even words, she couldn't tear her eyes from Ian's muscled shoulders, chest, and abs. So beautifully tanned, so hard, and ... dripping wet. Her mouth went dry as her eyes traced the dark tapering *V* of chest hair that disappeared into his low-slung jeans.

"Well, I guess this shoots my coat-and-tie image all to hell," he said.

"Huh?" Paige looked up into his amused sea green eyes. "Mmm ..." His chestnut brown hair was much darker wet with the reddish highlights erased. Her mind snapped back to coherency. "Uh, sorry. Sorry to disturb ..." She took a step backward her face reddening. "Oh, I'm so embarrassed."

"Really? I never would have noticed." He ran his hand down her cheek, continuing to grin." "There's no reason to be embarrassed."

"But, I've never seen you without ... That is, I only came to ask what to wear for lunch." She couldn't seem to stop the words from tumbling out. "And you have such a hard ..." Nor could she keep her eyes from wondering downward, only to quickly look up, mortified that he'd obviously seen where her eyes had been. "Chest," she squeaked. "Your hard chest, not your ..." She clamped a hand over her mouth, her face now crimson. She wanted to run away, to hide forever. Lord, what must he be thinking of her?

His gentle but passionate kiss came without warning but was oh so welcome. She sank into it molding against him. He reluctantly ended the embrace, leaving himself aching and her breathless. "Dress casually." He spoke softly. "Meet you downstairs in fifteen minutes, and we'll go to lunch."

"Uh, okay," was the best she could manage with her whole body pulsing. She took one last head to toe look before turning away.

She closed her bedroom door and fell backwards against it with a broad dreamy smile. "Oh my God, he's gorgeous." Sure she was reacting like a lovesick fifteen-year-old girl, but she was simply too happy and excited to care.

Lunch went well, with no indication of the women's animosity continuing. A tiny place, the restaurant was on the water. There was cold beer, friendly service, and crab cakes to die for, as good as the men had promised and a hit with the women. Dessert was out of the question and two beers seemed to be everyone's limit, so Ian went to pay the tab.

Bob suggested a round of golf before dinner, but both women all but turned up their noses. Shannon said it seemed like a stupid game, and Paige gave a disinterested shrug. It was ultimately decided the men would play golf while Paige and Shannon went to a nearby tennis center to "hit the ball around," as Shannon put it. They also realized they needed to coexist in the same house for the week, and they might as well find some common ground. Therefore, tennis it was.

It was a typical Hilton Head summer day, sunny, 94 degrees and humid. They drove to the Palmetto Tennis Center in Shannon's Mercedes convertible. Since neither had brought tennis equipment or appropriate attire, a shopping spree in the pro shop was the first order of business, with each buying things they thought would impress or irritate the other. Shannon's eyebrows and curiosity went up when she overheard Paige tell one of the pros, "I'll take the Prince 500 Composite Graphite in a 4 1/8, and string it at 68 pounds with natural gut."

An hour later, they walked onto the court suitably dressed and equipped. Both had mentioned how rusty they would be since they hadn't played in years. Shannon held up a couple of balls and yelled, "Want to just volley some?" Paige raised her racket in agreement and Shannon put a ball over the net with a rather casual forehand that came back via an equally casual backhand.

Five minutes later, however, neither had missed. The pace and power had picked up considerably as had grunts and mumbled curses on both sides. They had lost count of how many forehands and backhands they'd hit in the protracted, now intensely competitive rally. Each realized the other was not very rusty at all. Both women were rapidly tiring, but ignoring the heat and humidity, each was hitting as hard as they could, intent on making the other miss first.

"Damn Amazon," Paige mumbled under her labored breath. She stepped into a forehand with her full weight, took it early, and rocketed the ball toward the baseline corner. To her chagrin, however, Shannon sent it screaming back like a bullet. *Freak—arms six feet long.*

She's so quick! Shannon had stretched her five feet ten inches full out and barely reached the ball, somehow sending it back perfectly up the line. "Try to get that one back," she muttered with a nasty grin. But, she notice too late that Paige had cleverly come to the net. Shannon could only watch helplessly as Paige deftly dinked the ball across the net at a wicked angle. It dropped dead just inside the sideline and rolled slowly off the court. Grinding her teeth, Shannon walked forward mouthing indistinguishable curses and kicked it.

Each wanted desperately to say something snide and cutting, but both were too exhausted to do anything but gulp air and groan. Paige's hair was tangled, damp, black yarn against her flushed face. Shannon's new outfit was soaked and marked with irregular perspiration stains. Both women had dropped their rackets and were bent over, hands on knees, gasping for breath.

After draining a bottle of water, Shannon finally looked up. "For someone who's rusty," she grabbed a breath. "You've got one hell of a forehand ... and some mighty quick moves ... Miss Muffett."

"I thought," Paige began. "You were going to ..." Her words spilled out through ragged breaths. "... run me to death." She swallowed some water. "You're like ... hitting to a backboard."

Shannon just eyed her for a moment, then said, "Okay, you little wimp, you're no week-end player." Combing back sweat-soaked hair with her fingers, she leaned on the net, starting to breathe almost normally. "What's the story; how good are you?"

Paige had her head between her knees. "To begin with," she said, looking up and wiping moisture from her gritty, glistening face. "I wouldn't look like a wimp playing against a normal size person ..." She grinned at Shannon. "I played varsity tennis at Vanderbilt. Seems like a long time ago. And you?"

"My parents insisted I learn the game. Had to be properly athletic in polite society and all that." Shannon came around the net and plopped down next to Paige on a bench. "So, I played Girl's juniors, and then four years for Yale."

Paige looked Shannon up and down and surveyed her own sweat-covered arms and legs. Both women were mottled with damp, gray clay dust from their knees down and wringing wet from head to toe. Paige started to snicker. "Lord, we look awful."

"Yeah, your hair ..." Shannon pointed and chuckled. "Looks like crap, all stringy and wet."

"Yeah, well, your broad butt is so soaked I can see through your shorts. Not a pretty picture, Sprinter."

"My butt's not broad …" Shannon smiled cautiously. "How about making it Shannon, Paige?"

"Okay … Shannon," Paige replied with a wrinkled brow. "I think you might just be all right, after all." She grinned mischievously. "For an Amazon."

"Off your butt. This time we keep score, you little wimp. Shake?"

They clasped hands firmly each focusing on the other's eyes—two strong, competitive women acknowledging one another. Both smiled warmly sensing things had just changed considerably between them.

"Paige?" Shannon said.

"Yeah?"

"I just had a delightfully nasty idea."

"You, with a nasty idea?" Paige grinned. "There's a shocker." She canted her head. "Okay, let's hear it."

"How 'bout we challenge the men to play us tomorrow? Losing team cooks dinner for the winners. Bringing their egos down a click or two might be good for them. What do you say?"

16

Weaving Tangled Webs

"Son of a bitch!" The computer screen indicated it was 10:18 PM and Richard Billings was screaming into the emptiness of his office. He'd gone online to read McBride's expected response only to discover the threatening note he'd sent hadn't even been opened. He kicked the trash can across the room. "What kind of professional doesn't check his goddamn e-mail?" This was supposed to be the simple part, he thought. Billings poured three fingers of bourbon. "Shit."

He considered the situation, trying to steady himself. The PI had said McBride and Fowler had women with them at the beach house. Probably whores they hired for a few days, he reasoned. Calming a bit, he decided that was the answer. They were on vacation and screwing around with the broads. He'd give McBride one more day to respond. If he didn't by then, Richard would have to make the blackmail demand by phone. Damnit, that meant more risk.

He downed the bourbon, sprinkled cocaine onto the small mirror, and began to form it into thin lines with a razor blade. "One more day, McBride ..."

Mark Redding had followed the foursome to a posh restaurant and then to the local performing arts center. They were sufficiently tied up for the night and he needed to swap rental cars anyway. He decided to give himself the rest of the night off and was soon at a strip club drinking a beer.

Deep in thought, he paid little notice to the topless g-stringed woman strutting down the runway. As the hoots and whistles of the other male patrons rose, Redding glanced up and gave the stripper a brief appraisal. "Listen to those idiots," he said to the bartender. "Going nuts over a tattooed, skinny bitch with plastic tits." He shook his head.

Redding had a more important matter on his mind and, as usual, it involved making money. He went back to his investigative notes, reviewing each of his conversations with Richard Billings trying to decide what the lawyer was up to. It had to do with that kid, John William McDonald, now known as Ian McBride ... Something about McBride and his past.

He ordered another Coors and continued to think as the music and whistles got louder. All the records indicated McBride had a crappy childhood, beatings, arrests, and incarcerations, not to speak of having a whore for a mother and an alcoholic pimp father. No wonder he changed his name and bailed out when he was seventeen. Redding considered the news clips and book reviews he'd seen about McBride and his millionaire playboy lifestyle. Hell, he was doing fine now, his image all aces. Fame, women, money. No one would ever know he had such a shitty past.

A slightly overweight blonde with sagging breasts and a caesarian scar wrapped herself around a brass pole and slanted Redding an inviting smile. From experience, he knew she was only angling for money. Damn floppy-tit bimbo tease. She made kissing and humping movements in his direction. He knew if he even patted her ass, the bouncer would toss him out. He gave her the finger and watched her scowl and back away.

Redding chugged the remainder of his beer and began picking his way through the crowd moving towards the men's' room, still thinking. This all seemed to be focusing on McBride's reputation, his image, and ... Redding stopped abruptly. "Billings, you son of a bitch ..." He made for the parking lot. "It's friggin' extortion." Billings was planning to blackmail McBride. *Well, we'll see about that,* Redding thought. He pulled a cell phone from his pocket and dialed Richard Billing's office number. "Sneaky son of a bitch has been using me."

During dinner Paige casually brought up tennis and asked the men if they played. Both men said they'd played some. Shannon proposed a boys vs. girls match and smiled at Paige as Bob and Ian agreed, springing the trap around their own unsuspecting necks.

"We'll hold back some to make it fair," Bob said. "But when do we choose what you cook?"

"Never, since you'll be cooking." Paige winked at Shannon. "We'll choose the menu."

Ian rolled his eyes. "Bob, how can such intelligent women be so misguided?"

It was almost eleven when they returned to the beach house. Ian excused himself and returned a few minutes later with two large wicker picnic baskets. Each contained a frosty bottle of champagne, flutes, chocolates, a red rose, and a beach blanket. He handed one to Bob and turned to Paige.

"Would you care to join me for a moonlight walk?" She smiled and laced her arm through his and they made for the door. Ian spoke over his shoulder, "I won't wait up for you children. Do behave yourselves, now."

Paige looked back and laughed to see Shannon making a face and sticking out her tongue.

It was a near perfect summer evening, the ocean relatively flat except for the waves charging the beach and retreating in soothing rhythm. The air smelled of sea salt and the moon washed deserted beach was theirs. Paige glanced at the basket Ian had prepared. How romantic.

They walked hand in hand carrying their shoes, Ian still wearing a blazer and tie and Paige a chic blue print sundress.

"What a wonderful place," Paige said. She extended her arms and threw back her head with a childlike smile as the wind tossed her long silky hair.

Ian was once again taken by her appealing combination of vulnerability and sensuality.

She stopped her turn, tenderly kissed his cheek, and ran her fingers through his hair. "Tell me about you ... about when you were younger. I want to know everything ... all about your parents, school, sports, everything." Paige smiled with anticipation.

There was a long, uncomfortable pause however. Why hadn't he prepared for this moment? His usual practiced responses seemed so dishonest with Paige asking. For the first time, he was considering what had been unthinkable before. But no. She wouldn't understand—how could she?

"I didn't have a very pleasant, normal …" He could not believe he had said that. "That's not something I talk about." He made a clumsy attempt at changing the subject. "I'd rather talk about you. You're much more interesting."

"Come on, Ian, we've talked about me but never about you." Paige's smile had changed to a look of puzzlement. "I've already shared personal things with you I have never told any man. Now, I want to know more about you."

"I can't. I'm sorry." He shifted his weight from one foot to the other and back again. His palms were sweaty. "I just can't talk about that." His stomach was in knots. "I'll tell you anything else you want to know about me. Anything else."

"You said you have feelings for me and I certainly care for you," Paige said. "Why shut me out?" Then she began to back away, shaking her head. "You don't trust me. Or there's something in your past and you don't trust me enough to share. I'm right, aren't I?"

Ian only looked at her, squeezing his hands together, hoping she'd somehow understand.

Paige angrily kicked the basket, spilling its contents onto the sand. Tears were streaking her cheeks. "Well, just keep your secrets." Her shaky voice went icy. "Keep your closed-off life. But, deal me out, damn you!" Fuming and sobbing, she stormed off.

Ian felt small and like a fool, but he couldn't make himself go after her. Doing that would mean disclosing long-buried, painful truths to her. If Paige knew, she'd never respect him again. He couldn't bear the thought of that.

Shannon and Bob had talked, embraced, and kissed for some time. She was thoroughly enjoying the passion but was determined to stay with her agenda. She pulled away, and worked at catching her breath. "I think we need to back off the sex thing." There, she'd said it, set the boundaries, as she'd planned, was telling him the way things were to be, taking charge. She watched Bob's face, expecting surprise, thinking he'd be upset and peeved—she saw none of that.

"I agree," he said in a serious control tone. "We've been moving too fast. Actually, I wanted to talk to you about our first night together."

Whoa ... What was this? She'd anticipated anger, frustration; but no. Whatever. She stuck to her strategy, and forced herself to respond as she'd planned. "Yes, I got carried away that night. But, from here on, I'm going to ..."

"No, it wasn't you." Bob cut her off. He held her by the shoulders, and looked into her eyes. "I took advantage, was out of control, acted like an animal. I apologize, Shannon. You're a classy lady, and I didn't show you the respect you deserved."

Uh-oh. He wasn't supposed to be considerate and nice about this. Where was his predictable bravado, his hard sexual come-on? He was screwing up everything. She was supposed to have the upper hand here, but he had wiped out her whole plan with a simple stupid apology. Being sweet and calling her a lady when he very well knew how much she'd enjoyed it, how she wanted him. What was going on here? Shannon stared at him in befuddlement. Her clever strategy, the one he'd just turned upside-down, now seemed shallow and mean. She felt growing respect for this man, admiration. At that moment, all she wanted to do was hold him, kiss him … trust him. Should she take the chance?

What the hell was she thinking? Sure didn't seem impressed by his apology. He stood looking into her eyes, not knowing what else to do or say. Why did he care so much? He knew the answer, but it … well, it scared him. She was worthwhile, different from the rest, and he knew it.

He drew a deep breath, put his ego on the line, and asked, "Would you believe me if I told you I have deeper feelings for you than I've ever had for any woman?"

She was taken aback and moved, but responded quickly, honestly. "Maybe. I'd like to believe that. But can I believe it's true tomorrow or next week? Tell me."

He wasn't that surprised by her reply, but it still unnerved him. For the first time a woman was making him feel vulnerable. He could retreat with some joking riposte; say he was just testing her, something like that. On the other hand … He paused, swallowed hard, and went with his gut. "It's true, Shannon. I'm not sure I'm comfortable with it, don't claim to understand it. But it's the absolute truth."

The simple declaration dealt her a jolt with more punch than all the roses, champagne, and gifts he could have delivered. She saw the unalloyed sincerity in his eyes, and realized what an emotional risk he had taken. Coming from a man like Bob, it was the clincher. She'd run out of reasons for not trusting her heart to Robert Fowler.

He kissed her and then took her hand and began walking toward the beach house saying nothing. Shannon squeezed his big hand and dabbed a tear from her cheek. She knew their lovemaking that night would be special, deeply meaningful for both of them.

Ian stared down the moonlit beach, watching Paige disappear into the darkness. He dragged his hands through his hair and sighed. It wasn't that he didn't trust her, as she said, but he'd never even considered telling anyone other than Bob. Did he really want Paige to know?

Love had never been more than a fantasy for him, something that existed only in novels and movies. Something he'd accepted years before he was not destined to experience. He'd never felt the soaring, intense emotions people talked about … Before Paige, that is. Still, it had never crossed his mind that the unique, powerful feelings he had for her could be love. So why was he hurting so? He looked up into the black starry sky. "Why do I have to be so screwed up?" he asked.

Paige was wonderful, so normal, and decent. Certainly deserved better than the son of a whore. Nevertheless, he desperately wanted her trust. But if he told her, she might leave. *She's leaving now, you idiot!* Damning the consequences, he began to run yelling out, "Paige, stop." He tore off his blazer and broke into a full sprint. Running as hard as he could, he cried out again, "Paige … Please stop."

She turned, fists on her hips, chin defiantly set. Ian stopped before her, breathing hard. "Wasn't sure … you'd stop …" He continued between deep breaths, "I have things ... many things I want to tell you ... If you'll give me ... another chance."

She studied him questioningly, caution and reticence evident in her expression.

17

Unexpected Tides

They returned to the beach house and went upstairs to Ian's bedroom to talk in private. Paige sat in a wingback wicker chair and watched as he poured them wine—he looked nervous and a little pale. What could be so terrible? She studied him, wondering what he was thinking, what he was going to say. The strain on his face troubled her.

"This isn't an easy thing for me to do," he began. "It's both painful and humiliating for me ... especially with you." He paused, looked down. "Bob is the only other person who knows what I am about to tell you. I've gone to great lengths to keep it that way."

"If telling me ... whatever it is makes you uncomfortable, you don't have to ..."

He touched her lips. "I want to do this, want you to be aware." He shook his head, prayed he was doing the right thing. "People have no idea how I grew up. I want you to know, but ..." He looked away and said, "God, this is tough ... I don't want to destroy your opinion of me or push you away."

"Ian, if you'd rather not ..."

He cut her off with a wave of his hand. "I must do this." He stood, took a deep drink of wine, and began pacing again. "It's important you judge me for who and what I really am."

He sat and started telling her; talked for more than thirty minutes without stopping, pouring out intensely personal, hideous details of his childhood and adolescence. Not just the beatings and physical hardships, he described the psychological pain as well.

Initially Paige was speechless. The picture he painted was so shocking and terrible, hard for her to take in. He continued, sweating, looking more drawn than before, and telling of his prostitute mother and her alcoholic, pimp husband. His voice dripped venom when he used the words mother and father.

She thought her heart would break with sympathy for him. "Oh, Ian. How horrible for you."

He waved off her comment and pressed on, telling of how his father training him to be a petty criminal and how the man pummeled him if he didn't steal enough. The degradation, the injuries, the terror and fear, the absence of parental feelings, human respect, or love … he told it all.

"Lord, I am so, so sorry." His obvious pain had enveloped Paige. Tears streamed down her cheeks but she had become angry. "Such meanness … to a little boy." Hearing about the horrors of the juvenile detention facilities made her cringe and become even angrier. "Damn them," she muttered. "How could they be so cruel, so crude?" She moved to comfort him, only to be rebuffed.

"Sit down, Paige. Let me finish," he said, looking down rather than facing her. He segued into changing his name and entering the U. S. Marines Corps at age seventeen, told about how difficult it was for him to handle things that were meant for older males with normal life experiences. Paige was stunned to hear the Marine Corps provided the first new clothes he'd ever had. However, she saw unconcealed pride when he referred to himself as a Marine.

Finally, he spoke of Desert Storm. Paige knew almost nothing of war, and Ian's vivid descriptions shocked her. The heat, the miserable conditions, the brutality of combat, and the ferocious firefight in which he had been wounded.

"My God!" she cried, her face going pale. "You were shot?"

He didn't answer for a moment, then said, "Yeah … and I killed men there." Ian paused, looking morose. "Many men," he intoned and watched shock once again registered on her face. He told her about the gut-wrenching fear he'd felt, said he hadn't seen it as heroic when he saved three of his fellow Marines. Thought they'd have done it for him, probably. Regardless, he was given medals for his actions.

Paige struggled to reconcile all of this with the suave, caring man she knew to be Ian McBride. Lord, he'd even said there was a bizarre rush, a surreal *enjoyment* to combat. It all seemed so incongruous—could this new image be the same man she knew? How was it possible he had done those things, lived through such experiences, and yet put all of the ugliness behind him? Oh, but he hadn't. She listened and cried as he told of the recurring nightmares about his childhood and the war. How they still haunted him.

Then he looked at her and said simply, "That's all of it. Now, you know."

He appeared spent, and Paige wanted only to comfort him. She sobbed and held him, kissing his face and his eyes, and whispering in his ear while stroking his hair. In light of what she'd just learned, Paige marveled at what he had made of himself, all alone, with no support at all. To have suffered and endured so much, and yet have conquered and risen above it all, and be sane, was amazing to her. She held his face and looked into his sea green eyes with loving wonder.

What a decision it must have been for him to share such personally painful things with her. Yet he had, an unmistakable confirmation of his feelings for her. How could he think this would diminish him in her eyes? Nothing could have been farther from the truth, because at that crystalline moment, Paige knew ... She was hopelessly in love with Ian Michael McBride.

Both were more worn from the stressful experience than they realized. They fell asleep in each other's arms. Paige held him close; happy to lie with the man she loved.

Paige awoke just before dawn, took off her wrinkled sundress, and snuggled back against Ian in her panties and bra. She kissed and nibbled on his ear until his eyes crept opened. When he smiled, she took his mouth in a gentle but passionate kiss that brought him ever so fully awake.

"Wow! And hello to you, too, Miss Brittany."

"Morning," she purred, stroking his stubble. "I have my own secret. And this seems like a good time to tell you."

"Oh?" He propped himself up on an elbow.

"I want to make love with you, want you to be my first," she said. "And whether you think so or not, I'm ready ... completely ready."

"What?" Ian's gawked at her. "Did you say ... your *first?*" He swallowed hard. "You're not saying you've never ...?"

"Yes, that's right, and I've decided. It's final. It's going to be you, Ian."

Dumbfounded, Ian sat bolt upright, his body and mind swamped with arousal and a crushing sense of personal responsibility. He just sat staring at her, eyeing her tanned legs and small, pale breasts only half covered by sexy black lace.

She knew she'd taken him by surprise, but she was amused by this normally witty and charming man's nonplussed, flummoxed state. But, oh, when he did speak ... He looked into her eyes, traced a finger down her jaw line, and began describing his powerful feelings for her, saying how they had grown steadily stronger since their first meeting.

"I confess they confuse me—so intense, so deep. I've never felt this way before ... nothing even close." He paused and took a slow breath. "When you walked away from me on the beach, the thought of losing you was so painful ..." Then he went silent again.

His words, so heavy with sincere emotion, had her eyes welling with tears. Now knowing of his complete unfamiliarity with love, Paige believed Ian was struggling to describe that very emotion ... love for her. She threw her arms around his neck. For the first time in her life she wanted to surrender everything, body and soul. She smiled broadly. "Ian McBride, I'm in love with you," she proclaimed. "I love you so much I can barely stand it." She grinned and watched his facial expressions that seemed to hopscotch from shock to relief to unbridled joy.

It wasn't that the words were unfamiliar to him; he'd often woven them into his novels. But no one had ever said them to him, *no one*. And it was Paige saying it. Happiness swept Ian away like a flood. He took her mouth with a deep kiss. The desire in him was already raw and strong, forcing him to fight to control his hands and impulses. Her eyes had gone dark, full of question and unmistakable desire.

He skimmed his hands over her shoulders and down, stopping teasingly on the sides of her breasts. He heard her little gasp; part alarm and part delight as he released her bra. Her breasts were so firm, yet soft. He could feel her heart pounding with what he suspected was both want and anxiety. God she was beautiful, so small, delicate, and so very ready.

Oh, did he smell good, so sensually male. She could sense his hunger, and suspected she was feeling those wild and tangled emotions that fog women's minds just before ... Lord, the growing heat and tightness in her chest was almost painful. He traced her lips with his tongue before taking her mouth in a slow passionate kiss, blurring the edges of her mind, the taste of him seeping into her blood. "Ian," she breathed on a low moan. These had to be the desperate feelings that drive women to madness.

He held her face in his hands. "I'm going to make love to you and see that you enjoy every pleasure and that you never forget your, no *our* first time."

She felt light-headed and could only stare and tremble as his mouth took her breasts, teasing, tantalizing until her whole body felt hot. His hands moved lower over her hips, sliding under her remaining lace. Oh, if he touched her there ... He did—such knowing fingers—intense new sensations seared through her, making her cry out. Her eyes flew open, then clenched shut as the marvelous sharp spasms struck a scant moment later. Whimpering through clenched teeth, she bowed up and writhed against him until falling limp.

"Good ... Lord." She looked up into his face joyfully bewildered, gulping air, and quivering with aftershocks. She embraced him tightly. "Oh, Ian ..."

She looked impossibly alluring, the sight of her in climax having almost done him in. He groaned, and prayed for control. "Only the beginning," he managed. "There's so much more." He'd vowed he would be gentle, do this slowly, properly; show her what was in his heart. But God, he wanted her so badly he was aching.

Time seemed to disappear as he brought her to pleasured plateaus with his mouth and hands, showed her wondrous things she didn't know existed. She moaned under his magical touches rocketed to another wondrous climactic peak.

"My God," she panted. Had her bones turned to putty? She was awed. Her breast rose and fell as she struggled to fill her lungs. "What you did to me ... I just ... never imagined."

"I know." He strained to keep his voice calm. Pressed against him, her anxious wanton movements were nearly torturous. "Just feel ..." He pulled her close, buried his face in her hair, and whispered, "Just feel and enjoy, Honey."

"But ..." Paige was craving the ultimate bond, thought she might die if she didn't have it soon. "Ian, Please," she pleaded. She looked into his tormented but determined green eyes, reached down, and guided him to her need. "Now. Please ..."

Almost mad from holding back, he couldn't have said no if his life depended on it. He was all but lost, nearly beyond control as he linked his fingers with hers and began easing into her. So warm and deliciously tight, she squeezed down on him, the feeling almost overwhelming. He pressed farther meeting her virginal barrier causing her to stiffen, gasp, and clutch his fingers. He froze and held perfectly still. Then, sensing her willingness and anticipation, feeling her quivering desire, he tightened his fingers in hers and pushed his hips forward, plunging slowly but fully through the hymen.

The pain was sharp—she screamed—eyes going wide at the shocked glory of it. Her body reactively tried to pull away, but she held on. Sucking air, she gripped his shoulders, bit her lip and squirmed against the burn that was mercifully beginning to ease.

Of course he'd heard her cries, felt her tense around him, and sensed the pain in her strangled trembling groans. He held still and stroked her face, allowing her to adjust further. "Am I still hurting you?" he whispered.

"Uh huh, some," she murmured breathlessly. "But please ..." Stretched, as she would not have thought possible, she tried to move her hips. "Don't ... don't stop," she pleaded.

"Don't think I could. But ..." He caressed her tenderly and drove in a fraction more, slowly, gently. "I hate hurting you." Fully in, he paused again, and then began to move within her.

She marveled at the hot mixing friction of pleasure and diminishing pain rolling over her, a cascading kaleidoscope of newfound feelings. She sobbed and shuddered under the growing exquisite sensations, felt as if she was spiraling. He filled her completely, penetrating and withdrawing in a slow delectable rhythm. Just as she felt she might faint from his heavenly movements, his plunging tempo increased. Ever deeper into her ...

such pleasures! By instinct, she pushed upward against him, her hips arching off the bed as she fought to breathe.

"Wrap your legs," he commanded. "Stay with me."

She clung helplessly as his driving hips moved faster and harder until she began to buck and shake. She saw lights behind her eyes, felt an overwhelming rush of sensual heat. The galvanic orgasm erupted. "Ian!" she cried. Such intense melding pleasures—her entire system seemed to explode in molten jolts as his relentless thrusts continued.

Ian suddenly tensed, began to shudder, and called out her name. She heard pleasured male groans, and felt his wondrous warmth pulsing deep within her. They collapsed together. She lay panting, and exhausted, yet feeling a great reluctance for the ecstasy to end.

"Incredible," she gasped. "Thank ... you." She struggled to speak. "... for being ... so wonderful," she sobbed, feeling such joy. He pulled her close. She shivered as he kissed her neck, and murmured endearments.

Every cell in her body was energized, humming. She'd expected crude animalistic movements, terrible pain and perhaps some limited enjoyment. However, resting there so replete with him embracing her, Paige could only sigh in contentment. How could she have imagined the passion, heat and soft tenderness tearing at her heart? Or fathomed emotions layered on desire, want woven in need, and giving coupled with taking in warm love? She felt so alive ... and oh so much a woman.

She ran her hands over Ian's chest as he drifted in sleep. What a wonderful thing the male body was. Hard and powerful, yet capable of such gentle fulfillment. For a while, the new, transformed Paige Ann Brittany just grinned into the darkness.

Paige was glorying in the newfound morning after aches of a woman well pleasured. She couldn't remember ever being happier or more relaxed ... although a little upset with herself however. She'd so looked forward to sleeping with Ian, but their incredible lovemaking had left her so keyed up she had laid awake, couldn't sleep another wink. Explaining why she was in the kitchen at 7:00 AM, making coffee. She'd wanted to make love again, but he looked so peaceful that she couldn't bring herself to wake him. She had, however, been into some heavy duty fantasizing about her and Ian, when she looked up to see Shannon.

Barefoot, her hair tousled, and attired in an oversized man's bathrobe, the tall blonde padded into the kitchen. She rubbed her eyes and stifled a yawn.

"Good morning, Shannon. How are you this fine day? Want some coffee?"

"Huh?" Shannon's eyes flew open. She stepped backward, eying the petite woman beaming with happiness and joy. "Hmm, look at you," Shannon said, recognizing the unique glow on Paige's face, the sparkle in her eyes. "Uh huh, I'd love some coffee. Then I want to hear all about it ... every delicious detail."

"About what? What do you mean?"

"You've got that 'I just got laid' look all over you." Shannon smirked and folded her arms. "Now, just try to tell me I'm wrong."

"No ... No, that's not ..." Paige turned away, her cheeks ten shades of crimson. "Oh, Lord," she said, covering her face with her hands. "How did you know?" she mumbled through her fingers.

"Gotcha." Shannon pointed a finger at her. "And with that look, I'll bet it was fabulous."

Paige wordlessly filled a coffee mug for Shannon, being careful to avoid eye contact as she refilled her own.

"Well, it should've been great." Shannon let out a long breath. "He's gorgeous, that Ian."

Paige whirled to glower at her with a flash of something akin to fury. "What do you mean by that?" she snarled.

"Whoa, take it easy, Sweetie. All I'm saying is you're a lucky girl. Ian's a fine man."

"Oh." Paige looked down. "Sorry."

Shannon waved off the apology. "Believe me," she said, grinning. "I have all the man I want; almost more than I can handle." Her eyes rolled toward the ceiling. "Thank you, God." She chuckled and took a seat, joining Paige at the table.

Paige's head came up to meet Shannon's eyes. "Is it really that obvious with me?"

"Ohhh, yeah." Shannon could not help but laugh. "It'll fade, but you'll have women grinding their teeth in jealousy today."

"Hmm ..." Paige looked out at the Atlantic. "Interesting. I think I like that."

Shannon paused. No. Couldn't be her first. Offering to make toast, she reached to get two plates. Or, could it?

The thermometer read 90 degrees when they arrived at the tennis center for their 10:00AM game. The men were already making teasing remarks about how they would take it easy on them. "Yeah, Ian, we need to hold back so we don't damage these two delicate flowers." Bob said. "After all, we don't want them injured when they're preparing out feast."

Paige shot him a smile. "I'm not sure taking it easy is a good idea. Unless, of course, you've already planned out what you two are going to cook."

"Yeah, guys, Paige is right," Shannon said. "Give it your best shot. It still won't be good enough."

"That does it," Ian said with a mock snarl. "It'll be take-no-prisoners, cutthroat tennis. Right, Bob?"

"Right," Bob growled. "Bring it on, ladies. "

The men offered to warm up but Paige and Shannon said they didn't need it. They spun a racket to determine who would serve, and the men won.

Ian served a slow blooper to Paige that came screaming back, barely clearing the net and landing out of either man's reach.

Ian dismissed it as beginner's luck and served to Shannon with a little more oomph. Her scorching return whistled past Bob's ear like a bullet and skipped off the baseline.

"Sorry, Sweetie," purred Shannon. "A little too close?"

"Yeah, maybe a little," Bob scowled.

The women broke Ian's serve leaving the men plotting strategy behind their baseline.

"Look, let's drop the good guy thing and get ahead before we ease off," offered Bob.

"Sounds good," Ian said.

All four were soon soaked in sweat but the women still retained the lead. Ian called Bob to the baseline for another talk. "My friend, we have been hustled. These gals are good."

"No shit." Bob wiped sweat from his eyes. "Running us around like two yard-dogs—this just won't do. Let's go."

Bob's years of training and athletic ability carried him fairly well while Ian's physical conditioning and sheer guts kept him in it. The women were impressed with their crude but aggressive effort against two college level players. However, in the end, the final score was 6/2 and 6/3. Ian and Bob were soaking wet and filthy, having each gone sprawling on the clay attempting heroic diving saves. Handshakes, hugs, and kisses came from the women, who also offered to buy cold beer for the losers.

After the first beer and a barrage of grumbling from the men, the women finally admitted to their expertise and experience.

"Okay, so we played a little college tennis," said Shannon. "Shouldn't be a big deal for a hitherto football hero and a well-conditioned runner."

"Come on," said Ian. "You should have told us."

Paige smiled. "You guys could have always backed away from playing a couple of girls."

"No way," countered Bob. "But you're NCAA. Hardly just a couple of girls ..."

Ian didn't take the bait, but shot Bob a look. "We're toast, big guy."

"They hustled us," Bob carped. "Come on, you two, admit it."

"Ooo, hustled is such an ugly word," said Paige with a pout.

"A nasty word," Shannon agreed. "We prefer to see our non-disclosure as an error of omission."

Both men groaned. Shannon grinned mischievously. "Actually, Paige, I think the men did well considering their *hard* concentration last night on other things. They seemed a little *drained,* if you get my drift." Paige chuckled at the double entendre.

Bob and Ian sought an honorable retreat by insisting the women buy another round. It was good-natured fun, and they were all laughing on the way back to the beach house. They agreed they would clean up and work for a few hours before meeting downstairs for cocktails at five.

Redding had tailed the two couples to the tennis complex earlier that day and decided their game would give him sufficient time. With the house empty; he slipped inside and removed the needed hairs from McBride's brush and comb. He was sneaking out the back as they pulled into the driveway laughing and singing along with the radio.

Redding Fed Exed the DNA-laden material to Billings that night.

Ian took a long, hot shower and donned some comfortable Levis and a faded Boston College T-shirt. He plopped down at the computer, planning to write for an hour or so after checking his e-mail.

He was scanning the e-mail subject lines, when his eyes stopped abruptly halfway down the list. It was like seeing a ghost, the shock nearly paralyzing.

18

Stormy Alliances

Ian's shaking hand hovered over the mouse as he reread the e-mail caption. There was no avoiding it; taking a deep breath, he double clicked and watched as the message appeared.

Hello, John William McDonald, or Ian Michael McBride as you now call yourself. Yes, I know all about your past you have worked so hard to conceal. I am betting it is very important to you to keep that past a secret. That is why you are going to pay me $500,000 to not disclose what I know to the news media.

You would be very foolish to think I am bluffing. You will pay me what I say, how I say, and when I say, if you want to go on with your charade. Without that payment, I will ruin you; destroy your life within hours.

Some info to help convince you: Your mother was June Alice Martin, a drug-addicted prostitute who married Willard P. McDonald, a petty criminal and alcoholic who pimped her for years. I know where you lived, went to

155

school and much more. I have documents the press would love. Think of it: 'Playboy Author is Son of Drug Whore and Alcoholic Pimp.'

I want payment in cash. You will be contacted to arrange the time and place.

"No!" Ian reread it, envisioning his whole life crumbling, everything he'd made of himself wiped out. His fear however began to change to anger, a grim sense of determination growing within him. "I'm Ian Michael McBride. Nobody's taking that away—never."

So he wanted to arrange payment. Fine, thought Ian. He would meet the sleazy bastard face-to-face and ... Mindless anger flashed, followed by a strong right hook. The sheetrock gave way as Ian's fist hit the wall shooting pain through his wrist and forearm like a burning arrow. "Damnit!" he yelled, shaking his bleeding hand. "Probably broke the damn thing," he grumbled. Ian printed the extortion note and stalked out of his bedroom, headed down the hall, cursing and rubbing his swelling hand.

Bob, Shannon, and Paige had heard the thud, and Ian's ripe curses. Bob was the first to confronted Ian in the hallway. Moments later Paige and Shannon burst into the hall with looks of concern.

"What was that loud noise?" asked Paige. They froze when they saw Ian's pained expression.

"What's going on?" Bob asked. He grabbed Ian by the shoulders with a look of brotherly concern. Ian thrust the sheet of paper toward him.

"What's this?"

"I'll kill the son of a bitch!" Ian shouted. "Kill him before he does this …"

"Whoa," Bob said. "Kill?"

Bob focused on the paper with Paige and Shannon forced to stand by questioningly as he quickly read the note. They saw his face redden, veins suddenly throbbing in his neck.

"Goddamnit," Bob exclaimed, crushing the note into a tiny ball. "The low-life mother …" Brushing the three aside, he took five or six steps down the hall, stopped, and paused for an extended moment. When he turned back toward them, he had changed; his face was dead calm, gone from raging fury to coldly stoic in one controlled, self-managed heartbeat.

Bob took Ian by the shoulders again, caging his eyes. There were no words exchanged but Ian became visibly calmer. Bob turned to Paige, and nodded reassurance. She intuitively moved to Ian's side and watched Shannon move to stand supportively by Bob.

"We'll handle this, Ian," Bob said, his voice like ice water. "We'll handle him." "I've got a couple of preliminary ideas for a plan to neutralize this *individual*." The four of them stood together for a moment saying nothing until Bob turned to face them.

"Paige, Shannon, this is an extortion note. It's intended to blackmail Ian and demands $500,000 or the sender will destroy his personal and professional reputation. I have reason to believe you're aware Ian's past is something he is dedicated to keeping private. That's the basis of the blackmailer's threat."

Paige's expression had been one of sweet concern over Ian's hand, a moment before, but after Bob's explanation, her countenance had morphed into a look of determination and anger. When she spoke, Bob and Shannon were taken aback by the petite woman's ferocity. "He can't do this to Ian," she scowled in a low voice. "Yes, Bob, we need a plan, because by God, we'll fight him. We will stop this bastard," she declared with a scowl

Shannon was impressed by Paige, and had caught the word *we*—found herself nodding. Her mind had jumped to overdrive. She had recently been surprised at the growing affinity she felt for Paige, and watching Bob's calmness, she was impressed, almost overwhelmed with emotion. She glanced at Paige, protectively embracing Ian, her jaw defiantly set. It was evident she was in love with him. Shannon looked again at Bob and thought there seemed to be a lot of that going around.

She knew now she'd been right about the significance of Ian's background. Of course, she was curious and as a journalist, wanted to know all about his covert past. However, if she wrote it, couldn't she destroy him as the blackmailer threatened to do? At that moment, her priorities changed. There was no real conflict, her story was secondary. She would help Ian, Paige, and Bob however she could.

"I'm okay now," Ian said. He looked at the three. "I know I went sort of crazy there. I want to thank all of you for … Well, for this, for your … Oh, hell. Thanks guys."

"You look better," Bob said. "But I want Paige to take you to a clinic to get that hand and wrist looked after." He put his arm around Ian. "I need you clear-headed and well." He smiled. "Besides, I want you out of my hair so I can get a plan together. Paige, get him to a doctor."

Ian offered no protest as Paige took his car keys and directed him toward the door. As they left for the clinic, Bob overheard Paige, and smiled. "Hitting that wall was really stupid, Ian."

When the front door closed, and Bob heard the car leave, he exploded. "Damnit! Isn't this some shit? That son of a bitch! I could kill the goddamn mother ..." He closed his mouth when he saw Shannon quietly watching him. He gazed at her. In the midst of this storm, she stood supportively by, calm and beautiful.

Shannon knew he'd held it together for Ian's sake ... had done it as well as anyone could have. However, she was not displeased to see him venting. *So, Fowler, you're not superhuman after all*, she thought. However, in her estimation he didn't miss it by much. She watched him pace back and forth, saying nothing for quite some time. Finally, he stopped to face her.

"Have a seat, Babe." He cleared his throat and pulled his shoulders back, hoping to look as composed as she seemed to be. "I have an idea that involves you and your professional expertise in the media business. Sort of a preemptive strike."

Redding had observed McBride and the small, dark-haired woman for the better part of a week. They seemed mighty tight to him. The little broad really cared for this guy. He watched as Paige slid behind the wheel of the Boxter while McBride got into the passenger seat, cradling his right hand. Curious, he wondered what kind of injury McBride had, but it was only idle curiosity. All he wanted from the man was money. Once they were inside the Palmetto Urgent Care Clinic, Mark Redding began writing in his journal.

Confronted Richard Billings night before last by phone about his little blackmail scheme. First, he tried to deny it, but he couldn't stop bragging about how cool he'd been setting it up. He was pissed but finally agreed to give me half of what McBride paid.

This cokehead is a babe in the woods who thinks he's James Bond. The man's desperate. Desperate men don't think clearly and sometimes make bad decisions.

Redding paused to consider the possible ramifications of Billings' poor decisions and then began writing again.

There's a good chance he's going to screw this up. I'm not even convinced McBride will pay. Guess I should have thought of that before I got myself involved. If Billings gets caught, he'll give me up sure as hell. But if it does work, I walk away with 250 grand.

He chewed on the cap of the ballpoint pen, focusing, as usual, on money, and thinking again of the close relationship between McBride and his woman. An idea began to form. The ballpoint pen moved again over the page.

I need a backup plan in case Billings messes up the extortion. There's too much money here to ignore the opportunities. McBride's pretty little woman might just be the answer to my needs.

Redding watched McBride walk out the clinic with his hand bandaged. He tossed the pen on the seat and started the rented Pontiac Firebird. Billings was going to make the call that night to set up the payoff. He decided he would wait and see how that went, before he made any other plans.

Richard Billings grimaced and sat back gingerly, thankful they'd stopped punching and kicking him when they did. The throbbing in his ribs, lower back, and gut were their calling card, reminders of his overdue drug debt. He had to get money to pay them … very soon.

At least McBride had read the note. His plan was back on track, working as it was supposed to. He'd run through how he planned to handle the call to McBride several times—covering the phone's mouthpiece to muffle his voice, the accent he'd use, exactly what he planned to say, and so forth. He'd be firm in demanding the money, and the rich playboy would pay. Yeah, he'd pay.

He was pacing his office repeating aloud what he intended to say on the phone, when he turned and looked straight into her face. Wearing a purple mini skirt and red mesh stockings, she stood with one hip cocked to the side, smoking a Marlboro.

"What the hell?" he exclaimed. His stomach tightened and sweat popped on his forehead. He stalked across the room glaring at Martha McDonald. "How long have you been …? What did you hear?" He clenched his fists. "You can't just walk into my office like that."

"Sure I can. You're my lawyer, and I'm paying you." She smiled knowingly. "Besides, what I just heard was very interesting."

Billings told himself it probably didn't matter what the simple-minded bitch had heard—dumb as a post. Still, he blew out a long breath to steady himself. "What do you want?" he asked.

"Came to get the DNA stuff." She moved to within inches of him, smiled, and blew smoke in his face. "But now, I want to hear about your McBride shakedown. Sounds like blackmail to me, Sweetie."

"You stupid meddling whore," he growled. Half drunk and fogged by cocaine, Billings was furious. "Your precious DNA *stuff* just arrived." He snatched a manila envelope off his desk and thrust it at her. "But he's not going to pay you shit. Might as well get that straight," he added.

"The hell, you say." She glowered at him. "McBride owes me for all my misery … and for just being his sister. Where is he, anyway?"

Billings pointed off into space in the general direction of south. "He's way down yonder in Dixie." He smiled at his pun, figuring it had gone right over her empty head. "Hell, you wouldn't know where or even what Hilton Head was if I told you." His voice shot up, all but screaming at her. "He's paying you nothing! Now, get out of my office."

She scowled. "If you screw me out of what I deserve from him, I'll go to the cops. I swear I will. Tell them all about what I heard. Tell them about your blackmail scheme."

"Get out!" He grabbed her, pushed her hard toward the door. "Get the fuck out of my sight and don't come back!"

He slammed the door, locked it, and poured another bourbon. "Stupid whore," he muttered. "Not enough brains to pour piss out of a boot." Still working up his courage, Billings decided he would call Ian McBride as soon as he finished his drink.

Martha McDonald had always avoided them. Now here she was in a huge one, the New York City Metropolitan Library's Main Branch, and feeling very uncomfortable. The enormous room with its high ceiling seemed like it belonged in a castle with knights and all that. It wasn't cold, but it felt like it should be and was it ever quiet. And it smelled like books. Thousands of them were all around her, and all sorts of odd people just sitting at tables and reading. Damn, it was quiet ... downright spooky.

The more she had mulled it over, the more she'd decided to confront Ian McBride face to face. Looking at his pictures in her old clippings, she thought he looked like a reasonable person. He'd probably pay what she rightly deserved. Besides, if he sent her packing, she'd do the DNA thing with *The Inquirer* as she'd planned. But confronting him meant finding out where that strange-named place was. She figured libraries knew that sort of thing.

Martha had seen the head librarian watching her suspiciously. However, the woman ended up being friendly enough, even though she laughed when Martha asked where she could find a Hilton's head and how far away it was. The woman showed her a big book called an Atlas, of all things. There was a whole page showing South Carolina with roads, rivers, lakes, and stuff.

"That's Hilton Head," the librarian said, pointing to a small piece of land near the ocean's coastline.

"An island, huh?" Martha visualized grass huts and natives with spears. Why would a rich person live in such a place? "That's a long way away, isn't it? Damn, I need to get there quick-like ... Emergency, you know."

The librarian pointed to a tiny silhouette of an airplane on the island, and said that meant an airline serviced the island.

"No shit?" Martha watched the astonished woman's eyebrows jump into peaks. "I can fly there?"

She decided to spend some of the money she'd put aside, and fly to that island, see Ian McBride.

The next morning, she felt as if she were embarking on some kind of an adventure when she boarded U.S. Airways flight 2298. Her first time on an airplane, meeting a half brother, and getting lots of money. She took a deep breath and clinched the airsickness bag in her lap.

The wind off the Atlantic was stronger than it had been since they arrived on the island. Paige and Shannon's long hair streamed over their shoulders and tiny grains of sand blew against their bare legs. Already knowing the controversial parts of Bob's plan, Shannon anticipated fireworks and had talked Paige into joining her on a beach walk while Bob outlined his proposal to Ian.

They'd said little as they walked into the wind, until ... "You love him, don't you?"

"Yeah ... I do," Paige said. Well aware of Shannon's perceptiveness, she was only a bit surprised by the query. "But it's a little scary." They stopped walking and faced each other. "I would ask if it shows, but you seem to read me pretty well. That's the second time today."

"It's obvious you've got it bad for him." Shannon smiled. "I'm happy for you, Ian's a good one. He's a keeper."

"Thanks." Paige was touched. They started walking again. "I'm worried ... really upset and concerned about this extortion situation."

Shannon gave her a sympatric look but said nothing. They walked on in silence until Paige stopped and turned toward the ocean. "Bob's quite a guy. Talk about cool and solid in a crisis. He's impressive."

"I believe he'll do whatever it takes to shield Ian from this." Shannon looked away and began walking again. "Loves him like a brother." Still averting her eyes, she paused, a hitch in her voice. "Yeah, Bob's something special, all right."

Paige noticed the change in her inflection. "Shannon, we don't know each other all that well, but it seems very good with you two. Are you and I in the same emotional state?"

"It's damn presumptuous of you to ask me that," Shannon snapped.

"Oh ..." Paige was taken aback. "I didn't mean to pry. I just ..."

"Oh, shut up, Paige," she interrupted. She wiped at the tears running down her cheeks with the back of her hand. "No reason to apologize." She paused. "Yeah, I'm in love with the big ox ... although, I sure don't want to be." She looked down at the sand. "It's just that I'm not sure Bob's a long-term-commitment sort of guy. I think your words were 'It's scary.'"

Paige moved to Shannon and hugged her tightly. "Has he told you he loves you?"

"No," Shannon whispered while looking down at the sand. "But I'll bet Ian was firm on that point with you?"

"Well ...," Paige shrugged and shook her head. "He hasn't actually said the L word."

"He hasn't told you either?" Shannon rolled her eyes and held her head. "Good Lord, how do two intelligent women get into such a mess? How'd we let this happen?"

"Don't know ..." Paige shrugged again and smiled. "But I'm willing to go with it. You?"

"Yeah ..." The tall blonde kicked absent-mindedly at the sand. "Me too, I guess." She sighed audibly. "Damnit," she muttered as they started walking again. "Two pathetic love-at-first-sight twit women with non-committal men," Shannon grumbled. "Aren't we a pair?"

"Shannon," Paige walked on with a smile. "Are you happy? I mean, happy loving him?"

"Yes, God help me." Shannon shook her head. "I think I am ... You?"

"I am." Paige's smile widened. She chuckled. "Yep, we're a real pair, all right. But, I believe these men are both keepers, as you say."

Shannon just nodded and gestured at the ocean. "It's pretty dark out here. And we've gone quite a way—couple of miles, I'd guess." They turned and started back.

Ian was impressed. He looked out at the ocean and drained his bottle of Sam Adams. Bob's plan, as usual, was organized, logical, and convincing. He'd pointed out the precise wording and the tone of the e-mail, convinced the extortionist was an educated, but inexperienced criminal, probably a first-timer. On another point, they reluctantly agreed the two women needed to be included in the plan and decided what parts they would play.

"I like it, Bob. I didn't know you had a friend who was county sheriff here."

"Yeah, known him for about ten years ... used to practice law in Boston."

"Really? From Boston lawyer to South Carolina county sheriff; that's kind of different." Ian looked at his empty beer bottle and headed for the refrigerator. "So, he's coming by tomorrow morning?"

"Yeah." Bob took the cold beer Ian offered, and sat down. "To set up and tap the phone, I would think. I wouldn't be surprised if you get the demand call very soon. We'll all listen in and take careful notes." Bob paused to take a long drink of beer. "There is one more part of the plan we haven't discussed."

Bob was about half way through the last, and the most important part of the plan, when Ian exploded, just as Bob had expected.

"Are you fucking nuts?" Ian shouted. "Going public?"

"That is exactly what I'm suggesting," Bob said.

What a bullshit idea!"

"Ian … at least hear me out." Bob waited until his friend reluctantly plopped into a chair before continuing. "You might get through this one unscathed. Or maybe only parts of your past will get out." He paused. "However, if this asshole can get the info, others can and probably will, eventually. Do you want to roll the dice on your reputation every few years? Wouldn't you rather control how and what goes public and who says it for you?"

"Hold on. Stop right there," Ian said, studying Bob. "Are we talking about Shannon doing this?" Bob nodded.

"Come on, man—you really trust her that much?"

Bob stood, walked to the window, looked into the darkness, and spoke without facing Ian. "Yes. I do trust her. Shannon won't screw over us on this. I *know* she won't. She'll help us, Ian."

"Really?" Ian watched him, not saying any more for several moments. "Mind telling me why you're so convinced, so sure of this?"

"I have deep feelings for her," Bob said. "It's serious for me this time, very serious."

"God, Bob." Ian looked amazed. "Are you saying you're in love with her?"

"You, my friend, are no more surprised than me. But, yeah, I believe so. This could be terminal."

"Wow," Ian said, staring at his friend. "Damn, Bobby, I don't know what to say."

"Say about what?" Shannon asked as she and Paige walked in.

They spent the next thirty minutes discussing the plan in detail. When they finished, each knew the parts they would play in its execution.

The four agreed to try for normality, as best they could, while waiting for the blackmailer's demand call. That meant the men had a debt to pay. They had to cook dinner, and cook they did.

A couple of hours later, the first course, crab bisque, had already been cleared; they were finishing their salads on a candlelit table. The quality and presentation of the entrée, veal scaloppini with colorful vegetable side dishes, left the women awed. Strawberries over vanilla ice cream finished things off, and the men served coffee in the great room.

It was Paige who finally said it. "You guys can cook."

"You noticed," Bob said. "How flattering."

"A very good dinner," Shannon added. "But were you two ever going to tell us you could cook or just let us assume we should handle it all?"

"No comment," Ian said with a conspiratorial grin. "Right, Bobby?"

The phone rang, breaking the happy mood. They all suspected who and what it was. Paige answered the phone as planned, while the others hurried to extensions.

"Mr. McBride's residence," she said. "Whom shall I say is calling? Oh, yes, Mr. *Smith* … Your e-mail was received. I'll connect you with Mr. Fowler. Please hold." Paige listened and then said, "Oh, he's Mr. McBride's attorney and has been asked by Mr. McBride to handle you. Sorry. I should say handle your proposal." She paused again; now well into her officious secretary role. "No, I'm afraid that is quite impossible, Mr. McBride is not available. As I said, his attorney is to deal with you. He maintains an office here. I will connect you. His name is Robert T. Fowler. Please hold."

Paige smiled at Shannon and motioned for her to pick up.

"Mr. Fowler's office," chirped Shannon. "No, Mr. McBride isn't available, but Mr. Fowler should be available shortly." Playing the ditzy blonde, Shannon feigned puzzlement. "Yours was some sort of money thing wasn't it? You're Smith, right?" She began humming a tune. "Oh, dear, I've misplaced the memo about you … Hmm, where did I put that little 'ole thing?" She grinned at Paige and batted her eyelashes. "I'll just have to put you on hold. Uh, what was your name again? Who were you calling for?" She held the phone away from her ear, pursing her lips into a pout. "There's no need for that nasty language, Mr. Jones. It is Jones, Right? Whatever, I'll put you on hold. Mr. Fowler … or somebody should be with you before long."

The caller's loud curses and the sound of his receiver slamming down preceded the dial tone. Shannon smiled triumphantly, and was giving Paige a thumbs-up sign when Bob and Ian came trotting down from upstairs.

"He sounded sort of … maybe, drunk to me, or half stoned," Shannon offered. "What did you think, Paige?"

"Yeah, I agree. He was also really …"

"Really pissed and frustrated to the max," Ian interjected. He gave Paige a kiss on her nose. "Maybe a few blasts of liquid courage before the call, I think. Man, did you two mess with his mind." He turned to face Bob. "So, what do you think big guy?"

Bob seemed as if the other three weren't there, deep in concentration, scribbling on a yellow legal pad, making check marks and circling items. Ian tried again, "Looks like your analysis of him was right on the money, a first timer."

"Uh, what's that?" Bob said, looking up at Ian. "Oh, yeah … well done, ladies. Excellent." His eyes refocused on his notes, but muttered, "Obvious talents for getting under a man's skin."

Paige and Shannon smiled at each other, accepting that as a backhanded compliment.

"I've got to call Jim Bowling," Bob said. "Need to fill him in on this. Are we all agreed? Sounded drunk or high; bogus accent; well educated; and used to having people agree to his demands? A professional or executive type, maybe?"

Ian, Paige and Shannon all nodded, and Shannon put her arm around Bob as he picked up the phone. "So far, so good," he said to Ian. "But it's time for us to back off—we want this asshole arrested and prosecuted. Time to get Jim Bowling involved; get his professional opinion; see what his department's experts think should happen next. Besides, having this bastard in handcuffs would make a good strong ending to Shannon's story."

"Well, that sounds like my cue," Shannon said. "Time for me to get things rolling on my end."

Shannon went upstairs, placed several phone calls, and lined up interviews with a magazine, a major newspaper and two network TV anchors. Each had tentatively agreed to carry her Ian McBride piece.

After the Mister Smith call, she, and Ian spent two hours outside on the balcony and walking the beach. She took careful notes and asked questions to fill in details about his past. She'd found her professional composure strained to near breaking listening to his story. It was impossible not to admire and respect the man, and to her surprise, she'd come to truly like Ian. Shannon easily understood how Paige had fallen for him. He was impressive and she knew his life was powerful material for a story.

She'd already promised Bob, Ian would have final approval before she submitted the story for publication. She smiled knowingly and agreed when Ian asked if Bob and Paige could also look it over. She wondered how the four of them had become this close in less than two weeks.

Richard Billings is a damn train wreck. With all the coke and booze he does, it's a wonder he can even walk. He called me a couple of hours *ago saying he was going to make the call to McBride, as if he needed my approval or something. He was so nervous I could almost hear him sweating. Seems he's gotten steadily worse in the last three weeks. But what the hell? He's still paying. So I'm still here watching McBride and company for $250 a day.*

Mark Redding put down his ballpoint pen and journal and lit a cigarette. He'd already decided to knock off the surveillance at 10:00 PM, have a beer or two at the strip joint, and get some sleep for a change. His cell phone rang, the caller ID screen indicating it was Richard Billings. "Again?" He glared at the phone lying on the dashboard. "Jesus, Billings!"

"Yeah, hello?" He smelled trouble immediately. Billings was strung out or drunk, hanging by an emotional thread.

"It's all gone to hell, all wrong. God, I don't know what to do. It's all screwed up."

"Easy, Billings. What's all screwed up?"

"The McBride thing—what do ya' think I'd be talking about? It's all fucked up, couldn't even talk to him. They're going to kill me, Redding. You hear me? I'm a dead man without this money … They'll kill me."

"Hold on. Start at the beginning. Tell me what happened. I'm assuming you made the call, right?"

After two or three minutes of listening to Billing's frantic recounting of his call to McBride, Redding had the picture. They'd figured Billings out easy enough and turned his brain inside out. Redding shook his head. *The battle of the amateurs, and I'm backing the loser. Shit.* Redding drummed his ballpoint on the steering wheel and let Billings rant.

"Okay, enough. Now, calm down, Billings. They're just messing with you. It's a stall. They're buying time, maybe to get the money together, or whatever. Try to relax."

"Oh, God, Redding. They'll kill me, I tell ya'. I've got to have this money. What are we going to do, now?"

"What's this *we* shit?" Redding punched the seat. "You're asking what we are going to do, you asshole? You came up with this bright idea. You sent the e-mail, and you made the call. I would say *you* have a problem."

"You've got to help me. If you don't, I'll, uh … I'll go to the cops. Tell them it was all your idea, you made me send the e-mail and make the call—said you'd kill me if I didn't."

Redding sensed Richard Billings was desperate enough to do just that. *Son of a bitch!* The guy was a basket case, but Redding was tied to him, couldn't back off now. Damn, what a mess.

"Okay, okay, just a minute. Let me think," Redding said. "We can probably salvage this and walk away with a pile of money. Tell me how you left it when you hung up." He listened, and paused a moment. "We've still got McBride by the balls. Okay, here's what we do …"

19

A Lull Between Storms

Bob looked at his watch. 2:10AM. He knew she was working on the piece about Ian and knew it would be good. No, it would be excellent. He was confident her story would blunt the extortion threat and preserve Ian's reputation and career.

He smiled remembering how furious she'd been to learn he had hired a private investigator to look into her background. The report indicated how she had a prickly personality but was otherwise all aces. It also confirmed that her writing was quite good, mostly pieces with an edge that sucked readers in and tugged at their feelings. She had a reputation for being fastidious, factually accurate, and weaving in layers of emotion. If Shannon Collins wrote it, it was true and it was going to hit you in the gut.

He just could not stop thinking about her. And at that moment, he was thinking about having her warm and naked. He knew that was nothing more than fantasy. *Not tonight, Bobby.* He released an elegiac sigh. Knowing her work ethic, he felt sure she would hammer at the piece until morning.

How had she become such a part of him? Like a narcotic he had to have. The inescapable, disquieting truth of it had settled over Bob. He was in love with Shannon Collins. It scared the hell out of him, but he could deal with that because he had plans for their futures. Plans including a step he thought he would never even consider.

Tomorrow night, he thought. Maybe then, he'd tell her ... lay his feelings bare. A huge step. A risk he had always carefully avoided. A number of women had told him they loved him ... But not Shannon. Still, he thought he knew how she felt. So why was he so nervous about it?

"That still doesn't work," Shannon grumbled. She deleted the entire paragraph she'd written several different ways, to get just the right tone. "Maybe better on the other page," she debated with herself. "Come on—concentrate. Think!"

She was accustomed to deadlines, but this deadline was short and the stakes very high. The need to produce her best piece ever, in one night, had her feeling pressures that were heavy with risk and importance. She was personally invested in this story, its success important to her in many ways.

Shannon worked through the night and into the wee hours of the morning like a woman possessed, writing, editing, and rewriting. To her it was vital that this piece not just tell Ian McBride's life story, but that it move the readers emotionally, make them *live* what he endured. Therefore, she wrote some sentences over and over, seeking to convey a soaring emotion or a tearing pain. Tired but driven, she downed more half-cold coffee and continued to pour her thoughts and feelings into the computer keys, one page leading to another.

Strong winds had brought a storm from off the sea that evening with loud thunder and flashing spears of lightning. The winds continued, lashing rain against the beach house in sheets. Paige assumed some probably cursed its noisy ferocity, however, she'd seen it as perfect background music for wildly romantic lovemaking with Ian.

Only one of the four candles she'd lit hours ago remained, its wavering light bathing Ian's tanned, toned chest and chestnut hair. Paige cuddled next to him, relieved he was finally resting after an exhausting day of anxiety and anger. She stroked his face and watched him sleep, feeling a little guilty because her deep concerns about the extortion had slipped into the back of her mind. For now, filled with love and lying with him, she felt wonderful.

Once again too keyed up to sleep, she lay awake thinking. In love? Absolutely. But there was also the physical intimacy. Oh, the incredible sex. It seemed as if some wild woman had invaded her body. She was astounded by how she, Paige Ann Brittany, was acting. But she didn't intend to change her behavior one bit. No, with Ian she'd just let go and enjoy. There was one issue, however. She just had to learn to sleep after making love … or, willingly become Ian's sex zombie. *Hmm … Decisions, decisions.* She grinned into the darkness.

She studied his face, conceding she'd perhaps gone a little crazy over sex. Nevertheless, she doubted a woman could be any happier or more in love. The recurring erotic thoughts she'd been having since their first lovemaking session were her private little fantasies. Lord, she found it impossible to even be in his proximity without wanting to jump him, was amused how many times since that first marvelous morning she'd envisioned sex with him in this place or that. She watched the last candle flicker out remembering what had taken place a couple of hours before, how different this bout of lovemaking had been from their very first time.

She had seen what a toll the day had taken on Ian, it was obvious to her, he needed to unwind and rest. With Shannon locked away working on the bio piece, Paige would encouraged Ian to tell Bob he was going upstairs to bed. She would bring along a relaxing glass of wine for him. Then, she'd insist he take a nice warm shower to further relax. While he showered, she'd turn out the lights and set the mood. Then rub his shoulders and back to relieve his tensions. That might lead naturally to making love, which would also help him sleep. Yes, she had planned it all out. However, this man had a knack for surprising her … in many wonderful ways.

She did talk him into going upstairs early. They did have their wine and he'd gone to the shower. She turned off the lights and lit candles, all according to her plans. But …

He stood enjoying the feel of the hot water pounding his back and shoulders as he worked lather against his scalp. "I love you," Ian intoned, rubbing shampoo into his hair. Yep, she'd said those very words. A broad smile lit his face, and he spit suds. Paige had said 'I love you' several times, in fact. He repeated her wonderful declaration and grinned, careful to keep his lips together this time. He'd spend quite a bit of time pondering his deep feelings for her. But, at that moment he was focused on her with quite erotic thoughts. He tamped down the sexy images with considerable concentration. Maybe later, he told himself, ruffling his wet hair with a towel. He resolved that if they made love that night he would be gentle, taking her from one plateau to the next, as he had previously.

However, when he walked into the romantic candlelit bedroom minutes later a towel wrapped round his hips ... Paige's lithe body and inviting look launched his libido into warp drive, erasing any thoughts of gentle. He strode across the room and without any preliminaries, yanked her into his arms. He noticed a heated frisson flicker in her eyes before he took her with a hot possessive kiss.

The visceral want in Ian's eyes had caused her breath to hitch. A determined expression she'd not seen before—primal, reckless. "Ian?" She sensed this could be very different than before, when he'd been so careful and tenderly methodical. Sure enough, the instant she pressed her body to his, something strong, almost animalistic seemed to seize and consume them both. A hot lush wave of desire blurred her consciousness. She was lost, immersed in the exhilaration of it, her hands rapacious, almost frantic, stoking his hunger. She balled her fists in his damp hair, pulled his mouth to her breasts. "Want you," she breathed.

The air was soon thick with the sounds and smells of passion as he suckled hard, rasping and pulling needy nipples with his teeth. He pushed her forcefully against a wall, and was rewarded with a pleasured moan. Ripping away her panties, he thrust a hand between her thighs. "So hot and wet," he muttered appreciatively. His fingers cupped her, roughly probed, tantalizing, as he took her lips with a searing kiss. He returned his mouth to her breast as his skilled fingers continuing to work and tease her toward frenzy.

"Oh, God," she cried, squirming and bucking against his hand; panting out his name before coming and wilting in his arms on ragged gasps.

Watching her smoky eyes flutter in orgasm, and feeling the spasms course through her had him wild with need. "You're so beautiful," he said, his voice hoarse with want.

She was weakened and breathless, yet still desperate for more, wanted all of him. "Please," she said, part plea, but more demand. She tore the towel from his hips, and bit down on his shoulder, a feral sound coming from deep in her throat. "Now—can't wait ..."

He gripped her bottom and took her where they stood, ramming upward and fully into her. She shrieked in delight and wrapped her legs—lifted and thudded against the wall on each of his savage growling thrusts.

"Open your eyes!" He panted out the command. "Want to ..." He pulled her head back, fixing her eyes with his. "... watch you feel it."

She was already at the brink again, her breaths coming in grunting bursts, could only gaze into those determined green eyes and shudder as he exploded deep within her. "Yes ... Oh, yes!" she sobbed, and joined him in blissful delirium.

They clung to each other, fighting to breathe, slowly returning to reality. Paige was dizzy and trembling, her knees rubbery. "Oh ... Ian," she managed, through labored breaths. "Not sure I can stand ... right now."

"Yeah ... Understand ..." He gulped air and pressed her against the wall to keep from losing his balance. "Hold on. Can't move ... just yet." Mustering all his remaining strength, he lifted her in his arms, made two faltering steps, and collapsed unceremoniously onto the bed. Still breathing hard, they both lay on their backs laughing at their condition.

"Wow." Paige's eyes were liquid with wonder. "That was wild." She paused with a dreamy look. "And so lusty ..." Her lips brushed against his. "I loved it."

"You may be the death of me, woman," he said. "I want you all the time, and you never seem satisfied, always want more."

"Oh, Darling, you certainly satisfy," she purred. "Do you ever!" She shot him a mischievous look. "But, you may have created a monster, Doctor McFrankenstein."

"A terrible problem, for me." He grinned wolfishly. "Pretty cute monster, though."

Wondrously tired, they held each other and drifted into their own pleasant thoughts. Ian was soon asleep.

Paige laid thinking about Ian and the promises she'd made herself ten days ago. Promises definitely fulfilled. But being wanted and desired by a man ... yes even treasured by him, was almost overwhelming. One thing she knew for sure: She had never felt more like a woman, in every possible way. She was very contented ... and deeply in love.

"Oh, you look awful." The mirrored face staring back at her looked worn and tired. "More like exhausted and butt ugly," she corrected. Shannon had worked the last eleven hours without stopping and hadn't slept in more than a day. But damned if she'd greet her handsome lover, the ever-perky Paige, and a troubled Ian looking as if she'd been ridden hard and put away muddy. No, no way would she go downstairs in this condition. "Jeez ... just look at those red eyes," she groaned. This might take all of her womanly tricks, but she was resolved.

Shaving her long, tanned legs while the warm shower water cascaded down her back, she evaluated what she had written. She liked it. After much work and torturous editing, a biographical piece had emerged that Shannon pronounced quite good. She'd decided to call it *Yesterday's Shadow.* Its length and depth were perfect for a magazine story. For newspapers, it would probably have to be a multi-day series or a special Sunday piece. In addition, a good fit for a one-hour TV celebrity bio special.

She liked her idea of telling his life story in reverse, thought that should both disarm and grab interest because of the public's familiarity with the Ian McBride they knew. Previous stories of the war hero turned author had been popular copy. Since readers and viewers liked and felt comfortable with the handsome, jet-setting bachelor, they'd be shocked when she abruptly introduced his shocking, well-hidden past. They would embrace him. She began toweling off. *Yeah, it's good all right.*

Shannon was starting to feel energized when something dawned on her. Her stomach tightened as she thought of the review/approval process she'd agreed to. She'd dealt with many editors, was used to tolerating their unfamiliarity with topics, and even the limited writing skills of some. This time, however, her editors were two best-selling authors and a publisher/lawyer. But one was her lover and the others her friends. Yeah, but they were depending on this piece to preserve Ian's reputation and career, to shield him from extortion. They had no choice, had to be critical. She'd be critical if she were in their shoes. Bottom line—if they didn't approve, *Yesterday's Shadow* wouldn't be published.

Shannon envisioned their overriding concern was Ian's comfort level and sensibilities. She imagined her work being reduced to a bland, weak mess that wouldn't protect Ian and make her look sophomoric. "No," she said, glaring into the mirror. "It's my best work ever, and I'll fight them to keep it intact."

Shannon refocused on the reconstruction task at hand. After brushing her teeth and hair, she created makeshift ice packs for her face and eyes from her room's mini refrigerator. Dabbing a strong astringent cream under her eyes magically erased the puffiness and dark circles. Antihistamine eye drops restored the blue gray luster. Eyeliner preceded the final lipstick and lip liner treatment. She eschewed any additional aids, instead patting her cheeks hard for color. Then, a critical check in the mirror. Not quite the same as the debutante who'd walked an Atlantic City runway as Miss Connecticut a decade before. "But you scrub up pretty well for a gal looking at thirty-one next month."

She tossed her hair, lifted her chin to just the right angle, and headed toward voices in the kitchen. She pasted on a determined smile, and readied for battle. "Nobody's screwing up Shannon Collin's work," she whispered.

"Well, look who decided to join us." Ian got off his stool at the breakfast bar and bowed. "Could I interest the tireless Miss Collins in a cup of coffee?"

"Yes, kind sir, lest I swoon," she said, dramatically putting the back of her hand to her forehead, before shifting to demand

and desperate begging. "Coffee, now! I'll be your slave for a cup of coffee."

"I don't think I'll go along with the slave thing. But getting her coffee is okay," Bob said. "I have something else for her."

Their hot kiss lasted several moments as Ian and Paige exchanged looks and raised eyebrows. When Bob finally broke the kiss, Paige applauded. "Now, there's a breakfast appetizer for you. Wow."

"Whew," Shannon said, grinning at Bob. "Let me guess what you've been thinking about while I worked all night." She pretended to fan herself. "You certainly know how to get a girl flustered."

"I like flustering you."

"Yeah, you told me that once before."

He smiled knowingly. "Still true, only more so now." Bob turned to Ian and Paige. "Worked all night and just look at her. Doesn't she look fabulous?"

They nodded in agreement but Ian grabbed her hand. "The man is a barbarian, Shannon." Ian went to one knee. "Ditch the brute and run away with me to Tahiti." His head lurched forward as Paige delivered a smiling forehand smash with a stool cushion to the back of his head.

"Easy on the testosterone, McBride."

"Poor baby." Shannon pursed her lips and waggled a finger. "Looks like Tahiti will have to wait."

Bob took charge, as usual. "Have a seat, ladies. Scrambled eggs and bacon okay with everybody?" Without giving anyone a chance to answer, he was cracking eggs. "Good. That's what it'll be."

The women rolled their eyes. Ian patted Bob on the back, chuckled, and set about pouring orange juice and making toast.

Paige turned to Shannon with some concern. "How long have you been awake?"

"Hmm," Shannon glanced at her watch. "Coming up on thirty hours."

How do you do it? Beautiful and fresh as a daisy after working your butt off all night."

Shannon just shrugged and smiled.

Paige took a sip of coffee and decided directness was best. "How'd the piece turn out?" Paige saw her go tense, her expression suddenly stern.

"You tell me." Shannon handed her a copy of the bio piece with something just shy of a sneer. "Ian wants approval from you and Bob before it's released."

Paige stared straight into the blonde's challenging eyes while putting the copy face down on the table. "What do *you* think? How would you rate it against other things you've written?"

Shannon wasn't ready for that; the question threw her. She looked first at Paige then at the copy she had plopped face down on the table. "Well ..." She laced her fingers, fidgeted, and cleared her throat. I think it's pretty good, actually ..." She paused a moment, then set her chin. "No, it's damn good! My best ... The best thing I've ever written."

Paige studied the woman's defiant face. Then, without breaking the intense eye contact, she pushed the copy back to Shannon, still face down. "That's all I need to hear. It's a go with me."

Shannon sat speechless. She'd expected Paige to be the toughest since she and Ian were ... Shannon's eyes suddenly widened, Paige's unspoken message of trust and friendship crystal clear. "Oh, my God," she whispered. She looked into Paige eyes, feeling tears beginning to burn her own. "I know you love him. And yet you're placing your trust in …" Paige simply nodded. Shannon squeezed her hand. "Paige, I …" She chewed her lip and shook her head. "I'm not going to cry, damnit." She dabbed at her eyes. "I'm not."

"All right, ladies," Bob's big voice rang out. "Breakfast time."

They stood and Shannon pulled her friend into a hug. "You're a sweetheart and a real piece of work, you little wimp." She smiled through moist lashes. "Let's eat before you get me all blubbery."

"Bob, I'd like to have your opinion and Paige's before I read this." Ian had only thumbed at the pages of the copy Shannon had given him. "You two will be more objective than me."

"Okay, I'll read it now," Bob said. He stood, picked up his coffee and a ballpoint pen. "We need to hustle. I expect the sheriff will be here within the hour. I'll be on the balcony."

Paige turned to face Ian. "Shannon and I have already talked about it. She's quite confident that it's her best work ever."

Feeling uncomfortable, Shannon excused herself. "Tell Bob I went to get some air … out front."

Twenty minutes later Bob came out of the front door and found Shannon leaning on the mailbox, watching the ocean. "Hey, Babe. I have some changes."

"I'll just bet you do," she said. The statement came out harsh, and she immediately regretted it.

Bob just looked into her eyes. "You must be exhausted."

She pulled away from him, wanting to get it over with. "So tell me about these changes." They talked for maybe three minutes, going over each page. Shannon was so tired she had trouble concentrating.

"That's it? That's all you want to change—commas, a semicolon, and two typos. That's it?"

"Shannon, it's a great piece of writing. It's terrific." Bob looked puzzled. "But you already knew that; wouldn't have it any other way ..." He took a step backward. "Oh, I see. You thought I was going to go lawyer and publisher on you and pick it apart." He looked down. "That hurts, Shannon."

"Oh, Bob ..." She felt like a real bitch. And as if things couldn't get worse, she knew tears were pooling in her eyes, again. "I'm sorry." She couldn't make herself look into his eyes. "I'm a stressed-out mess right now. Jeez, I feel like a fool."

"You're no fool, Honey." Bob studied her, standing there looking like a reprimanded little girl. She had to be exhausted, struggling just to stay awake. He pulled her into his arms. "What you are is one hell of a woman and an outstanding journalist. The piece is wonderful, does all the right things for Ian. It's vintage Shannon Collins. Damn near made me cry, and that's saying something. It's very good work, Babe."

She looked up at him, stroked his cheek, and then shocked him speechless. "I love you, Robert Fowler. I love you very much."

The four of them sat in the great-room while Ian read the biography of his life. Paige watched and wondered what he must be thinking and feeling. Shannon sat with her legs pulled up under her, cuddled next to Bob on a loveseat. Her head rested on his shoulder.

Ian stood without speaking, walked out onto the balcony, and stared out at the ocean for quite some time. When he came back in he began to pace in front of them. "This step scares the hell out of me. But you've convinced me it's the right ... no, the necessary thing to do." Looking off into space, he waved the pages in his hand as he talked. "This is one excellent piece of journalism. I'm impressed and grateful for your work, Shannon. It makes me want to work hard to live up to the picture you've painted here. Thank you. Thank you for your support and for this wonderful biography of my life."

There were a few moments of silence before Bob cut to the bottom line. "What changes do you want to make?" Ian's response surprised even Bob.

"None. Change nothing. Let's launch it."

"I agree," Bob said. "Okay, then we go with it." Continuing to talk, Bob turned to face Shannon. "Okay, Babe. Looks like it's time to firm up the appointments you arranged, and ..."

But Shannon Collins was sound asleep with what appeared to be the trace of a satisfied smile on her face.

20

"The Best Laid Schemes o' Mice 'an Men ..."

Redding had discontinued his surveillance. Considering what a mess Billings had made of things, the cops almost certainly would be watching the beach house. The last thing he wanted was to be spotted anywhere near that place or McBride and his houseguests. Having observed them for days, Redding had decided these were four pretty savvy people. They had sure side-tracked Billings' master plan and stopped him cold. His ball-point pen moved over the page of his journal.

Clever, not letting Billings talk to McBride. Bought them time to plan how they would proceed while screwing with his brain in the process. But I know human nature better than Billings. No way do es McBride want his past made public. Hell, the thought must scare the shit out of him. He'll pay me, one way, or another.

They've probably called the cops, by now. What's to lose? Yeah, the cops will be on the look out, and tapping the phones, I'll bet. Well, it won't do them any good. Billings is a pitiful amateur but I'm sure as hell not. We'll still get McBride's money. And I'll finally be able to get out of this damn business. McBride will pay once I explain the way things are going to be. He'll be eager to pay.

Redding assumed his extortion call would be recorded. He resumed writing.

So what? They won't be able to trace it or ID me. If they cover the pay-off site, they'll arrest some stupid kid I'll pay to pick up the money. If they do that, McBride will pay more than money. I'll have Billings release just enough of his past to sting him good and tantalize the media. Then, he'll pay like he's supposed to.

He picked up the journal, thinking things over, weighing options.

Good thing I have my backup plan. If the extortion falls through, I'll still have McBride by the short hairs. I'm betting he'd do anything to keep that little woman safe and in his bed. To hell with Billings. I'm coming out of this with big money, regardless. The one fly in the ointment is that idiot Billings. Flying to Hilton Head to 'manage things' he said. Stupid asshole! Well, tonight I make the call and get things back on track.

Shannon awoke to bright sun in her face, feeling a bit disoriented and groggy, assumed she must have dozed off on the sofa with her head on Bob's shoulder. The thought of him had her smiling and stretching like a lazy cat. He must have carried her upstairs and tucked her in. *That sweetheart.*

She began replaying what had happened and felt good knowing they all liked her story and approved it. But she'd so misjudged how they would react to her work. Paige's unqualified act of trust had almost done her in. She'd never been one to make friends easily, yet there was no denying how uniquely close she felt to Paige.

And Bob had been wonderful. "Uh-oh." She sat straight up in the bed. "I told Bob I loved him." She tried to replay the scene, but she couldn't remember what he'd said. Well, there was one way to find out how he felt about her being in love with him. She'd just go tell him again.

She felt surprisingly rested, after only five hours of sleep. She ran a brush through her hair and redid her eye makeup tears had wiped out a few hours back. That set her to thinking again. What was it with these people? Ian, Paige, and Bob had each had her blubbering like a schoolgirl since they'd met. She'd cried more with them than in the past ten years. For some inexplicable reason, that had her smiling broadly as she finished dressing and headed out to find Bob.

She looked over the balcony railing into the great room below, hoping to see him downstairs. No Bob. However, there were two men in white shirts and ties, with pistols and handcuffs on their belts, and an array of small electronic devices on the coffee table and end tables. The detectives had arrived and apparently set up the phone recording equipment.

Back to her search—like Bob, Ian and Paige were nowhere to be seen. But, as she was walking down the hallway, she heard talking inside Bob's bedroom and assumed he was on the phone. She didn't pay much attention until she heard her name. She stopped, not really to eavesdrop … but she did want to hear what he was saying about her. She'd wave to him, and wait inside until he'd finish his phone call. The door was open just enough to allow her to see through. There was Bob looking out at the Atlantic, talking and gesturing with his hands, but he wasn't talking on the phone or to anyone else, for that matter.

"Shannon, darling, I have deep emotions ..." His hands went above his head in a frustrated gesture. "Come on, Bob." He stuffed his hands into his pockets. "Okay, here goes ..." He paused, took a deep breath. "I've loved you since I first saw your blue eyes over dinner. Yeah, that's better, but ..." He drummed his fingers on the balcony railing.

Shannon's heart had leaped into her throat. She could barely breathe, but she stood still taking in each and every word. Any remaining doubts of how much he cared were swept away in that moment. He was still facing the ocean when, without thinking, she walked into the room.

Engrossed, Bob balled his fists. "He pounded his hand on the balcony railing. "Just say it, Bob. Just say it." He paused, then said, "I love you, Shannon, and you're going to be mine." He smiled and nodded. "Yeah! That's it, straight and simple."

"Yes, Bob darling, and I love you too," Shannon said from behind him.

He whirled around looking as if he had been shot. "Shannon?"

Shannon thought he looked like a deer caught in headlights, as if he might either pass out or bolt and run. Completely unlike her take-charge Robert T. Fowler.

Oh shit," he croaked. "How long have you ..." His face was reddening. "You heard ... Oh, fuck." He closed his mouth and just stared at her, looking physically sick.

"Easy, Baby." She touched his cheek. "Everything's okay." She grinned. "Very good, in fact." Holding his face between her hands, she turned his head slightly and kissed him, a deep, sensual kiss. She looked into his eyes. "Darling, nothing you could do, say, or buy would make me any happier than what I just watched and heard. Bob Fowler, you take my breath away ... I love you so much."

Bob's knees almost buckled with relief and joy. He scooped her up in his arms, walked to the bed, and laid her down. He stroked her hair. "Oh, I do love you."

"Why did you think you had to practice to tell me? You must have said those words to many ..."

"Shannon ..." he interrupted, with that penetrating look she'd come to know so well. "I've never said those words to any woman. Well, other than my mother."

"What? I thought ... Never?" She had to physically close her mouth. She touched his cheek, brushed his hair with her hands. "Oh, how do I deserve you?" She just could not seem to stop smiling or sobbing. "Lay with me, Bob. Make love with me. Let me show you how a truly happy woman pleasures the man she loves."

Mrs. Fowler had raised no fool. Bob locked the bedroom door and allowed her to do just that. Actually, he *allowed* her to show him again about twenty minutes after their first time.

Later, as they lay blissfully quiescent, naked, glistening in sweat, Shannon traced a languorous finger over his chest. "Bob, Honey?"

"Hmm?"

"Earlier, I heard you say, 'Shannon, you're going to be mine.' By going to be *yours,* you couldn't have meant what a woman might possibly think that could mean. Now, did you?" She grinned at him teasingly.

"Yeah. That's exactly what I meant." His tone was matter of fact. "We love each other. I want you. And, you *will* be mine."

"Huh? Wh … what?" She sucked in air; felt her throat closing and thought fainting was a strong possibility. Shaken to her toes, her voice came out as a squeaking whisper. "Oh," was all she could manage.

It was just too much to take in. She felt lightheaded, willed herself to take deep breaths. Good Lord, what was she supposed to say? Another deep breath. He was talking marriage … Wasn't he? No. More than talking, he was claiming her. Rudely brazen and audacious, it was so Bob Fowler, completely straightforward and honest. Which was probably why she wasn't the least bit offended.

Overwhelmed, she had no idea what to do next. How could he be so casual? She wiped her sweaty palms on the sheets and once again, reminded herself to breathe. Oh, she had to give this some very serious thought.

Bob was delighted but worked to seem stoic. She was beside herself all flustered over his 'You'll be mine' thing. Outstanding, exactly as he'd hoped she'd be. "You look pale, Sweetheart," he said, casually. Propped up on an elbow, he grinned knowingly. "… like you could use a good stiff, drink."

Redding made the drive to Beaufort, South Carolina, a tiny, historic place about an hour from Hilton Head, arriving a little before 8:00PM. He thought it looked like a miniature version of Charleston, only seedier. Out of habit and as a precaution, he had once again exchanged his rental car and was now driving an off-white Oldsmobile sedan. He found a pay phone on the edge of a strip shopping center that was out of the way enough for the call he was about to make.

There had already been a couple of false alarms, a wrong number, and a call from Paige's publisher, Fred, trying to coax her to Philadelphia for a book signing. When the phone rang again, the planned sequence swung into action as it had each time before. One of the detectives activated the recording device and nodded to the other detective, who would listen and take notes as a backup. The larger of the two detectives nodded to Paige, indicating it was okay to answer the phone, which she did.

"Mr. McBride's residence."

"Yes, good evening. This is William Winston of the Atlanta chapter of the Veterans of Foreign Wars. May I speak to Ian McBride, please?"

Paige gave the thumbs-down signal to the others. "He's a bit tied up at present, Mr. Winston. What is the nature of your call?"

Mark Redding adopted a friendly tone. "We plan to name Mr. McBride as our chapter's Veteran of the Year, and we want to arrange an awards ceremony for next month, if possible."

"Hold the line, please, Mr. Winston."

Paige covered the mouthpiece and looked to the detectives who only shrugged and began to shut down the recording equipment. "Ian, you might want to take this. Seems the VFW wants to give you an award."

"Okay, I guess." Ian set down his beer and walked over to take the call. "Thanks honey." He took the receiver and cleared his throat. "This is Ian McBride."

"Ah, yes, Mr. McBride. You managed to brush off my associate earlier, but that will not happen with me. The figure is no longer 500 K. It's now $650,000, a penalty for not respecting us."

Ian swung around and waved at the detectives. Pointing at the telephone, he mouthed, "It's him." A flurry of activity followed. Ian's frayed nerves gave way to emotion. "That's crazy ... A lot of money. Why the hell should I pay you a cent?"

"Because we know all about your hidden past, John McDonald, and the news media will also if you don't do exactly as I say."

"Listen up, asshole!" Ian's temper flared. "You can't pull this shit on me. I'll ..."

Bob lunged out of his chair, gripping Ian's arm like a vice, shooting him a cautioning look.

Redding's voice went icy as he cut Ian off. "Oh, but we can. And we will if you don't do precisely as you're told. Oh, you'll pay all right. Or there'll be a few calls, a couple of faxes, and Ian McBride's reputation along with your future income will be destroyed ... all within an hour."

"Calm down, Ian," Bob whispered. "Play him. Follow the plan."

Ian nodded and took a deep breath before he spoke again. "Okay, but wait," he said into the phone. "I don't have that kind of money on hand. It'll take several days ..."

Redding cut him off again. "You have tonight and tomorrow. I'll contact you before noon, day after tomorrow, with the delivery instructions. You got it?"

"Yeah, I understand. But what if I can't get the money that soon?"

"Simple—we'll ruin you, of course—might be 'kinda' fun, actually. Oh, and as for the cops who are probably listening in. Too bad, guys. I'm at a pay phone in a different town. You've been on the job long enough to know that screws you. Get the money, McBride ... in cash and on time." The line went dead.

Bob turned to face Shannon. "We have little more than a day. Is that enough time to get your piece in the papers, magazines and on TV?"

"We'll make the papers ... I think the TV interviews will also work." Shannon had already considered contingencies. "Unfortunately, we'll miss the magazine—longer production times than the others. But ... the plan's going to work, Ian. I can feel it!"

"Bob, Honey, I've gotta' get moving. Need to call the paper, the networks, and some others. I really need to get to New York tonight. I know it's short notice, but ..."

"I chartered a Gulfstream G-100, their fastest. You can leave in an hour. Will that be soon enough? The plane will be waiting for you at the airport."

"Yeah, that'll work." She smiled. "I should have known you'd have everything covered."

Bob took her hands. "The pilot will wait at LaGuardia and fly you back after the interviews." He paused, stroking her hair. "You know I want to go with you."

"I know ..." The look on his face touched her. "But Ian needs you here. I'll be okay and I'll get back as soon as I can,

Hon. Gotta' get going." She yelled over her shoulder. "Want to give me a hand packing, Paige?"

With Shannon and Paige upstairs, Bob and Ian talked to the detectives. They now knew there was more than one extortionist. The younger detective had already determined the call's point of origin. A Beaufort police cruiser was on the way to check it out, but none of them thought that would accomplish much. Anxiously, Ian asked, "Well, what do you think? Can we catch these two?"

"Hard to say at this point, but we do have a lead, of sorts. This caller used a phrase, a very interesting phrase."

"Phrase?" Bob sat down, prepared to take notes. "What do you mean?"

"When he got cute toward the end, he used the phrase 'on the job'. He said, 'You cops have been on the job long enough to know.'"

"So what," Ian persisted. "I don't get it. What's the big deal?"

"It's an insider thing. Only a police officer would use that phrase, and only when talking to another cop."

The other detective looked up from his recording log. "Or a former cop," he offered. "This perp could be an ex cop, deputy, whatever. Maybe one who went bad and got the boot. Sounded like a Northeastern accent to me. New York or New Jersey, I'd guess. Worth checking it out."

"Yeah," said the senior detective. "I'll call the captain. He knows the politics of things like this, will know who to call up north."

The three of them accompanied Shannon to the airport. She brought them up to date as they drove. "I spoke to the news editor at the *Times* and also to UPI and AP. All three agreed to embargo the story and break it day after tomorrow at 6:00AM. I'm scheduled to tape an interview with Bill O'Reilly at nine tomorrow morning and another is scheduled with Barbara Walters for noon. Both networks will promo the interviews starting tomorrow night at 8:00PM and they will run simultaneously twenty-four hours later."

"Way to go!" Bob squeezed her hand as he turned the car into the airport. "Sounds great, babe." He glanced at her with a look of pride. "This will put you on the national map as a star. You deserve it."

Shannon kissed his cheek and turned to Ian and Paige in the back seat. "We're going to stop them. We won't let them get to you, Ian."

She watched the island slip away as the speedy little six-passenger jet roared skyward, pressing her back into the leather seat. Once it leveled off, Shannon looked down at the box lunch in the seat next to her unable to remember the last time she'd eaten. The pilot had left it in the seat, explaining they weren't much on frills but Mr. Fowler had arranged for the meal and asked him to see she got it.

Her thoughts drifted to Bob and then to Paige and Ian. The goodbye at the airport hadn't been at all simple. The discomfort she felt leaving Bob, even for a day, surprised her. Then Paige and Ian had pulled her into a joint hug, thanking her profusely for what she was doing. She tried to make light of it and almost succeeded until she looked into Ian's soulful eyes and saw tears welled in Paige's. As if that wasn't enough, she was still working to uncurl her toes from Bob's searing goodbye kiss. Then, of course, there was his marriage declaration to think about. *Jeez!* Bob had been right. She could do with a stiff drink. She was delighted to find two mini bottles of merlot in her box lunch. Smiling, she opened one and poured it into a plastic glass. "Here's to you Bob Fowler. Thoughtful, sweet, loving ..." She held her glass high. "To you, my darling man."

Leaning back, she sipped the smooth red wine, closed her eyes, and tried to force all emotional thoughts to the back of her mind. Not an easy task, but Shannon knew the stakes she was facing, and she was determined to excel in the important challenges waiting in New York. She was fully aware this was the biggest opportunity of her career, but was also ever so mindful Ian's reputation and future, at that point, were largely dependent on her.

Soon she was absorbed in preparing an outline for the two scheduled TV interviews. She had no way of knowing the dangers and stresses yet to come.

21

Plots and Revelations

"Where the hell is Redding?" he muttered rhetorically. It was just after 8:00PM when Richard Billings checked into the Westin Resort. His luxury suite's commanding view of the Atlantic was of no interest to him, it and all other things overshadowed by his obsession to obtain money for his drug debts.

"Damnit!" Almost sick with fear and worry, he kicked a trashcan across the room. Twice in the last hour, he'd tried, without success, to reach Redding on his cell phone. "My money, my plan, and I have no idea what's going on."

He rummaged through his briefcase and pulled open an inner seam revealing a small packet of white powder. Thirty minutes later, a cocaine fogged Richard Billings drove his black rental Cadillac out of the Westin Resort lot, once again dialing Mark Redding's cell phone number.

In the community of Bluffton, just off Hilton Head Island, another visitor was checking into a motel. Martha McDonald stood with a hand on her cocked hip, flirting with Ted, the night manager of the Motel 6. If things took what she saw as the normal course with men, she'd secure free lodging in exchange for a couple of quickies with this simple, horny dolt. Her room key in hand, she stroked Ted's cheek with a purple lacquered nail, and left him to ponder possibilities.

Martha's room was anything but plush, with its unspectacular view of six battered dumpsters in Burger King's rear parking lot. Closing the curtains, she checked the local phone book and was delighted to find an address and number for Ian McBride.

She stopped by the front desk to ask Ted for directions to the address she'd found ... and to steam him up a bit more. "You're a cutie, aren't you?" Martha placed a finger in her mouth and slowly withdrew it through pursed red lips. She heard his low groan and watched him shift uncomfortably in his chair. "What's the matter, sweetie?" Licking her lips, she stared blatantly at the distended bulge in his trousers. "Hmm ... Yummy," she purred.

"Well, gotta go." She turned for the door, grinning to herself. *Yep. He's a gonner.* She was all but certain Teddy would gladly cover the cost of her room and more for the next few days.

Mark Redding ended the demand call and walked about sixty yards to a restaurant with outdoor tables where he took a seat, ordered a beer, and waited.

A couple of minutes later, the first of two police cruisers skidded to a halt near the phone booth he had used. *Thought so. McBride called the cops.* He nodded, feeling pleased with himself. *Good. He's behaving predictably.* Redding ran a hand over the stubble on his chin, feeling uneasy, but unable to put a finger on why.

He absent mindedly watched two officers search in and around the phone booth, collecting gum wrappers and cigarette butts he knew would be useless. When the police cars left twenty minutes later, Redding sat perplexed and deep in thought. *Why's he stalling?* From Billing's e-mail and call until now, McBride had already had plenty of time to get money together. Yet, apparently, he had not. *He's buying time.* Redding chewed on a toothpick. *No, not just him. All four of them are working together just as Billings said.* Redding's PI instincts told him they were up to something, and he didn't like the smell of it.

He dialed Richard Billing's cell phone number.

Martha had driven onto the Island and along a few major roads getting a feel for the place. She found McBride's house near the Island's southern most tip; stopped fifty yards away, and parked by the curb. She sat in the darkness watching the big house, not really knowing why. Maybe she was hoping he'd walk out so she could get a look at him, maybe she was just working up her courage, or reconsidering the idea of confronting him, at all.

She had no way of knowing she was also being watched, through an infrared telescopic device held by a sheriff's department detective. He jotted down the license plate number, a brief description of her rental car, and notes about her face and hair.

It only took two phone calls for the detective to determine when and where Martha McDonald had rented the car; her complete physical description; home address; and details of her arrests and convictions. A woman with a California address sitting in the dark 3,500 miles from home watching the house of a man, who was being blackmailed, certainly aroused the detectives' suspicions. Arrangements were made to have her followed when she decided to leave. Before the night was over, they would also know where Martha McDonald was staying locally.

She drove north along William Hilton Parkway, heading back to her motel, unaware of the unmarked Mercury following her. Stopping at a traffic light, she glanced to her left and into the driver's window of a black Cadillac. She looked closer and recognized the man driving the Cadillac. The scene in Richard Billing's office snapped into her mind, as did what she'd heard him say, rehearsing actually. "Oh shit!" she muttered. *Bastard's here to blackmail McBride … and take my money.*

Billings was so absorbed in a cell phone conversation she knew he hadn't noticed her. She raised her right hand and defiantly extended its middle finger as the Cadillac pulled away from the traffic light. "Screw you, Richie! I'll beat you to the punch."

The three stopped at a small Italian restaurant on the way back from the airport. They'd agreed to try to talk and think of things other than the critical matter at hand. Some wine helped.

They shared a bottle and talked about Shannon, tennis, the beauty of the island and the close bond they'd formed. Bob was missing her already.

Two new detectives were in the great room, when Bob, Paige, and Ian returned to the beach house, watching the street, checking the recording equipment, and waiting for further contact from the blackmailers. Bob and Ian spoke to the detectives, who mentioned Martha McDonald only in passing, until Bob focused on the incident with her.

"What about the woman from California? And the name, McDonald? Seems suspicious; and a little weird don't you think?" Bob asked.

"It does," the younger of the detective agreed. "But, as cops, we're in the 'suspicious and weird' business." He chuckled.

"Probably just coincidence," the detective sergeant offered. "Maybe just one of your groupies, Mister McBride—no reason to think she's connected to our investigation—that's what our captain said."

"One of my fans? Hmm, I hadn't considered that," Ian said. "Possible; it's happened before. Right Bob?" Bob nodded and took a swig of Perrier.

"Most likely no big deal," the younger detective opined. "But we're following up on her anyway."

Bob told Ian and Paige goodnight and went upstairs to work. Ian motioned in the general direction of upstairs. "I'm still trying to deal with my confirmed bachelor friend having such a thing for Shannon Collins."

"Men!" Paige huffed, crossed her arms over her chest, and gave him a look. "You guys can be such blind, insensitive clods at times."

"Whoa! Where'd that come from?"

"Bob doesn't have a *thing* for Shannon. He's in love with her, and she loves him. Don't you see it? I think it's sweet."

"Oh, boy, there's that word again. I told you men don't like *sweet*. But, anyway … You really think he's in love?"

"Of course." She shot him another look. "Jeez! The way he looks at her and treats her … It's so obvious, Ian. And it is sweet, whether you like it or not."

"Hmm?" Ian looked uneasy, took a couple of steps away from her drumming his fingers against his wine glass. He cleared his throat, "Do you think I look at you … you know … that way?"

Paige had anticipated he might ask something along these lines, eventually. "Yes." She gave him a level look. "You look at me exactly that way."

Expecting a much less direct answer, he could only mutter, "Oh." He gulped down the remainder of his wine, and evasively asked, "Want some more wine?"

His obvious discomfort amused her. It also touched her deeply, but she kept her voice and expression neutral. "No, thank you."

Ian paced a bit before refilling his glass to the brim, and then downing half of the chilled Chardonnay. He turned and blurted out, "Do you think I'm in love?"

Paige moved to him with tears burning her eyes. "Yes, darling." She took his wine glass, set it on a table, and kissed him tenderly. "Even though I'm new to this, too, I think you're certainly in love. And I am so very happy it involves me."

"You really think so?" He looked taken aback but a smile filled his face. "Thought I was incapable. Not able."

"Yes, I believe you're in love with me." Thinking her chest might not hold her joyfully pounding heart, Paige stroked his cheek. "And you're doing a mighty good job of it." She pulled him down onto the balcony's wicker loveseat and wrapped her arms around his neck. "Oh, how I love you!" She kissed him deeply, and then gave him a mischievous grin. "Now, Mr. McBride, if you don't get me upstairs quickly, those two detectives are going to get a real eyeful when I tear off our clothes and take you right here on the balcony."

He ended the phone conversation with Billings more convinced than ever the man might screw this whole thing up. Billings was an emotional basket case, and if things kept going the way they had so far, they would get no money and Billings' bungling would land them both in prison. Redding had never been in jail and didn't plan to ever be. Nor did he intend to walk away from this empty-handed.

He made two decisions: One, he was going to run the extortion, leaving Billings to his cocaine and believing he was still in charge. Two, he'd start working on his own backup plan to get money from McBride. He wrote an old cop saying into his journal before he closed the cover. *Prior planning prevents piss poor performance.*

At Wal-Mart, he bought the things he needed for the night's work: black pants, a black long-sleeve shirt, and a mesh mosquito net to cover his head and face. The garb would blend him into any dark background and his face would be unrecognizable. Now he had to go shopping for one specific item that wasn't sold in stores. A little burglary was on his schedule.

Redding laid the phone book down, surprised such a small island had three practicing veterinarians. He jotted down the address of each, circled their locations on his map, and left his motel at 2:00AM, dressed head-to-toe in black. A small flashlight and gloves lay on the seat beside him.

The first veterinarian's office was in a small shopping center. No good. Finding the second to be on a main road, it was also rejected. He was growing concerned before he located the third on a dark, narrow road.

The office and clinic of Dr. Thomas C. Watson, DVM, was a converted one-story house with no alarm. Even though the nearest neighbor was more than a hundred yards away and barely visible in the darkness of the cloudy night, Redding parked a block away and walked to the house. With his entire body covered in cloth, netting, and gloves, the night's humid warmth had him soaked in sweat.

There was a small kennel adjoining the house with five or six dogs. He eased into the side yard. A couple of moves with a credit card and a small knife and he was into the house with ease. Redding was unconcerned when a couple of small dogs in cages began barking. The dogs outside were so noisy nobody would think anything of a few more barks.

Once in the clinic area, he began going through cabinets and looking on shelves, finding everything except what he sought. "Come on, Doc, where do you keep the good stuff?" Another examining room, more shelves, and more cabinets. Finally, he saw a locked wall chest with glass front doors. Focusing the beam of his small flashlight on the glass, he read the labels.

"Bingo! Paydirt." The cabinet held an array of narcotics, pain-killers, various anesthesias, and other controlled drugs. Among the bottles, he spotted his prize, chloroform. Splash it on a handkerchief, place it over the nose and mouth, and tell the victim good night for a while.

One rap with the flashlight broke the cabinet's glass, yielding access. He hated to mess up the Doc's neat, clean place, but necessity called for it. He tore the place up some to make it look like a routine burglary, scattered things from the cabinets and took several of the easily recognizable narcotics.

Back in his car and driving away, a satisfied smile filled his face. His plan was coming together well. *To hell with Billings. McBride will pay, and he's going to pay me.*

The Gulfstream's jet engines whined on and on, whisking Shannon back to Hilton Head from New York at 600 miles per hour. She was exhausted from negotiations with hardnosed editors and seemingly endless retakes for the two TV interviews, and she felt tense knowing success rested to a large degree on the deals she'd brokered. The whole plan would fall apart if one of the producers or editors got greedy and jumped the gun on the others. Nevertheless, she was about 90 per cent convinced she'd pulled it off, and things were going to go well. She refused to consider the other ten percent possibility.

She had provided almost fifty unique and candid photographs of Ian, some of which showed him shirtless in jeans or in swim trunks. The media folks loved those since he was seldom seen in casual clothes, and never shirtless. One of the female producers summed it up: "The women will drool over those pecs, abs, and that windblown hair." Shannon decided she wouldn't share that comment with Paige.

Yes, it had been a tiring but rewarding day including an unexpected development that was both flattering and disturbing. Barbara Walters' producer had offered her a position as a traveling journalist under contract to the network. It would require her to live in New York. The salary and benefits were substantial and she had to admit, tempting. It surprised her that she felt compelled to get Bob's opinion before giving the network her answer. Just one more complication to further muddle her already overworked brain she thought.

"Buckle up, Miss Collins," the pilot yelled. "Hilton Head Island Airport in five minutes."

It was 11:15 PM and all she wanted was to crawl into bed next to Bob's big warm body and sleep for a week, although the possibility of making love did cross her mind. She smiled, thinking what she'd like to do with that big male body ... if she still had the energy.

Ian lay on his back, his hands laced behind his head on the pillow and a lascivious grin alight on his face. A shaft of morning sun streaming through the windows was spotlighting Paige's perfectly shaped, petite butt as she bent over with spread legs to pick up her robe. He smiled at the contrast created by dark tan lines and bikini-protected pale skin.

Nude with her back turned to him, she lazily stretched, and shook her long black locks before donning the robe. The erotic sight had sent most of the blood in his head straight south. He bit his lower lip and growled. Turning, she noticed his blatant arousal and tortured expression. "Feeling frisky are we, Mr. McBride?" she asked with a sly grin.

He groaned. "You're incredible. Without even trying, you keep me constantly horny."

"I think I like you that way. However, be warned …" Paige leaned over and shot him a coy smile. "I'll only put up with your horniness about eight days a week." She snickered and slid away as he made a grab for her. "Oh, no. Not now, Mr. Horny. We're hitting the beach. I'll get my shorts and shoes from my bedroom and see you downstairs in five." She saw his mock pout. "You poor baby." She yanked the robe open, giving him a full frontal flash. Then laughed playfully and danced out the door. Ian just shook his head. He had finally admitted to himself he was hopelessly in love with her; thought he must be the luckiest man alive.

But the human mind can be a cruel thing, synapticly hop scotching from blissful to dreadful in a heartbeat. Today was the day he'd get the call … where and when to make the payoff. Every detail had been coordinated with the sheriff, but secretly, Ian still hoped for a few moments alone with the bastards before the deputies got to them. He pushed those dark thoughts to the back of his mind and went to meet Paige for what had become *their* daily run.

He knew she was concerned and worried about him, and he was touched she was doing everything she could think of to keep things as pleasant as possible for him. *The woman I love.* The words and reality of it still left him awed. He watched her stretching on the balcony, and marveled. She was amazing and wonderful in so many ways, certainly the best thing that had ever happened to him. Not having her with him had become unimaginable. He'd been giving all that a great deal of thought. The ultimate solution he kept coming back to was such a huge, daunting step. But he had an idea, an interim plan he thought Paige might like.

22

No Honor Among Thieves

It was a rainy day on Hilton Head Island. The gray sea and sky mirrored the mood of the four as they pretended to not be anxious. The extortionist had said he would contact Ian before noon, but it was 1:30PM and the phone hadn't rung all day. The detectives didn't know why there had been no call, but believed the payoff was still on.

Paige and Shannon absent-mindedly played gin rummy in the kitchen, as Ian and Bob sat preoccupied and edgy with the two detectives. Ian drummed his fingers on the coffee table, picked up his still full, but now warm Coke, and sat it down again. Standing, he began to pace. "So, what do you think, Bob?"

"Hell, I don't know," sighed Bob. He shrugged. "We just have to wait. I realize that's not your strong suit. Just try to hang in there."

When they'd talked by phone the night before, Billings had demanded they meet this morning for him to instruct Redding on how the payoff was to work. Redding, although aggravated, played Billings like a fish on a line during the phone call.

"Don't trust me to make the pickup, huh?"

"Hell no! I don't trust you or anyone else when it comes to this money. My ass is on the line here and only this cash will get me straight."

"Then I guess you'll want to pick up the package yourself."

"You bet your ass! Yeah, I'm picking up that money myself. I want you nearby, though, in case I need some muscle."

"Well, okay. You're the boss." Redding had smiled slyly. From his police days, he was positive officers would be covering the drop site to arrest whoever touched the money McBride was to leave behind.

Redding wrote in his journal, describing what he saw as a win/win situation.

I'll be a block or so away watching Billings make the pickup. If it goes smoothly, I'll have a bead on him so he can't split with the loot. On the other hand, if things go to shit, and they bust him, I just drive away and launch my own backup plan while McBride and his pals have their guard down, thinking it's all over.

Martha McDonald was busy in her tiny motel room. She smiled into the mirror and applied hair spray to her straw-like bleached hair. *Men are so predictable,* she thought. Just as she'd anticipated, the skinny night manager showed up after his shift ended that morning. She wasn't thrilled to be awakened at

7:00AM, but realized this was probably to her benefit. Martha was ever so cordial.

Sure enough, Ted had been looking to barter. So, for almost an hour, Martha *bartered* him to near exhaustion. She had only anticipated a standard straight quickie, but because he talked nice to her, and even seemed a little shy, she threw in a hard-driving freebie twenty-five minutes later, that almost did him in. He had gladly agreed to pay her room charges for as long as she wanted to stay, in exchange for them 'having coffee' each morning after his shift ended.

To her surprise, Martha had almost enjoyed the experience with Ted. Seemed like an all right guy ... for a South Carolina hayseed. She looked into the mirror and started to chuckle. "Poor guy could barely walk."

After shopping for some necessities and eating lunch, Martha refocused on her primary objective. She headed for McBride's beach house to confront him and demand the money she felt she deserved. It was just after 1:00PM, she'd be there by 1:30 or so.

Mark Redding was frustrated, increasingly apprehensive and pissed off! As agreed, he'd arrived at Room 1212 of the Westin Resort Hotel, right on time, prepared to call and tell McBride when and where to drop the $650,000. However, Billings didn't answer the door when he knocked. He pounded, but still no answer. Angry, he went to a house phone and called Billings' room. Finally, after twenty or so rings, a groggy-sounding voice answered. Richard Billings had been stoned, falling down drunk at 11:25 in the morning.

Redding paced the carpeted floor, with Billings, muttering curses under his breath. He checked his watch. *Shit! 1:45 already.* He'd already poured a pot of coffee down Billings, and still his demeanor indicated he needed at least thirty more minutes to be sober enough to handle the pick-up. Redding considered how much he would enjoy wringing the man's neck. Instead, he ordered more coffee.

The older of the two detectives watched from the window while his partner sat by the phone monitoring equipment and reading the newspaper. Scanning the nearby dunes and deserted street with binoculars, he was surprised to see something familiar. "Jim, I've got a car coming. Could be that woman from California." The other detective joined him and trained the binoculars on the driver's face.

"Sure is. That's her all right ... She's going to turn into the driveway."

"Mr. McBride, looks like you're about to have company, that McDonald woman we ID'ed the other night. Detective Jones and I will get out of sight and watch from the kitchen."

Ian answered the door. There stood a woman, saying nothing, but obviously studying him. Neither spoke—Ian looked her up and down. About five foot four, anorexic thin, and smelling of cigarettes and strong perfume, she had one of those faces that made it hard to guess an age. Somewhere between 35 and 45, hard years, lots of mileage on this one. A too short skirt, bleached out hair, false eyelashes, heavy makeup ... *Like a hooker*, Ian thought.

Martha continued to eye him, and quickly scanned what she could see of the room. Yep, he had money, all right. She set her chin and looked him in the eye. "You Ian Michael McBride?"

"Yes." He gave her a curious half smile. "And who might you be?"

"Name's Martha McDonald and I've come to talk about you and me. About when we were kids."

Ian looked puzzled. "What ... when we were kids?"

She handed him the stack of news clippings, photographs and book reviews with the handwritten note on top reading *Martha's half-brother. Same mother.*

Ian gave them a quick once over. "So, what's all this?" he said charily. Skeptical and on guard, Ian's voice went stern. "What's your scam?"

"No scam; I am your half-sister, sugar. That's what those papers show. That stuff came from my foster parents' things after they died." She handed him the private investigator's report. "This, too. It's all there, everything about our dear, sweet mother and your nasty-ass father in New York. Yep, I'm your kin."

"Sure you are," Ian said sarcastically. "That's ridiculous, impossible." He reached to close the door. "Good-bye."

"It's the truth. Read the friggin detective's report yourself." She thrust out her chin. "I ain't going nowhere." Her voice shot up. "You're my half-brother, and you owe me! You're gonna pay for what she did to me."

"You're nuts! I owe you nothing." He grabbed her arm. "You're leaving. Now!"

Bob, Paige, and Shannon looked at each other questioningly. Ian seemed to have things under control, but … The detectives hiding behind the breakfast bar gave them a sign to stay put. The younger detective was listening and taking notes as quickly as he could write.

"Damn you!" All but screaming, she tried to pull away from Ian's grip. "She threw me away like garbage and kept you. You owe me plenty! And if you don't pay me, uh … $50,000. Well, I'll uh … I'll go to the papers with my story."

"You're actually demanding money?" Ian's expression flashed from incredulous to angry. However, glaring at her, the illegal nature of her demands dawned on him. The detectives could hear everything she said. Ian shot her a menacing grin. "Are you threatening me?"

"Damn right!" Martha McDonald was red-faced, almost yelling. "If you don't pay me $50,000 … No, if you don't pay me $100,000, I go to the papers. I'll destroy you."

They'd heard enough. The two detectives drew their pistols and moved just before Bob did. Holding his badge high, the detective sergeant yelled a command. "Deputy Sheriffs—Put your hands behind your head and don't move!"

They converged on the astonished Martha McDonald, one detective holding her at gunpoint as the other grabbed her arms and handcuffed them behind her back. Furious, she cursed and struggled.

"Martha McDonald, you're under arrest for violation of SC1224, Extortion in the First Degree. You have the right to remain silent. You have the right to an attorney …"

The younger detective finished advising her of her rights while the sergeant placed a radio call to advise the sheriff of their

unexpected arrest. Their detainee continued to scream obscenities and wriggle against her bonds.

"Damn!" Bob exclaimed, turning to Shannon and Paige.
"We've got blackmailers coming out of the woodwork."

Ian stood skimming the report, shaking his head in disbelief.
Paige noticed his expression and put an arm around his shoulder. "What is it, sweetheart? It can't be what she said, right?" He
squeezed her hand and turned to Bob.

"I know her ravings sound absurd, but this info seems to
track. Take a look. Hell, considering my background ... not
that far fetched."

"What? Ian, the woman is just trying to blackmail you!"

"That's crap!" screamed Martha McDonald, who'd been
forced to sit on the sofa. She shot to her feet, yelling at Bob.
"Billings is the blackmailer. I'm just here for what I deserve."

Shannon stared in disbelief and Bob's jaw dropped as they
spun around to face the woman. Bob grabbed her shoulders.
"Billings? You can't mean Richard Billings?"

"Yeah, my damn lawyer. He's trying to do blackmail, not
me. Saw him yesterday night, in a big Cadillac, just a couple
miles from here."

Shannon felt shocked, sickened. Bob knew she'd dated Rich-
ard Billings ... maybe even suspects she'd done more with him.
But this. She stood with the others listening to Martha
McDonald relate how she had watched Billings rehearsing the
extortion phone call. Shannon cringed, feeling like a traitor.
God, she'd had sex with the bastard who was threatening to
destroy Bob's best friend. What Bob must be thinking of her?
She turned away, not wanting to face him ... or the others.

It was 2:15PM when the two uniformed deputies took Martha McDonald away. She would spend the night in jail and be arraigned the next day on a charge of felony extortion.

Ian, Bob and the detectives went over the plan again, and rechecked the box. The payoff package was ready. The detectives had used a chart to tell them how much $650,000 in $20 bills should weigh. The box was three-quarters filled with magazines and newspapers that were camouflaged with layers of banded money packets. Ian provided the $25,000. Atop Ian's money, there was $10,000 in Sheriff's Department marked bills. A thin GPS tracking wafer that would signal the box's location was placed into the container's cardboard bottom. It would be remotely activated later and monitored from the detectives' unmarked car. The two detectives each wrote 35 and their initials on the bottom of the box, thus certifying it held $35,000. Once sealed with duct tape, it looked and felt like a box holding a huge amount of money. All was ready.

The phone rang at 2:35PM. Ian swallowed hard and took a deep breath.

He followed what they had rehearsed, being careful of what he said and insuring the recorded words of the caller violated the law. The blackmailer's instructions were clear. When Ian agreed to comply, the phone went dead. Bob had listened in and told the deputies it was not Richard Billings' voice. The end game was afoot.

Bob hated that he could not go with Ian and felt he was somehow leaving his 'brother' unprotected. He would have to wait like Paige and Shannon, and only listen in on the sheriff's surveillance, and hopefully the arrests, via the police radio hooked up in the beach house.

Ian talked into a mic as he drove the Porsche through the steady drizzling rain and traffic. The tiny microphone transmitter concealed in his lapel allowed the detectives, as well as the three at the beach house, to hear his description of where he was and what he was seeing. He turned into the shopping center where the drop was to take place and drove to the southwest corner, as the caller had directed. The parking lot was crowded with the cars of people whose golf game or day at the beach had been rubbed out by the rain.

Ian finally saw the abandoned blue pickup with two flat tires where he was to leave the money. He eyed the box in the passenger seat and said, "Broadway," the codeword indicating he was at the drop site. It was raining harder.

Ian left the Boxter's engine running as he stood holding the box and peering into the driving rain. He looked in all directions but saw nothing out of the ordinary. He had been told there would be undercover deputies at the site. Were those two telephone repairmen them? What about the guy pushing a grocery cart? Deputies, hell any of them could be the blackmailers for all he knew. Frustrated, he went to the back of the battered pickup truck with rain running into his eyes. Still nothing. "Firestone," he said, indicating the drop had been made.

Hearing Ian's two key words over the monitor, Bob looked at Paige. He saw the look in her eyes and heard her sigh of relief. "He's going to be fine, Paige. We'll get the ones doing this."

Shannon turned from them and walked onto the balcony, feeling alone and ashamed.

"You okay?" Bob asked Paige.

"Yeah." She let out a relieved sigh. "At least better ... now that that part's done."

"Good." Bob patted her shoulder. "I'm going to get some air."

He had noticed Shannon's departure and her expression. He walked up behind her and wrapped her in his arms. "I know you were concerned. We all were ... But why do I think something else is troubling you?"

"You know what it is ..." She lowered her head and spoke while keeping her back to him. "I don't know how you can stand to look at me."

"What?" Bob whirled her around. "Tell me what's wrong."

She shook her head, covered her face, and started to cry.

"Shannon, what is it?"

Sobbing, she turned to faced him. "You know that I was ... with him ..." She lowered her head. "... the one who's doing this to Ian. I'm so ashamed, feel like such a fool."

"Oh, Baby." He paused, and then hugged her close.

"But ... but, I feel so guilty," she sobbed. "I should have seen it. Stupid! Should have made the connection, tied him to this ... I've let you and Ian down so badly."

"You've done nothing to be ashamed of or sorry for." Wiping tears from her blue eyes, Bob wondered how he deserved such an extraordinary woman. "The bastard fooled us all. Hell, I considered him a friend, was playing handball with him and buying him lunch a month after you figured out he was trouble and dumped him. You think I don't feel stupid and foolish?"

"I still feel bad about it." She sniffed and wiped her eyes. "I love you, Bob Fowler."

"YES!" Bob and Shannon's heads jerked around when they heard the large detective sergeant's booming voice. "Got him!"

Shannon and Bob dashed into the great room only to be assaulted by a jubilant Paige Brittany.

"They've got him! Arrested Richard Billings picking up the money—nailed him!"

There were smiles all around. Shannon and Bob hugged Paige and shook the detectives' hands. The big detective sergeant slapped Bob on the back. "He'll get big prison time for this."

"Prison?" Paige flashed a stern look that stopped the sergeant cold. "Prison's not enough," she exclaimed, her expression suddenly icy, vengeful. The petite woman shocked the room into silence with a venomous declaration. "The bastard should be castrated for what put Ian through!" She stalked out of the room, muttering obscenities.

Shannon smiled proudly, shook her head. Her diminutive friend's fierce loyalty to Ian and her friends was no secret, but she'd almost forgotten Paige's easily overlooked temper and grit.

Ian and Bob met with the Sheriff and his detectives the next morning at Jim Bowling's office. Their praise and thanks were effusive and heartfelt. A nasty situation had worked out quite well, thanks in huge part to Sheriff Bowling and the professionalism of his deputies. Ian was impressed and very grateful, spared no words letting the Sheriff and his men know it.

Richard Billings had garnered an additional felony charge because he had been stupid enough to have cocaine in his pocket at the time of his blackmail arrest. He, however, had been smart enough to give the detectives Mark Redding's name, eagerly volunteering how the whole thing was Redding's idea and that he only participated because Redding threatened him.

Still at large, Mark Redding was the only lose end. An APB was issued and a felony warrant was obtained charging him with extortion and conspiracy. However, Jim Bowling told Ian and Bob that Redding was probably already hundreds of miles away and using an alias. As a former police officer, he could make a wily fugitive.

Still, Ian and Bob drove back to the beach house with the Porsche's top down, relieved, buoyed, and singing along with Rod Stewart's CD rendition of *Maggie May*. They had already made dinner reservations at an expensive French restaurant for an evening of celebration with Paige and Shannon. The two men couldn't have been more relaxed or happier, life seemed good again.

When they entered the restaurant that evening, every male head turned as Bob and Ian escorted their ladies to a corner table at the posh Chateau de Pierre restaurant. Paige and Shannon looked gorgeous the striking contrast between the twosome all but igniting the carpet with sensuality.

The wine was excellent and their celebratory dinner was fabulous. There was much talk of how well Shannon's two TV interviews regarding Ian's life story had gone and how the piece she'd written for *The New York Times* had fan mail coming in floods. Shannon, of course, had to endure unmerciful teasing from her three companions about trying to upstage Bill O'Reilly and Barbara Walters.

When the women left the table for the powder room, Bob ordered coffee and B and B all around. He looked across the table at his friend. "Paige is fabulous, Ian. Obviously head-over-heels in love with you ... Pretty nice situation, Mister McBride."

"Yeah, I have to pinch myself occasionally to believe how lucky I am. Bobby, I haven't had even one of my nightmares since I've been with Paige. I never thought I could be in ... Feel this way."

Bob laced his hands behind his head and leaned back in his chair. "How'd this happen to us so quickly? His expression went serious. "I'm not ... that is, we're not misreading what's happening here, are we?"

"Don't think so. Seems like we're both into something very right. Now, what are we supposed to do about it?" Ian waited for a reply. "Bob?"

Obviously preoccupied, Bob's only response was, "Hmm?"

Paige and Shannon returned just as their table captain was overseeing the serving of coffee and after-dinner drinks. He handed Shannon a white envelope before walking away without comment.

Shannon settled into her chair and held up the envelope. "What's this?"

Ian and Paige shrugged, and Bob only smiled enigmatically.

"Come on. Open it," Paige said.

Looking at Bob for a sign, and receiving none, she tore open the envelope. The plain, white card had a handwritten inscription. *I love you, Shannon, and you will be mine. I hope.* Shannon swallowed hard and looked up at Bob. The note fell from her fingers, and her breath caught as she watched him stand and move toward her.

Ian's jaw dropped when his six-foot-four-inch, 240-pound friend went to one knee by Shannon's chair. His large hand was extended palm up with a glittering gold diamond ring. Paige gasped and clamped a hand over her mouth.

"Shannon, would you honor me by accepting this and becoming my wife?"

She stared at him, unable to speak or breathe. Scores of faces were trained on them, and the restaurant had gone very quiet. "Yes," she whispered while slipping the ring onto her left hand. Then, jumping to her feet, she exploded. "YES! YES! Yes, I will, you big ox!"

Bob grabbed her around the waist and twirled her around. They kissed passionately to rowdy applause, yells, and whistles from the normally reserved Chateau de Pierre patrons. When they broke from the kiss, Shannon leaned close and whispered into his ear. "Yes, I'll marry you. And you'll be *mine*, Robert T. Fowler."

Paige pulled Shannon into a big hug as a tear trickled down the tall blonde's cheek. "Well, congrats, Sprinter. Wow, I'm so happy for you, Shannon. He's a wonderful guy."

"Don't I know it!" They laughed and hugged again.

Shannon looked into her friend's eyes and grinned. "How come I end up blubbering so much around you?"

"My upbeat personality, maybe?" Paige chuckled. "And, as Ian says, I'm a hopeless romantic."

Then the two women watched with emotion as Ian moved to Bob, first shaking his hand then hugging him. "Congratulations, Big Guy. She's a real winner."

Paige turned to Ian with a hitch in her voice, "Come on, handsome. Let's get back to the beach house. I'm taking you on a long beach walk so these two can have some time to be alone."

23

The Root of All Evil

Mark Redding could not believe his good luck. He'd been prepared to watch for days, if necessary, waiting for just the right moment when she would be vulnerable. Amazingly, they were providing him the perfect opportunity. It was almost total darkness, the sky was cloudy, and the beach deserted. His hand fingered the grip of his Smith and Wesson 9MM pistol as he watched them kiss and begin to walk down the beach. "You'll pay this time, McBride, or you'll never see her alive again," Redding whispered. He prepared himself as they came nearer, furtively moving behind some sea oats.

Ian saw Paige's shock as he caught a flash of movement in his peripheral vision, and instantly sensed trouble. He had no time to react before the gun butt crashed into the back of his skull, driving him straight to his knees. Dazed and bleeding, he struggled to stand and fight. The second blow plunged him into blackness with Paige's scream being the last thing he heard.

Fired by a gush of primordial adrenalin, Paige's reaction was immediate and fierce. She reflexively tensed and launched her body at Mark Redding; the crown of her head smashing upward into the man's shocked face. Blood gushed from the unprepared Redding's mouth as he was propelled backward onto the sand, with items spilling from his backpack. Inculcated responses from self-defense classes suppressed logic and fear as Paige leaped onto Redding's chest with her fists flailing. Screaming incoherently and cursing like a sailor, she pummeled his head and ripped bloody gashes into his face with her nails.

"You bitch!" he yelled, as she landed another punch. Redding grabbed at her wrists, and wrestled to gain control. "Stop it, you little whore!" Flipping her to face away from him, he pulled her into a police-trained chokehold. "Damnit, be still!" He spit blood and tried to shake the dizziness away.

"You bastard!" Paige kicked and struggled to break his hold.

"No way for a lady to talk." He tightened his forearm across her neck, but Paige bit into his wrist and stomped down on the arch of his foot as she screamed for help.

"Goddamnit!" Redding cried out in pain. Paige broke free, only to be knocked to the sand by his powerful backhanded blow. Redding was atop her with his hand around her neck. She froze feeling the muzzle of a pistol against her temple.

"Now you stop that shit, or I'll put a bullet in your boy-friend's head." He quickly clamped a damp chemical-smelling cloth over her nose and mouth.

Fighting for air, Paige tore at his hands with her nails, as she felt herself losing consciousness.

Back at the beach house, Bob and Shannon lay languorous in a warm afterglow, talking of their happiness. Everything seemed so good and so right as they held each other close.

"Did you hear something?" Bob raised his head, not even sure he had heard it, a faint male voice calling his name. Then it came again, louder and pained. Shannon saw the look on his face as he leapt from bed. "Ian!" Bob yelled. "Where are you?"

Yanking on robes, they ran into the hallway and down the stairs. There, in the semi-darkened great room, they saw him leaning against the sofa. Pale and dazed, his hair, face, and suit jacket wet with blood, Ian was groaning in pain.

"Good God!" Bob dashed to his side. "What's happened?"

"Can't find her ... Knocked me out ... Heard her screaming. He took Paige."

"Paige? No!" Shannon gasped and sank backward into a chair. "Dear God! Not Paige." She held her head in her hands. "Please ... no."

"Shannon, go to the kitchen and get a towel for Ian's head. I'm calling 911." Bob reached for the phone.

Within 15 minutes of Bob's 911 call flashing red and blue lights and the crackle of police radio traffic filled half the block. There was an ambulance and numerous Sheriff's Department patrol cars in the driveway and on the street. Sirens of more approaching cars could be heard in the distance. Sheriff Jim Bowling ordered roadblocks set up on two main roads and on the parkway leading off the island, and he closed the Island's tiny airport. A dozen deputies fanned out and began a careful search within a half-mile radius of the house. The State Police was notified and technicians were reinstalling recording devices on the telephones. A temporary command center was established in the great room.

Bob and Shannon talked with the Sheriff as paramedics worked on Ian, who refused to go to the hospital. Bob had been asking Jim Bowling questions about the apparent kidnapping when the sheriff's cell radio/telephone crackled to life.

"2899 to Number One."

"This is One, Go, 2899."

"We've found the crime scene and some things out here on the beach, Sheriff. Think you'd better come take a look, sir."

"On my way, 2899." The sheriff turned to Bob and pointed to Ian. "Bobby, get him to a hospital right away. He looks terrible. I need him coherent for questioning and to talk to this bastard when he calls."

Shannon was worried sick about Paige but knew it was time to pull herself together and start helping. "Bob, you need to be here with the Sheriff. I'll get Ian to the hospital and look after him. I'll give you a status report, after I talk to his doctor."

Bob kissed her cheek. "Thanks, Babe. I'm sure Paige would appreciate that, too." He looked into her red-rimmed eyes. "We're going to get her back, Shannon." He paused. "I promise."

Three deputies were bagging items in plastic when the sheriff and Bob arrived at the site. A thick, well-worn, handwritten journal; a ballpoint pen; some antacid tablets; and a well-used map of Beaufort County, South Carolina, were found in and near a large clump of sea oats adjacent to the scene of the attack and abduction. A cloth smelling of chloroform and a woman's dress shoe were found about fifty feet down the beach.

"Damn," Bob muttered. "What do you make of all this, Jim?"

"Doesn't look good. A lot of blood, and from the looks of it, she put up a hard struggle. Seldom a good sign for victims."

"Well, what do you think?" Bob asked anxiously.

"Too early to say. But, I intend to pull out all the stops, Bob. We'll find her."

Detective Captain Raymond Fleming, a detail-oriented taskmaster, was placed in charge of the investigation. In a ten-minute meeting, he had issued a flurry of orders to the fifteen deputies, two evidence technicians, and four analysts. All of Captain Fleming's troops were occupied and feeling his imposed deadline pressures. The investigation was underway.

Technicians had already lifted fingerprints from the journal and the map, allowing handling by analysts without contaminating them as evidence. The prints were faxed to the FBI in Washington. The journal was photocopied and divided among three analysts who were given an hour to produce their reports, which would be combined into one. Another analyst was assigned the map that contained numerous inked circles and dots as well as handwritten notations. A handwriting technician determined the handwriting on the map matched the writing in the journal. A detective sergeant who oversaw the map analysis, dispatched patrol cars to every marked location. The officers noted, in detail, what was out of the ordinary or suspicious. The ballpoint pen had a logo reading *Days Inn, Bluffton, SC*. A patrol car was sent there to obtain the names of all current guests and those who had checked out during the past seven days.

Within two hours, a substantial amount of lead information was developed. The journal proved to be a treasure trove of valuable data. Its author had been a police officer with the NYPD, was wounded (specific date given) and was pensioned out of the force for medical reasons (specific date given). Part of the narrative mentioned the writer's ex-wife's name and their former New York address. Entries tied the author to Richard Billings' extortion plot and outlined the planned kidnapping. Thirty minutes after Sheriff Bowling phoned the NYPD Chief of Detectives and related the pertinent information from the journal, he received a return phone call that identified Mark Redding. NYPD faxed a photo of Redding. The Sheriff had a prime suspect.

The circled sites on the map identified three veterinarian offices. A computer check indicated a recent break-in at one of the three where chloroform was among the items stolen. The Sheriff's Department Lab had already identified the chemical on the recovered rag as chloroform.

The manager at the Bluffton Days Inn identified the man in the NYPD photograph as Mark Phillips, a guest who had checked out two days earlier. Similarly, the manager of the Cat Club, a local strip joint known as a magnet for unsavory characters, identified Redding from the photograph as a recent *regular*. Those two identifications, coupled with the fact that the beach house's location was circled on the map, placed Mark Redding in the area at the time of the extortion. Those things alone did not necessarily implicate him in the kidnapping, however, when added to the verification of his identity from the NYPD, the chloroform theft from a site marked on the map, and kidnap planning entries in the journal, they had more than enough for an arrest warrant. Their evidence showed motive, means, and opportunity.

An hour later, a fax from the FBI in Washington verified the prints on the journal and the map as Mark Redding's. A full-court press was mounted to locate and arrest him.

As with most investigations, there were findings that at first glance seemed irrelevant or useless. The analyst and the patrol deputies had verified three of the sites marked on the map as rental villa complexes on the island. Since Redding had stayed at the Days Inn for more than a week, it was unlikely he had also rented a villa. It also seemed unlikely he would have rented a nearby on-island villa as a place to take a hostage. However, ignoring any leads was not even considered.

Shannon returned with Ian at 2:30AM. He had a concussion and it had taken twenty stitches to close his scalp wounds. He was tired and sluggish from the pain medications but insisted on being present and being briefed on the investigation.

At 3:45 AM, Shannon, Bob, and Ian listened as Captain Fleming addressed a group of twenty-five Sheriff Department officers, analysts, and technicians. He had a portable white board he gestured toward. There was a timeline and an outline of evidentiary details on the white board showing the investigative findings. The man's organizational skills were impressive.

"Okay, people, we know who the perpetrator is, what he planned, and how and when he planned it. We know what has taken place. What we do not know is where this son of a bitch is! Well, I want to know, and I want him in custody. If any of you are thinking about going home or resting, think again. You should be thinking about Miss Brittany. We are going to find this young woman and ensure her safety, and we're going to do it soon. Do I make myself clear?"

There was a pause followed by a loud, "Yes sir!"

Pointing to the white board he said, "Our current leads as to his whereabouts are limited, but these villa complexes were circled on his map. Therefore, I want every villa in these three complexes checked out. Sergeant Brown, get in touch with the managers of these complexes. Wake them up and get keys to the units that are supposed to be vacant. The rest of you start knocking on doors and waking up the renters. If our hostage is in one of those villas, I want to know before daylight. Now move!"

"Ohh," she groaned. The headache was terrible and it seemed she was looking through smoke. *Where am I?* Confused, she shook her head and tried to blink away the mental cobwebs. It seemed to be a small bedroom illuminated by a single lamp on a nightstand. *Why was I sleeping here?* She tried unsuccessfully to sit up on the bed, and then saw the gray tape binding her ankles and wrists. "What?" she muttered. "Why would …" She glanced left then right around the room. Neat and clean with inexpensive furniture and carpet that looked practically new. *How'd I get here?* The door was closed and the silence was unsettling. Starting to feel frightened, she wondered what was going on.

Paige pushed back the fear and began an analysis. She wasn't seriously injured, although her muscles ached and she felt bruised. Her legs were splotched with dirt and her black dress was torn and filthy. She saw scrapes on her knees and elbows, and … Was that dried blood on her hands, under her nails?

Still groggy, Paige struggled to make sense of it. When it started to slowly come back, she was engulfed by dread. "Ian!" An image of him lying motionless and bleeding on the beach flashed into her mind. She looked at her bound ankles and wrists again, starting to remember more. He had clubbed Ian unconscious. Oh, Lord. Was Ian alive? Another fragment surfaced. She was fighting with a man ... A damp, medical smelling cloth. He'd drugged her. "Why?"

Her thinking was clearing and a terrifying realization dawned. "I've been abducted," she muttered. Some kind of maniac? A rapist? She tried hard to focus. Struggling and grunting, Paige moved her arms like levers trying to break or pry the tape apart. After a couple of minutes, her wrists were red and hurting. "Come on," she mumbled. "You can do this." Taking a deep breath, she twisted and turned her wrists forcefully against the bindings. She had to escape, had to find Ian. Groaning and cursing, she kept at it, the tape cutting into her skin, drawing blood. *Oh, God, please let Ian be okay. Please God.*

Bob was frustrated and worried. "You said Redding was probably hundreds of miles away. You don't have any idea where he or Paige are, do you?"

"Bob, what can I tell you? Believe me I want this bastard in the worst sort of way. We're doing the best we can with what we have." He looked into Bob's face and saw the disappointed look.

"Doesn't it seem illogical for him to be holding her here? It seems crazy, foolhardy."

"I've considered that, but knowing he's a former cop, it may not be illogical at all. You ever heard of hiding in plain sight? Really a pretty clever idea, *if* that's what he's doing. We just don't know at this point. We're covering every lead." He knew his answers were inadequate and not what his friend wanted to hear. "Bob, it's the best answer I have. Right now, I'm going to try to help by knocking on doors. I'll keep you informed."

"Jim, a favor? Would you mind if Ian and I rode along with you? I know he feels frustrated and sort of useless. He wants to be involved."

Sheriff Bowling smiled. "And you aren't at all impatient. Right? It's just McBride?"

Bob shrugged. "What do you say, Jim. Can we ride along?"

"Oh, hell, come on. But, you've got to stay out of the way, okay?"

Pleased, Bob motioned to Ian. "Okay. Yeah, sure, Jim. Whatever you say."

It was excellent law enforcement work, professional in every way. It had all been textbook. They had identified a subject, obtained a warrant for his arrest and an APB was outstanding. Yet, there was only disappointment and frustration. Another day had begun, and they were no closer to finding Paige Ann Brittany than they had been last night when the 911 call was received.

Captain Raymond Fleming ran a hand over his balding head as he paced the carpet of the makeshift command center. He and his troops had worked hard throughout the night. They checked out every one of the 142 villa units in the three rental complexes that were circled on Redding's map. Ninety-three of the villas had been occupied by renters whose reactions ranged from concerned cooperation to extreme irritation, when awakened. The deputies had shown them hastily made flyers with photographs of Redding and Paige. Nothing. They had searched the remaining forty-nine unrented or recently vacated units. Again, nothing.

It was 6:30AM. The deputies, analysts, and technicians had been sent home an hour ago to rest but were ordered to be available on short notice. Another, somewhat reduced, shift of deputies came on duty at the beach house, as did Captain Fleming's second-in-command, Lieutenant Fred C. Smith and his chief analyst. They conferred with Captain Fleming before he went home to get some sleep.

Ian, Shannon, and Bob sat silently in the kitchen drinking coffee. They were exhausted and increasingly worried about Paige's safety. Ian had a pounding headache, wanted to scream, or hit something. He desperately wanted to do something productive, anything to help find Paige.

Bob moved to his friend's side. "Come on, Ian. We all need to get at least a few hours sleep. Otherwise, we won't be able to think straight, and we'll be of no help finding Paige."

Ian didn't think he would be able to sleep, but he did not argue with the logic. Bob motioned to Shannon, who joined them, and kissed Ian on the cheek before they headed upstairs.

The fax machine woke Ian at 10:45AM. He rubbed his eyes and stared at the machine with its beeping alarm indicating an incoming fax. Ian turned off the fax alarm and staggered out of bed to use the bathroom. He swallowed one of the pain pills and one of the antibiotic capsules the doctor had prescribed. After washing his face and shaving, he was brushing his teeth when his tired groggy mind remembered the incoming fax. Still brushing, he walked into the bedroom to check out the curled piece of paper lying in the receptacle tray.

A picture of Paige holding the first page of the local newspaper in front of her was staring back at him. She looked frightened. The Island Packet newspaper bore the current day and date in its masthead, a welcomed indicator that she was alive. However, the fax also contained a chilling message:

She is alive for now. Pay me as I say or you will never see her again. Try screwing me like you did Billings and she dies for sure. Be prepared to electronically transfer $1,000,000 tomorrow. You will receive instructions.

Ian's stomach knotted. His composure was teetering as he stalked down the hallway, and pounded on Bob's bedroom door. Biting his lip, he silently mouthed a prayer.

24

Facing the Odds

Redding stood brooding, a Styrofoam cup of McDonald's coffee growing cold in his hand. He was seldom careless, but he surely had been during the abduction. *Stupid, Mark!* He assumed his haste and lack of thoroughness had probably already yielded his identity to the police. "Really stupid."

She was the cause of course. Pint-sized broad fought like a damn alley cat. Who would have thought? Looking into the bathroom mirror, he examined the raw, red gouges in his face. They were just as bad as the ones she had ripped into the backs of his hands. "Nasty little bitch." He glanced at the festering teeth-mark wound she'd left on his wrist, and shook his head. He knew her resistance was no excuse for his sloppiness. Leaving that stuff behind was a major blunder. The local cops seemed like pros. The journal would ID him sure as hell. And with ten years of personal thoughts and musings it was also like losing a part of himself. He picked up the McDonalds bag and started down the hallway.

He saw her body tense and tremble when he stepped through the bedroom doorway. There was deep apprehension in those blue eyes, yet she gave him a steely unflinching stare. "You back to take another photograph, to torture me?" He said nothing, just watched her raise her chin defiantly, swallow her fear and glower with disdain. "What are you going to do to me?"

"I brought you some food." He held out the paper bag. I'll undo your hands so you can eat." He noticed her bloody wrists and the stretched tape. There was sure no give up in this little slut. She couldn't hide the trembling as he took a knife from his pocket and came closer. "Take it easy. I don't intend to hurt you. Just stay calm, and do as you're told."

Afraid but defiant, Paige continued to glare at him. "Do you allow your prisoners to use the bathroom?"

"Oh." He looked surprised, almost embarrassed. "Yeah, sure ... I didn't think. Hold out your hands." He cut the tape.

She motioned to her ankles. "I can't walk unless you remove that too."

He cut that tape also, but held her arm, giving her a stern look. "Half bath's off the hall. Towel and soap if you want. I'll be just outside the door. By the way, there's no window, no way out. So hurry up and do what you got to do."

Sure enough, he was waiting to steer her back to the bedroom. She felt a little better after cleaning most of the dirt off. Famished, she made quick work of the Egg McMuffin and hash browns. She sipped at the bitter lukewarm coffee feeling him studying her.

"You got no reason to be afraid of me."

"Yeah, why should I be concerned?" Paige's cocky temper flared. "You contemptible bastard! Beat my Ian unconscious, then drug and kidnap me ..." Her voice went icy. "You don't know who you're dealing with. Ian McBride's killed men before. He'll make you pay for this. That is, if he doesn't kill you first."

"He'll make *me* pay?" Redding laughed. "No, sister, it's McBride who's going to pay ... Pay me to get you back. One million bucks!" He sat down on the bed. "This is just about money, sweet lips, nothing more. Look, all I'm saying is I'm no pervert, no rapist, I don't hurt women."

Why hadn't she seen it? The concept of using her against Ian seemed so elementary now. "So, you respect women, huh?" She scowled at him. "Yeah, right! You abduct me, hog-tie me, slap me around, and make me your prisoner. You attack unsuspecting men from behind, and kidnap their women for ransom. Yeah, you might make Man-of-the-Year, you repulsive, venal animal!"

"You bitch!" Redding lunged forward and slapped her so hard she fell across the bed. "I'm through being decent to you." He pushed her face down into the bed and bound her ankles and wrists again. "Now shut the fuck up or I'll put a gag in your smart-assed mouth!" He stormed out of the room and locked the door behind him.

Sheriff Bowling met with Ian, Bob, and Shannon late that morning to explain their dearth of leads. He wanted to alert the public and the media to generate productive information. Knowing they were all celebrities, he wanted to remind them a media circus could result. They asked if he thought it was the right thing to do and he said he did. They all agreed, Paige's safety was the only consideration, and they offered to help any way they could. By 1:00PM, press releases had gone out to radio and TV stations as well as newspapers in the area.

Redding's e-mail arrived just after noon. It instructed Ian to transfer one million dollars to The Royal Bank of Grand Cayman by 3:00PM the next day. The e-mail gave an account name and a routing number and said the transfer would be verified by 3:30PM. It concluded with an ominous warning:

Her life is in your hands, McBride.

At 4:10PM, the manager of Island Car Rentals called to say he had recognized Redding's photograph on the TV news. He remembered the man because he kept swapping cars. The manager said he was currently driving a light blue Ford Mustang. He gave the license number, which was sent to the radio, TV, and newspaper outlets for their next news edition.

Three callers reported seeing the car on Hilton Head Island during the last 24 hours. The most valuable caller said he saw the car leaving McDonalds at just after 1:00PM, heading south. Detectives went to McDonald's and found two employees who also remembered the car. An unmarked detective cruiser established a surveillance of McDonald's hoping for a dinner visit by Redding.

It paid off. They fell in behind the Mustang as it left the drive-in restaurant just after 8:00PM. Two other unmarked cars joined the surveillance. He drove straight to a small, neat, white frame house in an area of rental houses favored by tourists. Twelve other deputies' cars soon arrived.

The deputies parked several blocks away, cautiously approaching the scene on foot. They took up positions in a perimeter around the house. They had Mark Redding bottled up. Was Paige Brittany inside? How willing was he to hurt her? There would be no assault on the house. That could jeopardize her safety. Following Sheriff Bowling's orders, the deputies and detectives waited and watched throughout the night. The plan was to arrest Redding but to do it while eliminating the risk of having the hostage injured. They would be patient and hope his eating pattern held. They would take him in his car as he left to get breakfast.

Jim Bowling knew it was against policy and was tactically unwise. However, he had come to know and respect these four extraordinary people. He liked them. Therefore, he decided to ignore his own policy and allowed Bob, Shannon, and Ian to wait with him in his car a block away from the perimeter. There were sporadic status checks via radio as the surveillance was maintained around the small house throughout the night. It proved to be an uneventful ten hours. They were all tired and stiff from spending the night in the car.

It was 7:10 AM. Ian and Bob stood next to the patrol car stretching and Shannon was taking a bathroom break at a nearby gas station when they heard the radio. "Attention all units. Looks like he's coming out. He's alone. Getting into the Mustang."

Sheriff Bowling started his car and advised all units to maintain their positions until the car was at least fifty yards away from the house. The unit commanders acknowledged the order. The next radio transmission was Captain Raymond Fleming's familiar demanding voice. "Units Alpha, Bravo, and Charlie, initiate felony car stop! Execute, execute!"

Redding stopped at the end of the short access road, checked for traffic, and prepared to turn left. Shocked, he saw sheriff's cruisers suddenly racing at him from his left and right. A reflexive look in the rearview mirror showed more cruisers approaching from behind. Deputies seemed to be coming at him from all directions, running with their pistols drawn. "Shit!" was all he could mutter.

He seemed to be surrounded, but the thought of surrendering never crossed his mind. Crushing the gas pedal to the floor, he rammed the cruiser to his left before it blocked him fully. It worked. He had created a narrow escape route. Ignoring shouts of "Halt!" and commands of "Hold it right there," he backed away from the damaged patrol car and aimed the Mustang at two deputies running toward the car. As Redding fired his pistol at the deputies, the Mustang shot forward, tires screaming and smoking. The official response was instantaneous. A hail of pistol bullets and shotgun blasts tore into the Mustang, blowing two of its tires, shattering windows and hitting Redding in the left shoulder and arm.

Sheriff Bowling's cruiser skidded to a halt as Redding's car crashed headlong into a telephone pole. Bob and Ian jumped from the cruiser as Jim Bowling exited, pistol in hand. Deputies rushed to surround the smoking crumpled Mustang. They dragged the wounded and dazed Redding out and handcuffed him. The sheriff was immediately in his face demanding to know Paige Brittany's whereabouts. Redding only sneered. "Fuck you!"

Ian's temper flashed out of control. "No, fuck you, asshole."

Jim Bowling's reaction was an instant too slow to prevent Ian's fist slamming into Redding's nose. A gush of blood flew from the point of impact and the sound of cartilage breaking was unmistakable. It took two deputies to pry Ian's fingers from

Redding's throat. The deputies held him in check as Sheriff Bowling admonished him to cool down.

The Sheriff looked at Redding and shrugged. "Okay, Redding, same question. I suggest a different answer." Redding spit blood and complained about his nose but didn't answer. Sheriff Bowling grabbed his hair and yanked his head around. "You are beginning to irritate me, Mr. Redding. Tell me now. Where is she?" Redding only glared at the sheriff. Bowling gestured over his shoulder toward Ian. "You know, I'm not sure my men can hold Mr. McBride. Looks quite strong, and really looks pissed to me … And I suspect he'd probably like another piece of you. Think your nose can stand it?"

"Little bitch is in the house," Redding said. "Back bedroom."

Ian had already broken into a sprint and never heard Shannon's exchange with Mark Redding, which ended abruptly when he foolishly called her friend 'that nasty little whore.' Bob gasped as his fiancé vengefully propelled her knee into Redding's crotch. Two nearby deputies instinctively grimaced at the audible crushing thud of her knee finding its mark. As they dragged Redding away, howling in pain, Bob smiled and restrained a seething Shannon Collins, as the blonde continued to hurl ripe invectives after Redding.

First to reach the house, Ian saw the front door was locked. He turned to the two deputies who had run with him. One size 12 and a size 13 boot hit the door reducing the jam to splinters and propelling the door off its hinges and into the living room. They rushed in behind Ian and found Paige in the bedroom. Her ankles and wrists were bound with tape and a handkerchief had been stuffed into her mouth. When she saw Ian, her eyes filled with tears. Once free, Paige threw herself against Ian and sobbed. Ian's eyes were also moist as he picked her up in his arms. Kissing her hair and whispering into her ear, he carried her out of the house. They were greeted by the cheers of fifteen or so deputies and a number of reporters and TV cameramen who had learned of the ongoing drama.

Paige looked up at Ian sitting beside her in the ambulance. "I didn't know if you were alive." She held his face in her hands. "You were on the sand, not moving. I was so ..." She started to cry. "Oh, Ian. I was so scared."

He kissed her cheek, stroked her hair. "Thought I'd lost you—I was almost out of my mind." He looked at the bruises on her face and touched them gently as his teeth clenched. "I told myself not to ask this ..." He looked down, and then back into her eyes, his anger evident. "But I have to know ... Did that bastard do anything to you? I mean, did he *touch* you?"

She saw his white-knuckled fists, the restrained fury in his eyes and knew Ian would literally kill the man given a chance. "I'm okay," she assured. "Really. He didn't hurt me much at all after we fought on the beach." She kissed Ian tenderly, noticing the ugly stitches for the first time. "It's over," she said. "And I'll be fine. Let it go, Darling. Please. He's not worth it."

"Okay ... I guess." Ian exhaled deeply. "But, I may never let you out of my sight again."

"That wouldn't bother me one bit." She kissed his cheek. "I love you, Ian Michael McBride. I wondered if I'd have the chance to tell you that again."

"I love you, Paige."

"You said it!" Her jaw dropped and her eyes went wide. "You said the words." She looked into his eyes. "You've never told me … See, it didn't hurt that much. Now did it?"

"No. Relatively painless." They both laughed. "Who knows, I may tell you again sometime."

A warm smile swept her tear stained face. "Two or three times a day is good enough for starters." She thought of all they had experienced in such a short time. "Lord, my heart's about to pop. Let's get this hospital thing done so I can get you home and into a hot shower with me."

He shot her a wolfish grin. "Now, that's a deal!"

Paige's medical examination was much more extensive than she had expected or wanted, including one of her least-liked physical examinations. The chief resident explained that the exam had been ordered by the sheriff, "for law enforcement reasons." It was obvious there would be no speeding through this. Paige's mind wandered as she waited in yet another exam room, replaying every detail of Ian saying he loved her. His expression, the tone of his voice, feeling her hand in his—a wondrous, intimate moment she would never forget.

She remembered his grin when she said she wanted to go home. The word jumped out, jolted her. Home. She'd called the beach house 'home'. It had come off her tongue so naturally. What was she to make of it? Could she be 'at home' living in that house with Ian? Easy answer. Of course, she could be happy living there with him. Actually, it could be far more than … Good Lord! She was thinking about being married. She was surprised how casually, and quickly she had made that leap.

"All done, Miss Brittany."

Paige was yanked back to reality by the doctor's voice as he walked in smiling.

"We're going to spring you now. Except for the scrapes and bruises, you're a very healthy woman. I'll let the Sheriff know."

Slipping back into her dirty, torn dress, her mind went back to Ian ... and marriage. The idea should be frightening ... right? It wasn't. On the contrary, she seemed to have the same feeling about living with Ian, being married to him as she'd had when she agreed to accompany him to the Island. I just seemed right. As if it was supposed to be.

"No!" She had allowed herself to be carried away. *Get your head out of the clouds ... back to the real world.* This whole topic was crazy. He probably hadn't even considered marriage. There was no reason to think so. After all, she cautioned, the poor man had only just said 'I love you' for the first time. She reprimanded herself again. "Jeez Paige!"

25

And, then ...

Atlanta, Georgia
Three Months Later

The floor around her feet was littered with crumpled hand-written notes and discarded, edited pages from the printer. She sat at the desktop keyboard, a wooden pencil clamped in her teeth, deep in concentration, fingers deftly moving over the keys. Shannon Elizabeth Collins never neglected her appearance. Baggy jeans, an old paint-stained sweatshirt, and no makeup—her breath smelled of stale coffee and she was mutter-ing to herself. The tall beautiful blonde's state would signal any-one knowing her that this was one special project that had her serious undivided attention.

Three months before, Shannon and Bob had moved into Ian's apartment at his invitation and near insistence. The 2500 square foot luxury penthouse condominium that Bob once dubbed the ultimate in bachelor pads, sat atop a twenty-story office building in an upscale area of Atlanta. Shannon had been working on the *New Yorker Magazine* piece for those three months while Bob shuttled back and forth to Boston finalizing other matters. Her story-like piece, entitled "A Relaxing Week at the Beach" was scheduled to run in three sequential monthly segments. With her deadline looming, she was cautiously optimistic an expanded version of the *New Yorker* piece would become her first novel.

The extortion of one well-known author, followed by the million-dollar ransomed kidnapping of another, had grabbed the public's interest and generated a flood of media attention. However, when word got out that these victims, authors of romance novels, were in love, neither the media nor the public could get enough information about them and their harrowing exploits on Hilton Head. Ian McBride and Paige Brittany, and to a lesser degree Bob and she, were big news. Shannon's new publisher and fiancée had secured the deal with the *New Yorker* for her to tell the story of the four's planned 'relaxing' vacation on the resort island. That same publisher had also signed a contract with his fiancé to introduce her as a budding novelist.

Like a horse bound for the barn at feeding time, Shannon wanted it finished, and pushed herself to complete this final installment for the *New Yorker's* editors. As usual, she was obsessive about it meeting her critical personal standards. Walking into the kitchen for more coffee, she paused and looked out the picture window at a bright blue sky she had previously not noticed. *Like the Hilton Head sky,* she thought. She was soon replaying the last few days the four of them spent on the Island together.

They had become so very close. Sure, they might have become friends anyway. However, having shared so many remarkable events and feelings, their mutual trust and love was extraordinary. They were cemented into an almost inseparable unit. Their planned week at the beach, which turned into more than two weeks, proved to be a roller coaster of intense emotions. She and Paige had gone from a snarling catfight first meeting to becoming almost like sisters. All in less than three weeks. Amazing. Their last three days together on the Island had been wonderfully fun, romantic, and life changing.

After her joyful rescue, Paige rested and spent time alone with Ian until the next day. Bob and Ian insisted on preparing dinner for the women the next night. They had a lot to celebrate, Shannon's birthday and Paige's safe return. The women heaped praise on the guys for another fabulous dinner. They all seemed so relaxed and happy again.

After dinner, Shannon and Paige left the guys watching a baseball game on TV, and they cleaned the kitchen.

"I hate to see this end. It's been an incredible time," Paige said.

Shannon picked up a dish and put it in the dishwasher. "Yeah, know what you mean. You and Ian seem to be doing just great, in spite of it all."

Paige looked at her friend. "I guess you'll find out soon, but …"

"What? What's up?"

"Well, a moving van will be at my apartment in Chicago next week."

"Really?" Shannon smiled. "Fred finally talked you into moving to Philadelphia, huh?"

"No. I'm changing addresses, but not Philadelphia …" She forced a serious look

"Okay, so you've got my interest up. What's the big mystery? Let's have it."

"Well … The moving van will be bringing my stuff here."

"What? You're …" There was a moment's hesitation, before Shannon squealed, "Ohmygod! He asked you to move in?" She paused, looking suddenly questioning. "As in *live* with him?"

"Oohh yeah." Paige grinned. "As in live with him in every way. He …" Air gushed from Paige as she was crushed into a jubilant hug.

"Oh, Paige, that's fabulous! I am so, so happy for you two!" The blonde sniffled. "Damnit, you're going to do it to me again."

"Me too." Paige sobbed joyfully. "It's all sort of like a dream right now. But a real good one." She paused. "Are we two lucky girls, or what?"

"Big time lucky. But don't tell them that." Shannon chuckled, sniffled again. "Is he talking marriage?"

Paige laughed. "No, but … we'll see." She shot her friend a conspiratorial woman-to-woman wink. "Wouldn't bet against it." She batted her lashes.

"Oh, boy …" Shannon laughed aloud. "Yep. He's toast. Only a matter of time." She hugged Paige again. "He's getting the best."

Shannon checked her outline, fully intending to take up where she had left off. However, warm thoughts of how very happy Ian and Paige were together had her mind wandering again. She smiled and shook her head thinking how only Bob and those two could screw up her concentration like that.

She thought back to the day following Paige's revelation. It was a wonderful day together for the four of them. A picnic on the beach with too much beer, warm conversation, and playing in the surf.

That night, Bob said he had been checking on a few things and had an idea to run by them. His proposal initially shocked her, Paige, and Ian. Bob knew Ian's publishing contract was up for renewal and had found out Paige's current contract ran out in two months.

"Look, three of you are acknowledged, first-rate writers with established track records. I know publishing, finance, business, and the law. We like, trust, and support one another. Why don't we pool our monetary assets and share our talents to form our own publishing company? Since none of us likes cold weather, I suggest we base it in Atlanta."

His usual straightforward way of presenting complicated issues resonated with each of them. Because Ian, Paige, and Shannon trusted Bob's judgment so much, there was no more than ten minutes of discussion and questions among them. Handshakes and hugs launched F & M Publishing, on the spot, with one executive, no staff, and three clients who were also partners.

It was agreed Bob and Shannon would live and work in Atlanta. Ian and Paige would stay on Hilton Head Island, a great environment for writers, and only a four-hour drive from Atlanta's F & M "headquarters."

Bob and Shannon moved into Ian's condo three days later, where they would live until they could find or build something permanent. Bob was looking for Atlanta office space for F & M when he was not in Boston finalizing his exit from the firm there. He had even made Fred an offer to handle the firm's PR.

Lacing her fingers behind her head, Shannon leaned back, considering how to end it. The story, itself, was finished. However, she thought a few final touches were needed, dealing with what she regarded as remaining issues. She, therefore, began writing a postscript of sorts, to tie up lose ends.

Dear Readers:

So that is the story of four people who set out to explore romantic relationships and get to know one another better by spending a relaxing week at the beach. I suppose it goes to show, how one never knows what is around the next corner, or on the next page, so to speak. I thought you might be wondering what happened to some of the other characters you met in the story.

Sheriff James Bowling garnered glowing accolades from law enforcement officials, media analysts, and experts from coast to coast for his department's handling of the crimes against Ian and Paige. One would think his chance of being the County Sheriff for another term is all but a certainty. He is a good man.

Richard Billings' personal weaknesses lead to his self-destruction. He negotiated a plea bargain with the county prosecutor and another with the United States Attorney regarding federal charges. He is currently undergoing cocaine and alcohol detox in a prison hospital ward, and will serve seven years in that prison. Billings avoided federal charges by identifying his cocaine dealers and agreeing to testify against them. He will of course testify against Mark Redding.

As for Redding, he has recovered from his wounds and is being held in county jail pending trials on both state and federal charges of extortion and kidnapping. Surly and unrepentant, his first trial begins in January of next year. Prosecutors are confident of convictions with both Ian and Paige eager to testify. Some of you may think me heartless, but my pity for him is nonexistent.

And, oh yes … Martha McDonald. She continues to reside at the Motel 6 in Bluffton, South Carolina, assumedly paying her room rent in her own inimitable way. The county prosecutor dismissed the extortion charge against her at the urging of Ian and Paige. Rumor has it the loving couple set her up as owner/manager of a nail salon. My sources say if she works hard, stays drug free, and away from prostitution, her financial future will be assured. The same informants tell me Martha is often seen at McDonald's and the movies on the arm of a tall skinny man, thought to be the night manager of some motel. Who knows? Hilton Head is quite a romantic place.

Your correspondent and her fiancée are to be wed in Atlanta this winter. A certain wedding coordinator is going slowly mad dealing with not only the bride to be but also an equally strong-willed, Maid of Honor from Hilton Head Island. I shouldn't have to tell you Ian and Bob are staying as far from those matters as possible. Handsome and smart. Good combination.

The piece was finished. And none too soon since she had to pick Bob up at the airport in less than two hours. Shannon turned to look into a full-length mirror and gasped, mortified by her appearance. She dashed to the bathroom to begin necessary repairs and reconstruction, although not at all worried about the results. She smiled, knowing what low cut dress and sheer lingerie she would be wearing when she met her fiancée at the airport. After all, he had been gone all week. Shannon grinned vampishly into the mirror. "Better brace yourself, Bobby."

About the Author

Ray McElhaney was a career FBI special agent, a Fortune 500 executive, and a military combat veteran, prior to beginning his writing. Born in Tennessee, he did his undergraduate work in Memphis and his MBA work in Indianapolis.

The author was a Unit Chief at FBI Headquarters in Washington when recruited by IBM to join their corporate staff. Drawing on his varied life experiences adds credibility and depth to his characters and stories.

He lives and writes on an island off the South Carolina coast. When he's not engaged in his other consuming passion, golf the author enjoys fine wines, reading, and music.

978-0-595-48130-9
0-595-48130-2

Printed in the United States
103399LV00003B/175-186/A